MEMBERS ONLY

For more information about the author and her books, visit her website- www.shanteltessier.com. You can sign up for her newsletter on her website- www.shanteltessier.com
Photographer: James Critchley
Model: Andrew England
Editor: Amanda Rash
Formatter: Melissa Cunningham @booklovedesigns

GRAVE

THE DARK KINGDOM

PLAYLIST

"Swalla" by Jason Derulo
"Pour it Up," by Rhianna
"Mansion," by NF
"MONSTERS" by Shinedown
"Bloody Nose" by Hollywood Undead
"Numb" by 8 Graves
"Sail" by AWOLNATION
"Fire Away" by Chris Stapleton
"Bury Me Low" by 8 Graves

PROLOGUE

GRAVE

"SWALLA" BY JASON Derulo blares as lights flash in my favorite strip club. *Glass* has the best of the best women on the Las Vegas Strip.

My best friend, Cross, and I sit center stage with several stacks of hundreds in front of us while a dancer by the name of Mandi sits on his lap topless.

Natalie is face down on the black stage with her ass up in the air right in front of us. Her white G-string glows in the black lights. I toss a few hundreds while she bounces her ass up and down as though she's fucking an imaginary cock.

She sits up, turns around, and leans over the edge. Gripping my shirt, she yanks me to her, shoving her fake tits in my face, and I inhale the scent of strawberries.

She pulls away laughing, and I pick up my drink, downing what's left of it.

I whistle and lift my empty glass to signal I need a refill, knowing our waitress is watching us. I paid her two hundred when we sat down to ensure we never go without tonight.

As the song comes to an end, another drink is placed in front of me. Natalie licks her lips, looking at me. "Want a private dance?" she asks, shoving her hair off her bare chest.

"Of course." I wink at her. The girls know I pay well.

"What about me?" A man plops down in the empty seat to my left.

Her eyes go over to his, and the smile drops off her face. "What the fuck are you doing here, Randy?"

He leans forward, his forearms on the silver railing. "You've been ignoring my calls. I figured I'd come see you face-to-face." Her face tightens when he adds, "We need to talk."

"I have nothing to say to you." She starts to pick up the money that covers the stage. The place is packed this time of night, but most of what she collects came from Cross and me.

He stands and reaches out for her, but I'm faster. I grab his arm, stopping him. "The lady said she doesn't want to talk to you. I suggest you leave."

He looks at my hand gripping his arm and then up into my eyes. "Who the fuck are you?"

"Randy, stop," she warns.

I smile. "Doesn't matter who I am."

"Are you fucking my woman?" he demands.

I let go of him and pick up my glass. "I plan on it," I say matter-of-factly, "but it doesn't sound like she belongs to you."

"Randy ..."

"Are you fucking him?" he shouts at her.

My eyes shoot up to the DJ who stands in his corner booth, and he raises his hand, signaling to the security. They try to keep this place clean, but that doesn't stop the trash from getting in from time to time.

Cross shoves the stripper off his lap and gets to his feet beside me, knowing shit is about to get sideways. I place a hand on his chest

2

and push him back into his seat. I don't need his help fighting battles.

"We're not together, Randy!" She growls and stands.

"You fucking slut!" he screams. "You're nothing but a fucking whore!" He picks up my glass and tosses it toward her. She squeals as she jumps back in her six-inch heels.

Men crowded around the stage stand as what was left of my liquor splashes most of them.

I grip the back of his neck and slam his face down onto the stage. "Say that again," I growl.

Blood covers the side of the stage as his hands come to his busted face. He falls into his chair, and it tips over, landing on the carpet before rolling onto his side. I kick him. "Fucking say that again!" I shout.

I don't give a fuck what a woman chooses to do with her body. It's her decision. But for this fucker to come into her business and disrespect her like that is unacceptable.

"Speak, motherfucker!" I lean down and grab the back of his head, slamming his face into the dark blue carpet covered in purple and pink confetti. Standing to my full height, I step on his hand.

He lifts his head off the floor and cries out when I twist my boot, in hopes I'm fucking breaking the bones.

"Grave?" The security guard who works the front desk comes up to me.

"He threw a drink at her." I point at the stage. It's now covered in broken glass and alcohol. Natalie stands at the opposite end with her back pressed against the mirrored wall. She clings to her dress and the wet money. The DJ has exited his booth and is now walking up the side stairs to check on her.

"I saw." He places his hand on my shoulder. "The police have been called," he assures me. "Let them do their job."

I suck in a deep breath and then kick him one last time. "Piece of shit!"

He moans and rolls over, cradling his hand.

I look up to see Natalie walking down the stairs toward me. "Come on, Grave." She takes my hand and pulls me away from her ex.

I walk up the three stairs and pass the bar, grabbing a drink off it as she ushers me to a back room.

"You okay?" I ask once she shuts the door behind me.

"Yeah." She places her hands on my chest. "Thanks to you."

I fall into a chair in the corner, and she takes a step back from me. "When was the last time you saw him?" I demand, taking another drink of the rum and Coke, trying to calm my nerves.

"Last night."

"Jesus, Nat. You've got to quit seeing him." I remove the pill bottle from my jeans pocket because it's digging into my thigh and set it on the table next to the chair.

"We have a kid together." She sighs.

"So? That doesn't give him the right to disrespect you like that." I growl. What they have is complicated, to say the least. He doesn't want her but hates that she strips. He's a piece of shit lowlife who doesn't even help feed his kid. She does the best she can with the options she has.

"Hey, you need to calm down. I'm okay."

For now, she is. But I always worry about her and his ass. He's abusive. That's why she left him to begin with. "You need to get a restraining order against him." I growl.

"I have. You know that doesn't stop him."

"I have a friend who is a judge. I can reach out to him for you." I'm sure the fucker has a warrant. I can have his ass thrown in jail by morning.

She gives me a soft smile. "You're always watching out for me."

In general, I feel sorry for women in the same position as Natalie. They have no help and limited means. She makes great money, but kids aren't fucking cheap. Add in court and attorney fees and it's like running in place.

"Here ..." She drops to her knees before me and spreads my

4

legs wide. When her eyes meet mine, she gives me a reassuring smile. "I brought you something." Reaching down, she removes a baggie from her top that she slipped on after she exited the stage since her dress was wet. "Wallet?" She stands, holding out her hand to me.

I lift my hips to remove my wallet from my back pocket and hand it over to her. She opens it up, removes my black Amex card, and starts cutting the powder she pours out on the table next to my pill bottle. "You deserve it." She then removes a hundred-dollar bill and rolls it up before handing it to me.

I'm an addict to many things. None of which are good.

I FEEL MYSELF START TO RELAX AS "POUR IT UP" BY RIHANNA begins to play in the large room. Her white top is over by the small stage to the right. She dances before me in nothing but her thong and heels.

She stands and bends over, placing her face in my neck. My right hand goes to her bare ass while my other holds my cold glass on the armrest. She still tastes like my drink the bastard threw at her. She didn't even bother to take the time to wipe it off. *I don't mind.*

She's yanked from me. "Hey," she snaps, turning to face the man who interrupted us. Then her voice changes to interested. "I didn't know your friend was going to join us."

I look up, ready to beat the shit out of her ex but look into a set of dark blue eyes that match mine. *It's my brother.* They fucking called him to come and get me because I made a scene. It wouldn't have taken him long to get here. Kingdom—the hotel and casino we own— is just down the street.

"Let's go, Grave." He ignores her.

I run my eyes over her ass before I down what's left of the drink I took from the bar. Then I look up at him. "What's the rush, Bones? Stay. Play a little."

The man needs to let loose. He's too uptight. You would think for as much pussy as he gets, he'd be a friendlier guy. But nope.

He growls. "Grave."

I laugh, sinking farther into the chair. I run my hand over my T-shirt and grab my dick over my jeans. "If you don't wanna join, then pull up a chair. You can watch." I don't mind an audience.

He reaches down, grabs my arm, and yanks me to a standing position. "We're leaving," he orders, giving me no room to argue as he begins to drag my drunk ass out of the room. "Where is Cross?"

"He found a girl he liked and offered her some cash. They left." I overheard him telling Mandi that he wanted to take her home. Cross doesn't mind the private rooms, but he's always willing to pay extra for them to leave with him.

We make our way to the entrance, and I see his blacked-out Lamborghini Reventon still running at the curb.

"I don't know ..." a kid dressed in his tux says, sounding stressed. He works the valet. This place is as high priced as a strip club can get. "He just parked here and got out." He's gesturing to my brother's car.

"I'm leaving," Bones informs them.

"That's him." The kid turns and points at my brother.

The older man looks at us. "Bones. I apologize." He nods. "Have a nice night, sir."

I snort. My brother owns the place. He doesn't know that I know, but I do. He went in half with one of our best friends Luca Bianchi—he runs the Las Vegas Mafia. We've got ties all over Sin City. If you want to be untouchable, it takes an army, and we've built one that is indestructible.

"You as well," he says before we get into the car, and he pulls out of the parking lot.

I slump down in the passenger seat.

"What are you doing?" he asks with a sigh.

I pull my cell out of my pocket. "Gonna get fucked." I unlock it. "This hard dick isn't gonna suck itself. And you interrupted my plan for the night. I'm messaging Lucy." She never lets me down.

"When are you gonna shit or get off the pot?"

I snort at that. "I don't love Lucy. It's just sex." I start typing, but my phone begins to ring. **Cross** lights up the screen, and I answer it. "Hello?"

"Hey, there's a party going on tonight. Mandi and I are headed there now. Want me to come back and get you?" he asks. I can hear bitches screaming in the background over the music.

"Nah," I say. I'm not in the mood to chase down pussy. I want it to come to me.

"Okay, I'll see you in the morning." He hangs up, and I do the same. I go back to texting Lucy.

Me: You free?

My eyes start to get heavy. That pill I took earlier is starting to kick in.

Lucy: when and where?

ONE

GRAVE

I OPEN MY heavy eyes and roll over with a moan. "Fuck." My head pounds, and my right hand hurts. I look down to find cracked and bloody knuckles.

"The fuck?" I groan.

I sit up and run a hand down my face. I'm still dressed in my clothes from last night. Cross and I had gone to Glass like we always do to relieve some stress.

I reach into my pocket for my bottle of pills but come up empty. *Where the fuck are they?* I look over on the nightstand and then the floor, but they're nowhere to be found.

Where could they have gone? Did I drop them? I know I didn't take them all because it was a full bottle.

What time is it? I reach out, looking for my cell. I find it hidden underneath a pillow. The clock on the screen reads 4:30 a.m. I run my hand over my face and get out of the bed. Where am I?

I exit the room and know immediately where I am. Titan's—a childhood friend and business partner—house. How the fuck did I get here? And why ...?

"Titan." I hear a moan coming from down the hall.

Emilee. Titan's fiancée. The woman who just happened to fuck my brother in high school and college is now engaged to our best friend Titan. It's a fucked-up situation if you ask me.

I grip the banister to go downstairs for a bottle of water when she speaks again, bringing me to a stop. "Oh, God ... Bones."

What the fuck?

I decide to take a look because why the fuck not? I make my way to the end of the hallway and turn the knob slowly, gently pushing open the door enough to look inside the master bedroom.

Emilee lies on her back in the center of the bed. Titan lies on his stomach, his hands on her thighs, keeping them spread open with his face between them, fucking her pussy with his tongue. My brother straddles her face. He holds her arms down to the bed above her head. Her hips buck as Titan holds her down as best as he can while she moans around my brother's cock.

I watch her body fight their restraints as she comes from both of them pleasuring her.

Bones is the first to move, releasing her wrists and getting off her. She's gasping for air with her eyes closed. Titan then removes himself from between her thighs, and she closes her shaking legs and rolls onto her side.

"I'm not done, baby," Titan tells her, gripping her hips and flipping her over onto her stomach. Her hands grip the sheets, and she buries her face into them. "Bones?" He nods to the corner of the room.

My brother walks over and picks up a pair of jeans thrown over a chair, knowing what Titan wanted. He rips the belt from the loops and tosses it to Titan, who catches it midair.

He grabs her arms and pulls them behind her back, securing her wrists with the belt. He grips the extra and wraps it around his fist, pulling on it.

She whimpers while my brother stands off to the side, stroking his cock as it grows hard once again.

Titan spreads her legs with his knees and slides into her as she cries out. My brother walks over to the bed, grips her hair in his hand, and pulls her face up off the sheets and starts fucking her mouth again.

I close the door and make my way back to the spare bedroom. Lying down, I undo my pants and jack off, listening to them tag-team her.

TWO

GRAVE

YOU KNOW THAT saying what happens in Vegas, stays in Vegas? Everyone knows it's not true. Sin City is the biggest adult playground in the US. It never closes. People come from all around to spend every penny they have in hopes to hit it big. But me? I've lived here all my life. We were born and raised here. We, the Kings, don't talk about it, but we all had plans that didn't include Kingdom. Titan, Cross, Bones, and I didn't ask for this life or this empire. Kingdom was started by our fathers—the Three Wisemen. Along with that, we inherited clients and enemies. Just like anything else that involves money, you're going to have those who are jealous of what you have and those who want to take it. Then you have the ones who want to intertwine their business with ours. The Mason brothers have always been my friends. We grew up with them. They own the Airport. It's not what you think. Well, it used to be an actual airport back in the seventies, but it was shut down and turned into the most elite illegal gambling ring in Nevada. You can bet on anything at any time—day or night. Just like anything else here, it never closes.

Everyone knows about it—Judges, the Mayor, and the DA. What

it's about. They haven't shut it down because they depend on their cut. It's just another source of income for them that they don't have to pay taxes on. Money in their pocket seems to have a blinding affect.

After my fight at Glass last night, I wanted to get out tonight. Get some fresh air. Do what I do best. Race.

The night air is stuffy, making it hard to breathe. It's humid, causing my sweat-covered shirt to stick to my body. The woman standing before me digs her nails into the fabric, yanking on it.

She shoves her face into mine, and I bite her bottom lip. She growls like a fucking bitch in heat and then her hands connect with my chest, pushing me. The back of my knees hit the front end of my car, and the force of her shove has me falling back. My back lies on the hood as she climbs on top of me.

"I don't have time ..."

"I'll make it quick," she rushes out, placing both hands on my face and kissing me. My hands go to her jean shorts that have ridden up, and I dig my fingers into her bare ass cheeks. She moans. Her hips begin to grind against my hard cock.

Fuck! I don't have time for this. "Lucy, I need to go," I say but make no move to push her off or stop her in any way. My cock is fucking hard, and she is willing. What kind of motherfucker would turn pussy down? Not me.

"Just let me suck it real quick." She crawls off me and stands in her high heels. I peel my sweaty back off the already hot hood of my Dodge Demon.

I look over her as she stands before me panting. Her bleach blond hair is a fucking mess. Her roots have grown out longer than they should. She wears a pair of Daisy Dukes that barely cover her fucking pussy, and she has the top of them undone and rolled down once. Her white T-shirt has a black skull on it with a matching black crown. It sits uneven, tilting to the right, and blood runs down it, coating the skull. She has the shirt tied in a knot underneath her large tits with no bra. Her navel has a yellow and red sun tattooed around it with a string of diamonds that hangs down from the piercing. She's my number one cheerleader. My go-to fuck. The bitch can suck start a fucking Harley.

Before I can speak, she goes to my jeans. I raise my hands while her fingers fumble with my black studded belt. Once she gets it undone, she rips the buttons open and shoves my pants to my ankles along with my boxers. My hard dick springs to action, staring up at her.

"Bow to your king, my lady," I say with a British accent.

Chicks fucking dig that shit. Well, never met one who hasn't.

She laughs and bends at the waist, leaning over to take my dick into her mouth without wasting another second. I should force her to her knees, but we're standing in an abandoned gravel parking lot. And I'm not a total fucking dick.

I place my hands behind my head and link my fingers together. Throwing my head back, I look up at the dark sky and groan as she swallows my fucking dick like I'm throwing hundreds at her.

My tongue darts out and runs over my lip ring. "Fuck! Yeah, baby ..."

"Racers, take the stage for the last qualifying round of the night." Colt Tinsley's voice rings out through his megaphone from behind us.

Fuck! I shove her head away. She loses her balance and falls to her hands and knees in the gravel. "Grave..." She growls my nickname, her brown eyes glaring up at me.

"Sorry, babe." I'm hopping on both feet, trying to pull my boxers and jeans up as I round the car and almost trip myself when my shoes slip on the loose gravel. I fall into my Challenger, not even bothering to zip or button my pants before I start it up.

Lucy jumps to her feet, dusting her hands and knees off before stepping back when I rev the engine, shift it into gear, and take off, throwing gravel and dust up in my wake.

I speed over the gravel and onto the asphalt. I pass cars that just exited the once private airport strip.

Making my way up to the front line, I bring my car to a stop and look to my left to see a guy I've known for years. Jimmy Trust sits next to me in his new yellow fucking Ferrari. I smirk.

"Two nights in a row?" he asks. Cross and I were here last night before we hit Glass. "Don't you ever give her a rest?"

"Whores were made to be ridden." I rub the black dash. "Aren't you, baby?"

I've had the Dodge Challenger SRT Demon for two years now. She's the fastest production car out on the streets. Only thirty-three hundred were made. Three thousand of those were sold in the US. The other three hundred went to Canada. I had a friend who worked at a Dodge dealership and paid cash for her months in advance to make sure I was guaranteed one. She only comes out when I race her. Other than that, she is kept in the garage.

He snorts. "Just gonna warn ya, Grave. You're not ready."

A woman with big fake tits, fake tan, and fake eyelashes walks out onto the tarmac and stands. Our headlights illuminate her and the runway before us. People are lined up on both sides as far as you can see. Some have their cars pulled right up to the line, and they sit on their hoods or their trunks after placing their bets. Drinks in one hand, joints in the other.

"I'm always ready, sweetheart." I blow him a kiss. "I hear you like having your ass spanked. But what about accessories? Would you prefer rope or handcuffs? Maybe some zip ties? Oh, or a chain. Maybe a little whip action? I have it all."

His hand tightens on the black steering wheel, and he shifts in his seat.

"Aww, don't be ashamed, Jimmy. We all have our kinks," I taunt.

He shakes his head. "You sadistic son of a bitch," I hear him mutter.

"Racers, are you ready?"

Putting all jokes aside, I turn to look at the half-naked woman who stands before us. She has a green flag in her right hand. She parts her legs in her black heels. Leather straps run all the way up her calves to her thighs. She wears a black leather skirt that barely covers her pussy and a black lace bra. *That's it.* She pushes her right hip out, lifting the flag and then bringing it down. I let off the clutch and shift into first. Then second. Then third. I pull away from him right off the bat. I'm the quickest off the start and the fastest all around. No one can beat me. I'm not even sure why they fucking try.

My car vibrates underneath me, the sound of the roaring engine filling the inside. I have the A/C turned off and the windows down, and the wind feels good on my sweaty shirt.

When I cross the finish line, I see people jumping up and down on either side of the lanes. They know to bet on me. I've never let them down. Looking in my rearview mirror, I see his lights behind me, and I laugh.

I begin to slow down and make the turn that they have mapped out with orange cones.

My car comes to a quick stop right off the tarmac. He finishes, then goes to the parking lot. Once out of his car, he heads toward me. He looks down to see my jeans still undone. I make no attempt to fix it because they're about to come off anyway.

"How did that feel?" I ask. "Was it as good for you as it was for me, baby?"

He just shakes his head at me, shoving his sweaty hair back from his face.

"Next time, I'll bring the lube. Don't wanna hurt you too bad," I joke.

He comes to a stop, tilting his head. "You gay, Grave?"

I smirk. "Homophobic, Jimmy? It's 2020. Aren't we past that?"

"I think you have a crush on me," he mutters, disgust dripping off his words.

I smile at him and throw my arm over his shoulders, pulling him into my side. He stiffens. "I'll fuck anything with a hole, sweetheart. Why don't you get on your knees and open that mouth for me?" My free hand comes up and touches his lips.

"Fuck you, man!" he snaps and shoves me away. He digs into his pocket and tosses a wad of hundred-dollar bills at me.

"Aw, come on. Making it rain?" I ask, and he turns his back to me, walking away. "Don't you wanna see what else I can do for a stack of hundreds?"

"Fuck you, man," he shouts, flipping me the bird over his shoulder.

I laugh as I pick up the money from the ground.

"Grave!"

I spin around to see Lucy running toward me. Her legs wobble, like a baby fawn not knowing how to walk just yet as her heels take on the gravel, but I find it cute that she tries for me. I bend down and pick her up at the same time she jumps into my arms. Wrapping my arms around her, I spin us around.

"You won!" she says excitedly.

"Did you ever doubt me?" I ask with an arch of my brow.

She shakes her head. "Never! Now what does the king want from his queen?"

"Well, for starters, you can finish what you started before I had to run off."

She jumps out of my arms, grabs my hands, and is yanking me back to my parked car.

THE SMOKE FILLS THE SMALL ROOM RESERVED FOR HIGH rollers. I sit at the blackjack table inside the Airport. The Mason brothers don't actually own a hotel and casino like the Kings and I do. They're more of an underground, off the books type of gambling ring. Due to Nevada laws, this is the only place I'm able to gamble at. Being part owner of a casino has its cons. So when I have the need to blow some money, I come here.

A cigar to my right and a rum and Coke to my left. Lucy stands behind me. After she sucked my dick in my car, we decided to go inside and play for a little bit. I was on a high from winning the race. *Why stop then?*

The dealer hands me a new card and I inwardly cuss. Twenty-two. I fold my cards and he takes the five grand in chips I had sitting out.

"How much longer?" she whispers, leaning over to speak into my ear. "I need to..."

"Go ahead," I tell her.

She gives me a kiss on the cheek and then heads off to the women's bathroom.

"Mind if I ask how much your date is?" the guy sitting next to me asks.

I look over at him. He smiles at me. His dark eyes crinkle at the corners. He looks over and watches as she sashays her ass in those tiny shorts. I'm not the jealous type. Never have been. Plus, Lucy doesn't *belong* to me.

"Too rich for you," I answer with a smile. He's betting between five and twenty dollars a hand.

He laughs and then begins to have a coughing fit—like a smoker. "Son, back in the day, you could get a blow job for fifty cents."

"No shit?" I laugh.

He nods before taking a drag from his cigar and blowing it out. The smell of cinnamon fills the air. "Women back then were much more enthusiastic. I was in the Navy. Fleet week..." He trails off with a whistle.

I bet they were. I pick up my cards and look them over with a smile. I choose one to put down.

I feel her more than see her return to stand behind me. The dealer places the card down, and I jump in my seat. "Woohoo!" I won.

Placing my cigar between my lips, I sit up and dig into my pocket. I pull out five one hundred-dollar bills and hold them out to her. "Go play your favorite machine." Lucy isn't a girl you have to buy. No, she gives that shit up for free. But I don't mind sharing.

"Thanks, baby," she says excitedly and then bounces off.

The thing about being in any casino is that you lose track of time.

No clocks. No windows. You could literally sit there for as long as your bladder can hold on while you're on a winning streak. But when I finally stand from the table, I check my phone to see that I had been sitting there for three hours. I have two calls from my brother. One from Cross and two from Titan. I go to our group message and send a quick text.

Me: What's up?

Then I place it back in my pocket. I walk between the dinging machines, coming up to the one that has big red and yellow fish on it. Lucy sits there with one leg on her chair and the other on the platform the machine sits on. I plop down next to her. "How you doin'?"

She looks at me and growls. "Shitty. You?"

"Fucking fantastic."

She rolls her eyes dramatically. "Of course. You're always lucky."

"It has nothing to do with luck," I tell her.

She throws her head back with a laugh. "You're so full of yourself."

I lean into her neck and kiss her. "You're going to be full of me."

"Yes, please." She turns her head and places her lips on mine. "Let's go upstairs to my place." She breathes, pulling away.

She jumps into my lap with a squeal, and I slap her thigh. "Let's go," I order.

The Airport sits on about two hundred and fifty acres with the original five-story airport structure and an underground level, which is where the tables and machines are located. Connected to the Airport is the Mason Towers. Two towers that were once hotels for those flying in and out when the airport was still in service. The Mason Brothers have redone them over the years and turned them into apartments they rent out.

We make our way to the towers and take the elevator up to her penthouse. As soon as I open her door, she's pushing me toward her room. We start down the hallway when she shoves my back into a wall and digs into the pocket of her jean shorts. "I got a surprise for you." She sticks it on her tongue, then runs it along my lips. I capture her lips with mine and take the pill from her. She pulls away, panting.

"Yours?" I ask.

"Already took it."

Tossing her key to the floor, she rips my shirt up and over my head while I do the same to hers as we make it the rest of the way to her bedroom. She pushes my jeans down, and they get caught around my ankles, causing me to trip.

She giggles as she pushes her shorts down her legs before falling on top of me, not even bothering to wait for us to make it to her bed. Kicking my jeans the rest of the way off, I grab her hips and flip us so I'm straddling her.

She leans up and runs her tongue over the spike I have through my nipple. And I moan when she wraps her lips around it.

My hands grip her blond hair, and I yank her head back. Her mouth is open, and she pants. "How do you want it?" I ask. She goes to speak, but I say, "Never mind. I know how *I* want it." I crawl off her, grab her hips, and flip her over. Then I'm yanking her ass up in the air. My hand comes down on it—*hard*—leaving an instant red print. She buries her face in the carpet, releasing a moan.

"Grave." She pants, wiggling her ass up in the air for me because she knows exactly what I'm going to take tonight.

THREE

GRAVE

THE RINGING OF my phone has me opening my eyes to a dark room. I fall out of her bed and hit the floor with a thud, then moan at the pain that shoots up my side. It rings again, and I see it lighting up on the floor at the end of the bed. Crawling to it, I answer. "Hello?"

"Where the fuck are you?" my brother demands.

I had messaged the group text earlier, but I never checked my phone again after that. I was too busy with Lucy to fucking care what they wanted. "What time is it?" I ask roughly. My tongue sticks to the roof of my mouth. Feels like sandpaper.

"Are you high? Of course, you are," he growls, answering his own question. "Are you at Kingdom?"

"No." I run a hand through my hair, finding my way back into the bed. Lying down, I reach over to my right in the darkness to feel Lucy lying next to me, naked and sound asleep. "What ... What do you want?" I clear my throat. Fuck, I need a drink to wash down this taste.

He sighs heavily, his anger fading, and my body stiffens. "We've been trying to reach you. I got a call last night ..." He trails off, and my grip on the phone tightens. "It's Dad, he's ..."

I lie silently in the darkness, completely and utterly still, waiting for him to say the words that I already know are coming.

"I'm sorry, Kyle." He uses my real name, and my heart begins to pound in my chest. He never calls me that. *I'm Grave.* I've always been known as Grave, even to him. "Dad passed last night. He was found dead in his condo. They're saying it was ..."

I hang up.

The motherfucker is dead.

I saw him at our friend Luca's engagement party, but I avoided him. I haven't spoken to him in over six months. Before that, it had been at least three. He called to tell me that he was disappointed in the life I chose. That he didn't approve of the drugs and women. As if I should settle down and get married—give him grandbabies.

I snort at that thought.

He never wanted to claim me as his. He referred to me as my mother's child. Dillan was his favorite. He taught him everything he knows. Wanted to make a man out of him and groomed him for the family *business.* It never fucking mattered that Dillan and I do the same thing for a living. My brother may not do drugs, but he has his addictions. And my father knew them well. He just shared the same ones, so to him, they were a perfect father and son duo.

I get out of bed and use my phone as a light to make it out of her room, down the hall, and to her kitchen. The light streaming in from her floor-to-ceiling windows allows me to see better than the one on my phone. Grabbing a bottle of Jack, I remove the lid and then toss it back, trying to drown out any memory I have of him. He doesn't deserve my time.

"Grave?" Lucy calls out. Standing in the center of the kitchen, she's leaning up against her island. "Grave, what's wrong?" She walks over to me and flips on the light.

Her blond hair is wild, and she blinks several times, her eyes trying to focus on me.

My body shakes, and I take another gulp, the drink burning my chest. When her eyes finally find mine, she looks from my face to the bottle. She reaches out for me, placing her hands on my chest, but I push her away. "Not now," I mutter.

"What happened?" she asks, fear lacing her words.

My phone rings in my hand and **Bones** lights up the screen. I silence it and then turn it off before tossing the fucker on the counter. I walk back to her bedroom, shove open the French doors to her bathroom, then slam them shut behind me. Placing my hands on her white marble counter, I bow my head, trying to ignore the fucking hole in my chest that's growing by the second.

It's gonna be okay. I can turn it off like I did all those years ago after I lost the only woman I've ever loved. I'll never forget what that fucker told me when we lost our mother. The only parent who loved me for me.

Seventeen years old

I stand at the front of the church. My brother stands next to me. He stares down at our mother, not a single tear in his eyes. His face a blank canvas. He's like our father. Tears run down my cheeks, and my shoulders shake. I'm having trouble breathing, and my chest aches.

"Mr. Reed, we're about to open the doors to friends and family who want to pay their respects before the service," the woman says to my father.

He comes to stand on the other side of me and nods his head.

I can't look away from our mother. She doesn't look like herself. Her skin is yellow, and her face appears swollen. They didn't do her makeup how she wore it. Her hair is teased at the top and fanned around her face. She never wore it like that, though. It was always curled.

My brother waits another beat and then turns and walks away, heading back down the aisle. Probably to go find his fuck outside to suck his dick in a back room somewhere. The only thing he allows himself to feel is her. Anything else is just background noise.

Placing my hands on the wooden casket, I clench the satin lining that covers the sides. I go to lean forward to kiss her cheek, but a firm grip on my shoulder yanks me back, and I'm spun around. My father leans down to put his face in front of mine. Blue eyes glaring at me. "Pull yourself together!" he growls before roughly wiping my face of my tears. They just fall faster. "Death is a part of life. And you're making a spectacle of your mother's funeral. Turn it off."

"Dad ..." I sniff.

"You're seventeen. Not five! Turn it fucking off, Kyle! It's just an emotion. You have control of your mind to overcome something so insignificant," he finishes and then straightens. He doesn't even look back at my mother as he grabs my arm and drags me to our seats in the front row.

I lift my head to look at myself in the bathroom mirror. "I will feel nothing for you," I say to myself. A sick part of me hopes he can fucking hear me as he burns in hell. All he cared about was Kingdom. His precious fucking *club* that was there for him day in and day out. It gave him life. Money. Women.

I yank open the doors to find Lucy standing naked at the end of her bed with my phone in her hand. She can turn it back on if she chooses, but she doesn't know the code, so she can't unlock it. I grab her arm and push her onto the mattress.

"Grave, what are you ...?"

Gripping the back of her neck with my hand, I shove her face into the bed. "You."

Her body relaxes, and she gives in to what is about to come. I never did get the concept of feeling no emotions like my brother did. He was already pretty dead inside, but after Mom passed, he was a walking, talking zombie. I thought it was a shame, but my father praised him for it.

FOUR

GRAVE

"**W**HERE ARE YOU going?" Lucy asks, sitting up in her bed.

"I have somewhere to be," I lie, yanking my jeans up my legs.

She frowns but doesn't say anything else. She knows when I'm done, I'm done, and there's nothing she can do to make me stay.

"What are you doing tonight?" she asks.

"I don't know." I grab my shirt off the floor and slide it on. Fuck, I really need a shower and some clean clothes.

"Grave—"

"I'll call you," I interrupt her and exit her room. I make my way out of her penthouse and into her private elevator. As the doors close, I pull out my cell and press call.

"Hello?" Luca answers on the first ring.

"Hey, I'm out. You have anything?" I ask, leaning my head back against the wall. I get most of my shit from Luca Bianchi. My brother hates that he's my main supplier, but there's nothing he can do about it.

"Yeah, I'll swing by Kingdom later and drop some off."

"Sounds good. Thanks."

"Anytime."

We hang up as the door slides open, and I step off into the parking garage. I fall into my car, not really sure where I'm going but knowing I can't stay here any longer.

I'm not in love with Lucy and she's aware of that. Regardless of what she feels for me, she knows where she stands. And you have to respect a bitch who doesn't push something that she knows won't ever happen.

I drive through town, my radio blaring "Mansion" by NF on max volume to drown out all my thoughts. I haven't called my brother back, but he sent me a message an hour ago to call him. I didn't respond.

He's probably getting his morning wood sucked now. Since Titan is up for sharing his woman with him, he's probably drowning himself in Emilee. They have some fucked-up threesome thing going on.

I come up to a stoplight and sit there while a car with two girls pulls up next to me. They barely look sixteen. The driver smiles at me, and then her eyes run over my neck tattoo and sleeve, and her smile grows. I look away from her, staring straight ahead, not having the time to deal with a girl who has daddy issues. Most women who want to fuck me do it to piss off their fathers. The only flaw in their plans is that I don't ever stay around long enough to meet their dads.

The song changes to "MONSTERS" by Shinedown, and I rev my engine, waiting for the light to change as well. I look to my left and see a flower shop. It's got a blood-red awning and glass storefront. A red rose is painted on one of the windows. It reminds me of my mother.

Seventeen years old

The service is about to come to an end. We've only been to one other funeral before, and they had a picture of Aunt Beth and the front of the church was full of flowers.

My brother sits to my right, back ramrod straight. Emilee's hand in his on her lap. "Where are Mom's flowers?" I ask him.

He leans into me but keeps his eyes facing ahead. "Dad said no flowers. He didn't want them cluttering the house afterward."

I fist my hands. Dad hates them. Always said it's a waste of money to pay so much for something that is just going to die within a matter of days. "Mom loved flowers," I tell him.

He sighs heavily. Even he knows it isn't right, but he doesn't challenge Dad. I don't know why he cares so much about what Dad thinks of him. I guess if I were the chosen child, I would feel differently about the situation.

"Will you shut the fuck up, Kyle?" my father growls in my ear. "Show some fucking respect."

The light turns green, and I pull into a front row parking spot at the flower shop and come to a stop. Sitting in my car, I don't know what I'm doing. But without any more thought, I get out. I open the glass door that reads *Roses* and step inside. The smell of flowers hits me like a fucking punch to my face. It makes me nauseous. This is why my father never bought them for my mother. He hated the way they smelled and what they represented—life.

I don't want to be anything like him.

"Hello?" I ask when I don't see anyone behind the counter in front of me.

I look to my left and a row of glass doors holds all sorts of flowers inside. Each door is labeled with its contents.

"Hello?" I call out a little louder.

Still nothing. I look to the other side, and there are shelves of vases in various sizes. Some are just your simple glass, but others have been painted. I walk over and pick up one that has a beach scene on it. A big, bright yellow sun is setting in the background, giving the beach a soft yellow glow. The waves are rolling in, and the sand has seashells on it. It makes me want a vacation. I don't even remember the last time I went on one.

I set it down and walk over to the counter. There's a bell and a sign that reads—*ring if not at counter.* I ring it twice. "Hello?" I call out again.

My phone vibrates, and I dig it out of my pocket. It's a message from my brother.

> Bones: Where the hell are you? I'm at
> Kingdom.

I ignore him and put my phone away. "Anyone here?" I shout and ring the bell again.

Turning back to face the door, I double-check the open sign and see that they are. I push off the counter and walk past it farther into the shop. There's a door behind the counter, and I push it open, thinking it's an office. I storm in to go off on whoever has abandoned their duties but come to a stop when I enter.

It's not an office. It's a freezer of some type. A shiver runs over me as the cold hits me, instantly soaking into my skin and chilling my bones. I hate cold weather. But that's not what has me pausing. It's the girl in front of me. She faces me, but her head is down, and there is a glass vase in front of her on a white table. She is cutting the stems off a set of yellow lilies before placing them in the vase. Then she picks up the white ribbon next to her. She pulls it off the spool to where she wants it and cuts it.

I take a second to look over her. She wears a pair of faded blue jeans with the knees torn out. They sit low on her narrow hips. A white shirt that has a big red rose in the center. One petal has fallen off and lies below it by itself. And it reads *until the last petal* in black ink at the top. Her hair is a vibrant purple that she has pulled up into two messy buns.

Her hips sway back and forth, and her head bounces up and down gently. An iPhone sits next to the arrangement she is still working on and earbuds are in her ear.

She's listening to music. That's why she didn't hear me calling for assistance.

I stand just watching her. My body shivering slightly from the coldness. It doesn't seem to bother her.

She stands back and examines her work with a smile. Straight white teeth beam proudly at her work. Her plump lips are covered in the same shade as her hair.

Picking it up, she turns and places it on the fourth shelf. She has to stand on her tiptoes to reach, and the back of her shirt rides up, showing off two little dimples and sun-kissed skin. My eyes travel up over her back, and it's hard not to notice the straps of a black bra that you can see through her thin white shirt. If you're paying attention like I am. I get to her hair and see she has two braids on either side running up to the two messy buns.

She gets it where she wants it and spins around. That's when she screams, pulling me out of my trance. She shoves her back into the shelves, making them rattle, and rips the earbuds out of her ears. She places her hand on her chest, and her tits bounce up and down from her heavy breathing. Ice blue eyes meet mine, and she swallows nervously as they take in my face. Her gaze lingers on my eyebrow ring, before dropping to my lip ring and then moves to my neck tattoo that peeks out from underneath my shirt before they go to the sleeve I have on my right arm.

"Sorry," I announce, raising my hands to let her know I'm not about to rob her. Or worse. I know what women think when they first see me. Most don't like tattoos and piercings. They call us thugs. "I rang the bell ..."

Her body instantly relaxes, and she takes a deep breath. Then her laughter fills the small room. It's light and innocent. "I'm so sorry," she apologizes, her voice shakes a little from the near heart attack I just gave her.

"I didn't know we were open yet," she adds when I just stand here.

I frown and point my thumb back to the closed door to this ice box we're in. "The sign said open."

She stops laughing and steps back up to the table. "Have you been waiting long?" She places the scissors in her back pocket and then grabs the spool of ribbon.

"Maybe five minutes."

"I'm so sorry about that." Walking over to me, she opens the door and gestures for me to exit, and I notice the silver hoop—a septum piercing. A row of little diamonds. It's dainty and barely noticeable at first glance.

I place my hand on the door above her head and hold it open. "Ladies first."

She gives me a kind smile and walks out. She takes a hard right, and I follow her, taking us deeper into the shop. She comes to a new door and rips it open. A younger, teenage boy sits behind an old wooden desk. His mop of dark hair is covering his eyes. His arms crossed over his chest, and his head is back as the chair looks like he's about to fall backward. *The kid's asleep.*

She walks over to the desk and shoves his feet off the scratched surface. He jumps up, eyes springing open. "What ...?"

"We had a customer. What are you doing in here sleeping?" she snaps at him.

He pushes the long dark strands from his face. "It was an accident ..."

"Go make some arrangements in the cooler," she orders.

He nods once and mumbles, "Yes, ma'am."

She seems satisfied with that and turns back to exit but comes to a stop when she sees me. Her eyes meeting mine, and I instantly begin to back out. I didn't mean to follow her in here. "Sorry," I say again.

She walks out and goes to stand behind the counter. "What can I get you?"

"Uh ..." Words get lodged in my throat as my mind runs wild. *Why did I even come in here?* I'm not going to buy flowers for my father's funeral. And our mother is buried in another state, so it's not like I can go place flowers on her grave. She moved here when she was sixteen and met my father. They got married right after she graduated high school. When she passed, he had her body moved to her home state of Illinois. Like she'd know the fucking difference. I think he just wanted to get rid of her. Out of sight, out of mind type of thing. And a way to punish me so I wouldn't get to visit her grave.

I run a hand through my hair. "What do you suggest?"

"Is this for a girlfriend? Wife?" she asks, and I don't miss her eyes dropping to my left hand to check for a ring.

I almost choke at the question. Clearing my throat, I shake my head. "Neither." I've never bought flowers for Lucy before, and I'm not about to start now. The only time I've ever purchased flowers were for my mother. On her birthday. She died five months later. "My mom's birthday," I say and instantly tense. It's eight months away, and she's fucking dead.

What am I doing?

She beams at me, her ice blue eyes shining with excitement. Her purple painted lips pull back into a big smile. She's gorgeous. I've never seen anything like her before. So colorful. So real. I find myself leaning toward her. My hips pushing into the counter.

"What do you have in mind?" she asks.

"What do you suggest?" I ask again, my eyes following the line of her square jaw and full lips.

She begins to rattle off all the options of arrangements and various flowers, and it makes my head hurt. I'm still feeling whatever pill Lucy gave me last night. "Why don't you surprise me?" I offer.

Her smile widens, and it's beautiful. Reminds me of that sunset I saw painted on the vase when I walked in. "When do you need it by?"

"Thursday." I almost roll my eyes at that.

She nods and writes that down.

"I'm sorry if that's last minute." I add.

Liar.

She shakes her head. "No worries." Then she looks up at me through her long, dark lashes. They're lined with thick black liner that fans out to the side. Lucy refers to it as cat eyes. "I apologize you had to wait."

It was worth it sits on my tongue, but instead, I wave her off. "It's okay. I'm sorry I frightened you."

"Here." She gives me the paper that she had written on. "Write down your name and the best number to reach you at. I will give you a call as soon as they are ready."

I bend over and begin to write down my information.

"Will you need them delivered?" she asks.

I put the pen down and push it back over to her. "Nope. I'll pick them up." Then I turn and walk out, but one of the vases she has sitting on the shelf catches my attention. "Are these for sale?" I ask, turning back to her and pointing at them.

"Yes."

Walking over, I pick up a black vase that has a dark purple butterfly on it. The inner wings fade to a dark pink. It too reminds me of my mother. She loved butterflies. She had this picture that she kept in the family room of two butterflies sitting in a field. She loved it. My father had it boxed up and sold at an auction after she passed.

I place it on the counter. My eyes lift from the butterfly to hers, and I notice the purple color of the body matches her hair and lips perfectly. "I'll take this one." Before she can say anything else, I turn and get the hell out of the shop.

APRIL

I watch the man exit the front door and then I turn to the cooler door and barge in. "Just what do you think you were doing?" I bark at my little brother.

He stands behind the small table, trying to make an arrangement for the Blitz wedding this weekend. Stopping, he looks up at me and releases a sigh. His blue eyes are heavy, and he has bags under them. His band T-shirt and ripped jeans look like he picked them up off his bedroom floor this morning.

"What time did you get in last night?" I ask him. I went to bed at midnight, and he wasn't home yet.

"Late." Comes his clipped answer.

"Where were you?" I pry.

"At a party."

He's lying. "Ethan ..." My younger brother is my responsibility. I have to protect him, but he fights me every step of the way. I'm only three years older than him. Since he still lives with me, he thinks he's the man of the house and that he can do whatever he wants.

"Just stop, April. I don't need you going all mom on me. It's too early, and I'm too tired."

I refrain from rolling my eyes at him. "I'm gonna cook spaghetti tonight. Your favorite." I try changing the subject.

"I won't be home until late."

"Where are you going?" I ask through thin lips.

"Out," he says.

"Ethan, you need to get some sleep."

He just ignores me.

I run my hands over my jeans and close my eyes. "Are you in trouble?" I ask. It's been my biggest fear for a while now. He didn't always hang with the best crowd. Between getting thrown out of school on multiple occasions and his run-ins with the law, he's already on a dangerous path. He snorts, and my eyes spring open.

"No."

"I'm serious, Ethan. I'm worried about you. You're never home. You're sleeping at work ..."

He slams down the glass vase onto the table. "You wanted to keep this fucking store!" he roars. "Not me!"

I swallow nervously. "It's all we had left of Mom," I whisper, and my chest tightens. How could he not want to keep a part of her? This was all she had to leave us. Every time I walk into Roses, I think of her. I see her. I smell her. In a way, she lives on as long as I'm here. This was her life. Her dream. I couldn't sell it to someone else who would most likely close it and turn it into another coffee shop.

He places his hands on the table and bows his head. "I know." He growls, pushing off the table. "You wanted this, April. I didn't." Then he shoves past me and out the cooler door.

I follow him back through the flower shop and into the office. "Where are you going?" I ask when he yanks his jacket off the back of the chair.

"Out." Comes his clipped answer. "And don't wait up for me tonight."

It's seven in the morning. "Ethan?" I call out as he makes his way to the front door.

He doesn't respond or stop before he shoves the front door open and storms out. I walk back into the office and plop down into the chair. I rip both of my buns out and run my hands through the back of my hair to undo the braids, allowing my hair to fall over my shoulders and down my back. It was giving me a headache. Looking down at the floor, I see what looks like a key card to a hotel room of some sort. A black circle is in the middle with a gold K in the center. Then below that it says *Kingdom Members Only*.

It must have fallen out of his jacket pocket. I fist it in my hand and sigh.

FIVE

GRAVE

I PULL INTO the private parking garage at Kingdom and bring my car to a stop. Walking up to our elevator, I scan my card and step inside. I make my way up to the thirteenth floor and walk off the elevator, stepping onto the white marble floor. The receptionist looks up at me, but I ignore her and head straight down the hall to the back. The four of us each have our own office, but I'm headed to my brother's. He hates it when he has to hunt me down, so I might as well get this over with.

Shoving his door open, I refrain from sighing. My brother sits behind his desk. The black curtains behind him are pulled tight since it's a nice day outside. He has a problem with sunshine. Anything that has life to it, he likes to black it out. Just like our father did.

Titan leans up against the wall to his left. Arms crossed over his chest and ankles crossed. He wears a pair of jeans, plain black T-shirt, and a scowl on his face.

Cross sits in one of the chairs in front of the desk. Holding a Zippo in his hand, he flips it open and closed.

They all look at me as I shut the door, but no one says a word. "I didn't know we were having a meeting today." I fall into the seat next to Cross.

My brother leans back, the oversized black leather chair squeaking at his movement. "We need to talk."

"If it's about Dad, you can save it." I dismiss him. I have nothing to say on the matter.

"It's about you," Titan growls.

I turn to look at him, wondering what's up his ass. Ever since he got with Emilee, he's been much more pleasurable to be around. "What about me?" I ask, not caring.

"We need to talk about the incident last week," my brother answers.

"What incident?" I ask, but I already know what it's regarding. Do they think they can corner me and expect me to talk because of their half-assed attempt at an intervention? They don't know me very well if that's what they think.

Titan pushes off the wall, eyes narrowed down on me. "Emilee thought you were dead."

I run my hands down my shirt and jeans to where I grab my cock. It's still hard from seeing the woman with the purple hair at the flower shop. I never did get her name, but I've decided I'm going to call her Petal. She's as delicate as a petal. "As you can see, I'm very much alive."

"Goddammit, Grave!" My brother slams his hand down on the black desk. "This is a serious matter."

It's one of his favorite lines to yell at me.

"You terrified her," Titan adds, and I snort.

Cross and I sit in the living room of the Royal Suite—the suite the Kings and I share here at Kingdom.

Titan is working, of course, and Bones left earlier today to go to New York for whatever reason. He never tells me shit.

I throw back the glass of bourbon and stand. Swaying on my feet, my vision blurs. "Fuck ..." I slur.

"Yeah," Cross agrees, falling off the couch and onto the floor. We

both laugh. "This shit is good."

I take a step toward the open kitchen, but trip and fall on my face. My heavy eyes close, and I let out a long breath.

I woke up to Emilee kneeling beside me, shaking my body while screaming in my face. She called Titan, and he called Bones. I had passed out. It wasn't something new or life threatening, but she freaked the fuck out and tattled.

I lean back, crossing my arms over my chest. "Cross was just as fucked up as I was." I rat my best friend out like the child I am.

"Hey, don't bring me into this." Cross places his hands up in the air, surrendering immediately.

"Emilee didn't find Cross passed out on the floor. She found you," Titan growls.

I smile up at him. "Does she have feelings for me, T?" His nostrils flare. "Better make sure to keep her in check, or before you know it, she'll be asking me to join in while you fuck her." I wink at my brother. "Bones shouldn't get all the fun."

Titan lunges for me. His hands hit my chest so hard my chair falls back. We crash to the floor, and I roll to my right as Cross yanks Titan off me.

I sit on the floor staring up at an infuriated Titan. His chest rises and falls fast, and a growl comes from deep in his chest. His hands fist, and when I think he's about to hit me, he turns and storms out without another word, yanking the door open so hard it hits the interior wall with a thud before it slams itself shut.

I reach up to see if my nose is bleeding. I'm surprised when I see no blood. I think it was his elbow that connected with it.

"Give us a minute," my brother tells Cross.

He exits, and I pick myself up off the floor. I tilt my head back, still waiting for the blood to come oozing out. Bones comes around the desk and leans his ass against it, crossing his arms over his chest. His black button-down strains against his muscular, inked arms. "Why do you do that?" he asks.

I don't answer.

He sighs. "Why do you take a serious situation and ruin it by opening your mouth?"

I snort. "How did you think that conversation was going to go?"

He bows his head and runs his hand through his dark hair. "You have a drug problem."

My palms begin to sweat. He's never said it out loud before. We both ignore it. "Well, I'm sorry but not all of us can turn everything off."

"Is that what you think I do?" he asks, frowning.

"It doesn't matter what you do." I shake my head, not caring. "You deal with you, and I'll deal with me." I go to exit, but his next words stop me.

"You're all I have left, Grave."

I swallow and close my eyes. He and I were always close. Him and the Kings are only one year older than me, but he's always been my big brother. When our father wouldn't teach me to play baseball because he wanted Dillan to be the star, Dillan taught me. When it came time for me to drive, Dillan taught me how to in his car. He gave me my first beer. First cigarette. He was the one who showed me how to be a man.

"I want you to get help," he adds, filling the silence.

I straighten my shoulders, not bothering to turn to face him. "And I want you to stay out of my business."

"Kyle?" He sighs, and I swallow the lump that forms in my throat. "Mom's been gone for eight years."

My entire body goes rigid. He never mentions her. "Your point?" I snap.

"Now Dad is gone."

I spin around on him with my face scrunched in anger. "So you didn't feel shit when Mom passed, but now that that son of a bitch is dead, you're gonna feel something?"

"That's not what this is," he growls, his blue eyes narrowing on me.

"Then what the fuck is it? 'Cause that's how it sounds."

He looks away from me, and I see the tic in his jawline right where his neck tattoo comes to a stop. He took me to get my first tattoo when I turned eighteen. It was actually on my birthday. He already had his first one. I remember the next day when I saw Dad, and he was pissed at me. Said I was trying to be like Dillan and he didn't raise sheep. I shouldn't do something just because my brother did. I told him to go to hell and immediately went and got another one.

"You're going to hurt yourself if you don't stop," he finally says, avoiding my previous question about our parents.

I snort. "Yeah, because you're so cautious with your life."

"It's different," he growls.

"How is it any fucking different?"

"I'm not feeding myself full of drugs," he snaps, pushing off the desk.

"No. Instead, you're too busy killing people and fucking your best friend's woman." I turn toward the door.

"Grave?" he demands.

"Fuck you, Dillan!" I throw over my shoulder as I go to walk out of his office door, but he yanks me back by my shirt and slams my back into the wall. Both of his hands grip the collar of my shirt, and his blue eyes are glaring into mine. *He's pissed.* I've always known what buttons to push when it comes to my brother. I like the fight, and as much as he hates to admit it, he does too. This is one of his vices. We're the same—he and I—I just don't choose to hide it.

"Say that to my face," he growls as his nostrils flare.

I lick my lips, lift my chin, and smirk. "Fuck you ..."

He yanks me from the wall and shoves me away. My feet get caught up in his rug, and I find myself once again on the floor. I roll onto my back and close my eyes. *Fuck, I should have stayed in bed with Lucy.*

"Get the fuck up!" he shouts. "Go home and get some sleep. We're leaving first thing tomorrow."

I sit up and rub the back of my neck. I need something for the pain because my head is pounding. "Where are we going?" I couldn't care less.

"To Rio," he growls.

I start shaking my head. "I'm not going."

He walks over to me, standing at my feet, staring down at me still on the floor. "Yes, you are. We're going to go identify our father's body and then we're going to lay him to rest." With that, he storms out of his office, slamming his door shut.

I fall back down onto his floor and let out a long sigh. *Fuck my life.*

Getting up off his floor, I walk down the hall and see Titan standing in his office with his back to the glass on his cell phone. Probably talking to Emilee. Cross stands at the receptionist desk, leaning over it and looking down her white silk blouse.

When he sees me, he straightens and walks away from her while she's midsentence. "Where are you going?" he asks me.

"Out," I answer and punch on the elevator. If I'm going to be stuck with my brother for a few days while we take an eighteen-hour trip to Rio, I'm going to get fucked up.

It opens immediately. I enter, and he follows me.

"Wanna go to Glass? They're serving breakfast," he offers.

The best thing about strip clubs in a town that never sleeps means they never close. I open my mouth to say yes but pause. "What happened to you the other night?"

"I left with Mandi. Then I was gonna come back, but when I called, you were already in the car with Bones. He came and got you."

I lean my head back against the mirrored wall. "Did you take my pill bottle?" I ask.

He shakes his head, pulling out his Zippo and flipping it open and closed.

"Then it had to have been Bones." *Fucker!*

"Not surprised. They're worried about you."

I snort. "Not you too?"

He gives me a smile. "I said they."

That makes me laugh. Cross and I are a lot alike. We just don't give a shit about a lot of things. Titan and Bones are the serious ones, always crunching numbers and wanting to chase down men and demand payment in blood.

Kingdom doesn't deal with minor shit. From the outside, we look like a legit hotel and casino with hundreds of attractions, but on the inside, we're as dark as the fucking world can go.

We deal with drug lords, celebrities, heirs to billionaires. My brother even deals with the mafia. To him, money is money. Doesn't matter whose hand it comes from. That's our dad in him.

Titan is the same fucking way. That's how he got Emilee, and the bastard just so happened to fall in love with her.

The elevator dings, and the doors slide open. I push off the mirrored wall and walk into the underground garage. This elevator is for the four Kings only.

I unlock my car, and the lights blink. "Glass?" Cross asks.

I almost forgot he was with me. I look down at my Patek Phillippe watch and nod. "Sure. I could use some food." Maybe it will get rid of this fucking headache. "Then we can make another stop afterward."

He nods.

"Get in. I'll drive us." I pull my cell out and send Luca a quick message.

Me: Change of plans, I'm coming to you.

Luca owns the other half of Glass. His silent partner is my brother. Might as well get my shit from him there instead of him having to make a trip to Kingdom where Bones can see the exchange.

Luca: Sounds good. I'm here.

APRIL

"WHAT ARE YOU doing, Princess?"

I plop down on the barstool and look up at my best friend working the bar. She has her bleach blond hair up in her usual high ponytail and a smile on her face, but her green eyes look tired. Running two businesses will do that to you.

"Needing a drink," I answer. It's been a long day.

She frowns. "You mean you didn't come just to see me?"

I chuckle. "Afraid not."

"Sis, we both know that she only comes here to see me." Derek walks out of the fridge behind the bar, closing the door behind him. "How are you doing, sexy?" he asks, and I don't miss the way his dark eyes fall to my chest.

Derek and I went on one date. It didn't work out. But we're both adults and were able to stay friends. Thank God because his younger sister has been my best friend since we were in grade school.

"You wish." She smiles brightly, showing me those teeth that took three years of braces to straighten. She hated every second of it. I remember her having to cut up everything she ate. It took forever for her to eat.

"Always," I tease.

She laughs and turns to grab a frosted mug and pours me a Corona. Knowing what I like. She places it on the bar in front of me and then leans over on her forearms. "I'm slow. Fill me in on your day."

"It started off with me getting in a fight with Ethan this morning. It didn't get any better after that," I state and take a drink.

"Girl, I don't know why you don't just beat him into submission. We both know that you could take him."

I snort into my beer. "True, but I'm trying to teach him that violence is not the answer."

Now she's the one who snorts. "Since when? You beat the crap out of him when he got into your computer and stole your research paper and used it as his own."

"That's different," I argue.

"How?"

I set my beer down. "Because Mr. Walden thought I had just freely given it to him, thinking he wouldn't remember." I sigh.

"Anything you need me to do?" Derek asks. "Want me to talk to him about something? Is it girls?"

I shake my head. "I found a key card of some sort from Kingdom at the shop today. I think it fell out of his jacket pocket."

"What?" she asks. "How the hell would he get in there?"

I shrug. "I'm not sure what the hell he would be doing with that."

Derek's dark eyes look around before he leans forward and whispers, "Kingdom is bad fucking news, April."

I wave him off. "It's just a casino."

"No. I hear shit in here. Kingdom is into some bad shit."

I've lived in Vegas most of my life, but I know nothing about the casinos or nightlife. I have always lived in my own world. From the moment my mother opened Roses, I worked there with her. Before school. After school. Even after I turned twenty-one, I never ventured out onto the Strip. It's just not my scene. "Like what?" I frown.

"Yeah? Like what?" she asks him.

"I hear that the guy, Bones, is in big with the mafia. Whatever they want, he gets them. Vice versa. And they bury bodies in the desert."

"Mafia? Really?" I laugh. "Since when do you believe in that shit?" I know they exist. But in Vegas? They're in places like New York, Chicago, and Italy. "And what could this Bones guy get them?"

He shrugs. "I don't know exactly. I just know that anything goes there. I guess there's some sort of black market that the guys run."

"Illegally?"

He rolls his dark eyes. "That's what black market stands for."

I'm still not sure I believe it. But even if I did, I ask, "What would Ethan have to do with that?"

He shakes his head. "You need to find out. And better hope that it's not too late to get him out of it."

Alexa frowns. "He's a teenage boy. Maybe some friends of his had a party there or something." She shrugs. "Kids do it all the time."

"Or it's something much worse," Derek argues.

I sigh and tip back my beer as he goes to help a man who just walked up to the bar.

My brother better not be into some shady shit, or I will beat him so badly he won't be able to sit down for a week. He forgets that I can knock his ass out. I've done it before. Many, many years ago. But a woman doesn't forget how to fight. It's like sex. Another thing I haven't done in a while. When your body is put in that situation, it just knows what to do. Instincts take over. And cravings need to be satiated.

"What are you going to do?" Alexa asks me.

I shrug. "Not sure just yet."

"Well ..." She slaps the bar top. "How about we go out tomorrow night?"

"How is that going to help me?" I arch a brow.

"It won't, but you need to have some fun and let loose. When was the last time you went out and had some fun?"

I sigh. "I don't know."

"Exactly. I have this girlfriend who's having a party. I actually have a night off. It'll be fun."

"Girlfriend, huh? Have something to tell me?"

She laughs. "Trust me, April, if I was trading teams, you'd be the first one to know." She winks at me, and I throw my head back laughing.

SIX
GRAVE

I LOOK OUT the oval window in my brother's private jet. All I see are clouds, but it's better than the judging looks he's been giving me since he picked me up and dragged my ass onto his plane this morning.

"Here you go, Grave," his flight attendant, Nicki, announces as she comes over to my seat. "Sure you don't want anything, Bones?" she asks him.

He shakes his head once without even bothering to look up at her.

"Thank you," I tell Nicki and throw it back. Setting it on the table between my brother and me, I notice his eyes on mine. Then they drop to the now empty glass. "If you didn't want me to drink, then you shouldn't keep your bar stocked," I say matter-of-factly.

He runs a hand through his hair and looks away from me. He's clearly still very pissed.

"Why are you fucking your best friend's fiancée?" I come out and ask.

"What me and Emilee do does not concern you," he snaps.

"My other question is why would Titan allow that?" I go on

when he doesn't say anything. "I mean, if I was engaged, I wouldn't let you go anywhere near my pussy ..."

"Enough!" he shouts.

I cross my arms over my chest and smirk at him.

"Again, what we do is none of your business," he says in an annoyed tone.

My phone vibrates, and I look down at it to see a message from Lucy.

Lucy: I'm lonely. Come over and fuck me.

I type back a response.

Me: Can't. Out of town.

It vibrates immediately with a sad face. I lock the screen and place it back down on the table.

"I want you to go to rehab," Bones states.

I snort. "Stay out of my life, and I'll stay out of yours."

"Grave." He sighs and looks at me. His dark blue eyes look exhausted. My brother runs too much and rarely sleeps. "I made Mom a promise."

I throw my head back and laugh, my chest shaking. "And you're deciding now that you want to honor it? She's been dead for eight years, Dillan."

"Goddammit, Grave," he growls softly, shaking his head. "I'm trying here."

"No, Dad is dead, so now you're going to try to take over that role." The truth is, he has always been more of a dad to me than our father ever was. And I owe him everything for that, but I can't change who I am. I don't want to change who I am.

"I can't do this again," he whispers.

"Do what?" I look around for Nicki. *Where the fuck did she go?* I told her to keep them coming when I boarded his plane. "Act like you care?"

"Of course, I care." He slams his fist down on the table. "We buried our mother, Kyle. Now Dad ..." He sighs. "Is it so awful that I don't want to bury you too?"

I swallow the lump in my throat and avert my eyes.

"I know what you think." He fills the awkward silence. "That Mom's death didn't affect me, but it did."

I lift my eyes to look at him, and he's staring out his window.

"I did what I had to do for you. You needed me more than ever after she passed. And I'm sorry if I did a shitty job."

Just then, Nicki comes up to our seats and hands me another drink. I take it from her hand and say the only thing I can think to say. "It's too late to make up for lost time." Standing from my seat, I make my way to the back of the plane. I open the bathroom door, and slam it shut, locking him out. I dig into my pocket and pull out the pill bottle that I got from Luca yesterday when Cross and I went up to Glass. I pop the lid and wash two pills down with my new drink.

I can't handle this flight with my brother sober. Especially if he's going to bring up our past.

APRIL

I STAND IN the middle of a grand foyer in a black cocktail dress with a glass of champagne in one hand and my clutch in the other. "How long are we going to be here?" I ask Alexa.

"I just wanted to make an appearance. I promised her we would come," she whispers.

"Who?" I ask before taking another sip of my drink.

"Alexa," a woman calls out, coming toward us. She wears a white one-shoulder dress that comes midthigh. It has to be designer and cost a small fortune. Her red hair is cut short and parted to the side, tucked behind her ear. She raises her arms, opening them to welcome Alexa in for a hug. "I'm so glad you made it."

Alexa hugs her and then pulls away. "Of course." She steps to the side and gestures to me. "April, this is Jasmine. Jasmine, this is my best friend, April."

"It's nice to meet you." She surprises me by pulling me in for a hug.

"You too," I say when we separate. "How do you two know each other?" I ask.

"Oh, Jasmine knows everyone," a woman says, joining the conversation. She wears a turquoise minidress, showing off a set of long legs. It dips down low in the front, and she wears a black choker around her neck. Her dark hair is down in big waves. "Hi." She reaches out her right hand, and I don't miss the huge rock that covers her ring finger on her left hand that holds her champagne flute. "I'm Emilee."

"Nice to meet you. I'm April."

"It's true." Jasmine nods once. "I do know everyone. It's because I'm so relatable."

Emilee snorts, making Alexa laugh.

"So what's the occasion?" I wonder.

"I just bought the place." Jasmine smiles, holding her hands out wide. "Thought I'd have a party to break it in."

I nod. "Well, it's a gorgeous place." It's an understatement. The house is a fucking mansion with all the amenities that make places like this worth millions. Marble floors, crystal chandeliers, and expensive artifacts. Once you entered the gated property, they had valet out front to park the cars. Men in suits stood outside at the front doors, and two stood inside to greet the guests. Butlers walk around with trays of champagne and finger foods. The only thing the party is missing is puppies as party favors.

"Thanks." She smiles at me. "But let's be honest, it's boring, right?"

"Oh, no," I say.

"Not at all," Alexa adds.

"It sucks balls," Emilee tells her before taking a sip of her champagne.

Jasmine sighs. "I know, right? Let's say fuck it and go out."

Emilee smiles brightly. "Yes. I could use a girls night. It's been too long."

"What about your guests?" I ask, taking a quick look around. There aren't really that many people present that I see. But then again, this house is massive, they could all be in a ballroom somewhere. We've only made it to the grand foyer.

Jasmine shrugs. "I don't care if they stay. I have enough security here to make sure nothing gets stolen. And Lord knows a riot isn't going to break out with this laid-back crowd. Most of them are my father's friends anyway. Any chance he gets to show off to them, he takes advantage of." She snaps her fingers. "Let me get my purse and cell really quick."

Alexa turns to face me after they walk away. "We won't stay out late."

I shrug. "It's no big deal. I won't be drinking much tonight."

The girls return, and we walk out the front double doors, down the steps, and to the right. I almost trip over my heels when I see the black Mercedes Maybach G650. I've always wanted one. When Alexa opens the back door for me, I slide in and sink into the leather, biting my lip so I don't groan at the softness.

I wonder what this chick does for a living. The size of her house … the cars … it has to be Daddy's money, right? I'm twenty-two, and she can't be much older than me. She did say that he likes to show off.

The remix of "Roses" by SAINt JHN starts blaring through the speakers as she pulls out of the driveway.

"Where are we going?" Emilee asks from the passenger seat.

Jasmine shrugs. "Wherever."

The music comes to a stop as she receives a text message. Her Bluetooth begins to speak to us. "You have an incoming message from **Big Daddy Dick**. *Landing early tomorrow morning. You going to be home?*"

Emilee starts laughing. "Who the fuck is Big Daddy Dick?"

Jasmine looks over at her and smiles. "No one you know." She picks up her cell out of the cup holder and hands it to Emilee. "Text him back."

"What do you want me to say?" She looks down at the phone.

"Say, I'll snort two lines of birth control just for you, Daddy."

Emilee frowns. "But you're on the shot."

"Dear Lord ..." Jasmine jerks the phone from her hands and tosses it to the back, and it lands on my lap. "Text the man, please?" she asks, looking at me in her rearview mirror.

Nodding, I open the text and do as she asks. "Done," I tell her.

"Thank you." She says.

"Is this some guy you fuck for free?" Emilee asks.

My eyes widen at that question. What the hell does that mean?

Jasmine snorts. "Honey, I'd pay to fuck this one. He's that good."

I look over at Alexa and she just shrugs. I've never heard her speak of these girls before, so I know she's not close with them.

Her Bluetooth picks up again. "You have an incoming message from **Big Daddy Dick** *you better meet me at the front doors on your knees wearing nothing but your red heels.*"

SEVEN
GRAVE

"WAKE UP." I hear my brother's voice far away.

I ignore it, but then a hand slaps my face, and I sit straight up. "Huh?"

"We're here," he growls, standing over me.

After I took the pills in the bathroom, I made my way to his bedroom in the back and passed out. Decided to sleep as much of the flight as I could.

Rubbing my heavy eyes, I crawl out of the bed. After sliding my shoes on, I lace them up and then follow him off the private jet. The heat is stifling, the sun is blinding, and the smell of the salty ocean is intoxicating. I hate the beach and the water. That's why I live in the desert.

A black Town Car waits for us with the back doors already open, so I climb in and then so does my brother. When the driver speaks to us, I look out the window and allow my brother to communicate with the man. My tongue feels swollen, and my head's still foggy. I need some water to drink.

The car takes off, and thankfully, my brother stays silent as we are delivered at our destination. Exiting the car, we walk up to a back door. Bones enters, and I follow him.

The smell of death instantly hits my nose, and I feel vomit start to rise. I begin to cough.

"Keep it down," my brother orders, and I pull on the collar of my T-shirt.

We're ushered into a back room with a table sitting in the middle. A white sheet covers it, and a man stands to the right. "Bones." He shakes his hand. "Grave." I just nod, crossing my arms over my chest. "I'm sorry you had to come such a long way—"

"It's fine." My brother interrupts him. "If you don't mind, we're on a tight schedule."

"Yes, of course." He nods once and pulls back the sheet. "As I informed you before, he was found in his condo. A woman called it in ..."

I tune him out as I look down at the body lying on the metal slab. His color as white as the sheet that covers his lower half.

I sit on my bed, the house quiet. Who knows where my brother is when my door opens. I quickly jump to my feet and wipe my wet cheeks when my father enters my room. "Ever heard of knocking?" I manage to get out without sounding upset.

"I pay for every inch of this house, including this room. I don't have to fucking knock," my dad snaps.

My hands fist, and I spin around to face him. "What do you want?" I grind out.

"Where's your brother?" he asks, looking around as if he's in here.

"How the hell should I know?"

He lets out a long breath but ignores me. "I'm leaving. Dillan is in charge while I'm gone."

"Where are you going?" I ask. Our mother just died. We buried her yesterday and just arrived back in Vegas this morning. Where the fuck could he possibly be going so soon?

"That's none of your business," he snaps, then exits my room, slamming the door.

I yank it open and catch him exiting the front door. I run down the stairs and open the front door just in time to see him help a woman into the passenger side door of his Ferrari.

Anger boils inside me. He was never faithful. My mother was an angel. She gave everything to my brother and I. But my father? I know a part of her loved him in the beginning, but over the years, Dillan and I watched them both change. He lived for Kingdom, and she despised it. She hated how it took so much of his time away from us. His family. He didn't care. The house we lived in became a cold mansion. My mother was trapped. She knew she couldn't leave him. He'd fight her for us, just for spite, and our mother didn't come from money. Maybe she preferred him having women he could fuck so she wouldn't have to do it anymore. But that doesn't mean he has to disrespect her memory. Not this soon.

"It's him." I hear Bones confirm.

"Can we have him cremated?" I ask.

The guy looks up at me. "Yes, but ..."

"Good. Burn his body," I order, then turn to walk out.

"But what about the ashes?" he asks.

I turn back around. "Throw them where they belong, in the fucking trash." Then I walk out, heading back to the car. This was a total waste of a trip.

APRIL

THERE'S A REASON I'M not much of a drinker. I don't do well the following morning. I open my eyes and am thankful that I'm in my own bed. Last night is a little foggy. The girls and I ended up at a club. VIP status. I feel like that's the only way Emilee and Jasmine roll. We partied hard for about three hours, then everyone called it a night. Jasmine had a visitor coming over early the next morning, so she wasn't going to stay out all night. Emilee said she had to get home to her fiancé, and Alexa spent most of her night on her cell. Her ex blowing up her phone. We'd had so much to drink that we had to call an Uber to get us all home.

I've been up for four hours now, and I'm starting to feel more like myself. I just needed a shower and three cups of coffee.

I stand behind the desk at Roses when I hear the bell ring that hangs above the door. One of my most loyal customers enters.

"Hello, Luca." I smile up at him.

"Good morning, April." He walks up to the desk dressed in a black three-piece suit. He always looks like he just walked out of a courtroom. I don't know anything personal about him except he's married. And he didn't give that information out willingly. I just put two and two together. The wedding band on his finger along with the flowers and vase he buys at least twice a week.

"What can I do for you today?" I ask.

His dark eyes meet mine, and he gives me a kind smile, placing his hands on the countertop. "How about some violets. Do you have a solid black vase by any chance?"

"I have the perfect one." I nod.

He pulls his wallet out of his back pocket and begins to count out some cash that he lays on the counter. I walk away and go into the cooler and put together his arrangement. When I return, he's on his cell.

"Yeah, I can do that." He nods to himself. "I'll meet you at Kingdom in twenty. I'm going to run by the house really quick."

Kingdom?

"Okay. Sounds good." He hangs up.

"What do you know about Kingdom?" I ask.

His brown eyes look down into mine, and he tilts his head to the side.

I lower my eyes, instantly embarrassed by my question. I don't know this man personally. Maybe he likes to gamble. It is Las Vegas, after all. "I mean, uh ..." I stumble, looking for the right lie to make up. "Do you like to play the machines or the tables?" I ask. Then I add, "I prefer the machines." *Lie.* I don't even like to gamble.

"I don't gamble," he answers.

"Oh." Then why in the fuck would he be meeting someone at Kingdom? Maybe for an early lunch? I bite my tongue to keep from asking.

"Thank you for the flowers." He nods, picking them up off the counter.

"You're welcome," I call out as he exits the flower shop. I sigh and pick up my phone to call my brother. He never did come home last night, and he's three hours late to work.

The phone rings three times and then goes to his voicemail. Sighing, I hang up and immediately call him again. Straight to voicemail this time. The fucker turned his cell off.

Sitting my phone on the counter, I let out a growl. What the fuck is he up to?

EIGHT

GRAVE

I SIT IN my private locker room at Kingdom, waiting to go out into the ring. I can't say that I've always been a fighter, but I have always needed that adrenaline rush. The need to go faster, harder. I feel alive when I'm closest to death. It's another thing on my long list of addictions. And bouncing around in a ring getting hit while I knock the shit out of someone else feels good.

Cross stands before me, wrapping my right hand in tape. He throws the roll to the floor, then he sighs, letting me know he's about to bring it up. "How was your trip to Rio?"

My brother and I returned this afternoon. It was either get fucked up tonight or throw a few punches. "Fine." I jump off the table and start for the door, exiting the room and walking down the long hallway. I can hear the crowd already wound up. Their shouts and hollers fill the large space. "Bloody Nose" by Hollywood Undead plays through the speakers, announcing my arrival. And I hop from foot to foot.

A hand slaps me on the shoulders and then begins to massage them. "Go out there and kick some ass," Cross tells me. "Then we'll go out and celebrate."

I nod my head. "Sounds like a plan. I wanna forget this fucking week." *It's only Wednesday.*

I bounce down the narrow passage. Kingdom is always hosting fights. Some are televised and a big deal, but tonight is amateur night. Which sucks for whoever my opponent is because I do this all the time.

I come to a stop, remove my black silk robe, and the ref feels around me to make sure I'm not hiding anything that can hurt my opponent. Once he nods, giving the all-clear, I enter the ring, throw up my hands and bounce around in a circle in the center of the event center. I spot my brother at the top of the stairs. He stands there with his eyes narrowed and arms crossed over his chest. I ignore him. We haven't spoken one word since we identified our father's body in Rio. He didn't even fight with me about cremating his body and tossing his ashes.

My eyes find Cross, and he's nodding his head at me, trying to get me wound up. Letting me know I got this. Not surprising, Titan is nowhere to be found. Emilee and her best friend Jasmine have been ring card girls in the past, but they are both MIA tonight while other women fill in for them.

"Give it up for the one, the only ... GRAVE!" The announcer yells out my name, and everyone is up on their feet, shouting my name. I smile at them, soaking it up.

"And in the opposite corner, we have a newcomer who thinks he can take on Grave." People boo.

I smile. *Bring it.* I love virgins. Well, the ones I get to beat the shit out of anyway.

"It's his debut, welcome Marker."

I spin around to see a kid bouncing his way down his aisle. He has a white zip-up hoodie on that's covering half of his face. I snort. *Kids.*

He gets checked and then ushered into the ring. He pushes his hoodie back, then he turns around. His hands drop to his side, and his blue eyes widen on me.

Fuck!

APRIL

I sɪᴛ ɪɴ the silent living room with a plate of untouched lasagna on the coffee table in front of me. I couldn't eat. Derek's words aren't sitting well with me the more I think about it.

It's now past three a.m., and Ethan still hasn't come home. Calls to his cell have gone unanswered along with my text messages going unseen.

I wrap the blanket around me and lean my head back, yawning. I'm so tired. I gotta be up at six to be at the shop and have it open by seven. He acts like we both wanted this life. Like I didn't give up college or a life for him. I didn't have a choice. I did everything I could to make sure he had one, and he still resents me. I don't think anything I could have done would have been right.

I hear a car pull up outside, and I jump to my feet to look out the window. Ethan exits the passenger door of an old Saturn and begins to walk up the path to the stairs. My anger flares at him as I see he's looking down at his phone. That ungrateful son of a ...

The front door opens, and he leaves the lights off as he starts to walk up the stairs. I flip them on. "Where the hell have you been?" I demand.

He stops midstep but keeps his back to me. "Out."

"No shit!" I snap. "Where the hell were you, Ethan?"

"None of your business," he snaps back and begins to crawl up the steps.

I move and yank him around to face me, almost making him fall down the stairs. His eyes meet mine, and mine widen. "What the hell happened to you?"

His right eye is swollen and has a blue and purple bruise. His bottom lip is cut, and he has dried blood on his chin and neck. "Jesus. What did you do?" His mouth clamps shut, and he looks away from me. I dig into the pocket of my robe. "Did you get that here?" I hold up the key card, not sure what a room key would have to do with bruises. Maybe he got into a fight with some kids. That happens at parties. And I wouldn't be all that surprised because he's a mouthy fucker.

His eyes widen on it, and he reaches for it, but I pull it away. "Did he give you that?"

"What? Who?" *What is he talking about?* "I found this in the office. It fell out of your jacket pocket."

His shoulders slump, and he runs his hands through his shaggy hair. "Keep it," he says before he gives me his back and walks up the steps, slamming his door shut in the process.

NINE
GRAVE

I STAND INSIDE Roses the following morning. She stands behind the counter in a pair of black yoga pants and a shirt that reads *prick me* with a rose that has thorns on the stem. *It's adorable.* "I hope you like it," she says nervously.

"I have no doubt."

She walks away and goes into the side door behind the front counter. While I wait for her to return, I head back to the office. I smirk when I see the kid exit the office. He sees me and immediately turns his back to me, ready to run away.

"Come here," I order him.

He comes to a stop and turns to face me with a look of annoyance on his face.

"Does she know?"

He shakes his head before dropping his eyes to his feet.

"I don't wanna see you there again."

That gets his attention. "But I ..."

"I don't give a fuck! If I see you at Kingdom again, I will throw you out on your ass. *After* I beat the shit out of it." Kingdom is no place for a young kid like him. It's not meant to be a place where kids hang out. It was made for adults, for men who had more money than God and were bored out of their fucking minds, needing a place to spend it. He fits neither of those qualifications.

Of course, we have our customers who get a room for the night, but our hotel is just a front. Our event center brings in major cash along with the Queens service that Titan supplies the city with. Nothing good will come from him hanging out up there.

He opens his mouth to argue again, but April walks out of the cooler. He rolls his eyes and then turns back to enter the office before she sees him. I'm not even sure who he is to her exactly. He could be a brother, or he could be some charity work she's doing by giving him a job here. Doesn't matter. He was there to fight last night, but he won't be doing it again any time soon.

"Here you go."

I reach out and grab the arrangement from her hands. "Wow!" I say, looking it over. It has five kinds of flowers with multiple colors in the pretty butterfly vase.

"I hope she likes it," she says to me, and I swallow nervously.

What the fuck are you doing, Grave? "She's gonna love it," I tell her, forcing a smile and hoping she doesn't notice it.

She looks up at me with her ice blue eyes. They're lined in black again today. Her purple hair has one braid down the middle, and it's all pulled up into one big messy bun at the top of her head. She wears two chokers—a black one that has a silver heart in the middle and a solid purple one. And her lips are lined in that color that matches her hair. She looks like a walking, talking wet dream that I want to drown in.

I hear the ringing of the door, announcing someone has entered. "Grave!" Cross's voice snaps. "What is taking so fucking long?"

He comes up beside me and looks down at her. "Oh," he says as a smile slides across his face. "Now I understand."

I elbow him in the ribs. He makes an *oof* noise and reaches out his right hand to her. "Cross. Nice to meet you."

"April." She gives him a smile and shakes his hand.

It just became my favorite month of the year.

He turns to face me with a stupid grin on his face. "We need to go, man. Your brother is blowing up my phone." Then his eyes drop to the flowers in my hand. "Who are those for?"

"They're for his mother's birthday." She answers for me.

His brows raise to his hairline, and he looks from her to me with confusion.

"I'll be right out," I say tightly, silently telling him to fucking leave.

He gives me a look that I don't care to decipher, then pats the countertop. "Nice to meet you." Then he exits.

She turns her ice blue eyes on me. "Is Grave your real name? I noticed that's what you wrote on your information."

"No."

She tilts her head to the side, those gorgeous eyes falling to my tatted arm. "Nickname?"

I nod. "Something like that."

"I like it." She smiles up at me.

"Yeah, well, I have to get going." I pick up the flowers. "Thanks again."

"No problem." She picks her cell up off the counter and starts to walk back to the office. I watch her ass sway back and forth in her black yoga pants like the pervert I am. Once the door to the office closes, I let out a deep breath and exit the flower shop.

"Man, what in the fuck was that?" Cross asks as I fall into the passenger seat of his car.

"Honestly?" I look down at the flowers in my hands. "I don't know," I answer, noticing a white folded piece of paper. I pluck it from the flowers and open it up. It's a card.

I hope you have a wonderful birthday. Love, your son Grave.

My jaw tightens. I specifically left the message part blank when she had me fill out the form. Seeing it written out just makes my chest ache. "Let's get fucked up." I wad up the note and throw it to the floorboard.

APRIL

I sit at the bar as Alexa stands behind it mixing drinks. She's slammed tonight, but I needed to get out. My brother isn't speaking to me. He left the flower shop earlier today without saying a word, and my concern has grown tenfold. The silence. The bruises. They all have to mean something. I just hope I can figure it out before it's too late.

"Hey, girlie."

I look over to see Jasmine sit down next to me. "Hey. What are you doing here?"

She shrugs. "Was on my way out for the night and thought I'd stop by and see Alexa. Have to support my friends." She drops a couple of hundreds in the glass tip jar that sits on the bar. "What are you up to tonight?"

"Nothing." I take a sip of my Corona.

"Come out with me. I'm going to a party," she offers, fixing the thin shoulder straps to her little black dress.

"Nah—"

"Hey, you work at Kingdom," Alexa interrupts me, coming up to us. "We have questions." She looks at Jasmine.

"What? You work at Kingdom? What do you do there?" I wonder. Why didn't Alexa bring this up the other night when we went out? Well, I mean we ended up at a club. The music was loud, and the drinks kept coming. There wasn't much conversation going on. We were too busy dancing around and drinking it up.

She chuckles, shaking her head. "Sorry, ladies. I can't discuss that."

I frown, and Derek joins in the conversation while he pours a Miller Lite into a frosted mug. "See, told you some bad shit goes down there."

Jasmine squares her shoulders. "You know nothing about Kingdom. Trust me."

He tops off the mug and sets it down before placing his forearms on the bar and leaning into her personal space. "I know that Bones is in with the Mafia. I know that a lot of illegal shit goes on there." He pulls back and looks her up and down the best he can since she's sitting, and adds, "And I know you're a Queen."

"What's a Queen?" I whisper to Alexa.

She shrugs.

Jasmine places her hands on the bar and stands, leaning over it. They're nose to nose. "You seem to know a lot about nothing."

His eyes drop to her breasts that are poking out of her skintight dress. He licks his lips before his eyes meet hers again. "I know enough." Reaching out, he takes a piece of her red hair, freeing it from behind her ear. "How much does a Queen go for these days?" he asks her.

Her red painted lips turn up at the corners before she runs her tongue along her upper lip. "More than you can afford."

He lets go of her hair, his finger trailing down over her neck. "I don't know. I've heard pussy comes pretty cheap."

"Not the good ones."

"Hey, Derek? Where's my beer?" a guy shouts from the end of the bar.

He ignores him as he looks at her. It's like they're in a staring contest. Whoever looks away first will lose. "Let's just say our opinions differ on what's good," he finally says before pulling away from her and delivering the beer.

"What was that about?" Alexa asks Jasmine wide-eyed.

I'm confused too after that exchange.

"I gotta go," Jasmine states, picking up her clutch. "We'll do lunch next week." Then she walks away without another word.

"Derek?" Alexa yells out to him.

"Busy," he shouts back from the other end.

She looks at me and raises a brow. "Was it just me, or do they have something going on?"

I'm not sure what that was. I don't think they have a thing, but Derek wouldn't turn her down if he got the chance. "Don't ask me. That entire conversation confused me."

TEN

GRAVE

I'M SITTING AT my desk when my office phone rings. I pick it up. "Hello?"

"Sir," Nigel speaks. "I've got a Natalie down here wanting to speak to you."

"Send her up." I order then hang up the phone. I close out the emails on my computer and stand from my desk. I walk over to my door and open it just as she storms in.

She's got her head down and her hair covering her face. She's dressed in a pair of shorts and overly large t-shirt with tennis shoes.

"Hey," I run a hand through my hair. "I don't have much time." I've got a meeting with the Kings and Luca in twenty minutes. I can't miss it. I can't even afford to be a second late.

"I understand," she sniffs. "I can go …"

She turns to leave, and I grab her upper arm, pulling her to a stop. "I've got time. Just not a lot of it. What is it?"

She looks up at me, her hair falling away from her face and I see her black eye. I sigh, running a hand down my face. "Did Randy do this to you?"

She wraps her arms around her chest and nods once. "He came over last night to pick up Brent. I had a man over. Things got heated."

"And he still managed to touch you? With a man there?" The motherfucker didn't try to stop him?

"Yeah, he told my company to get the fuck out and he ran."

My jaw tightens. "Give me Randy's address?"

Her eyes widen. "No, Grave. That's not why I came here."

"Then why ...?"

"I was wondering if you could contact that judge?" She licks her busted lip. "See if he could help?"

I place my hands on either side of her face. "I'll take care of it."

Tears fill her eyes and she wraps her arms around me, hugging me. "Thank you." She sniffs.

I rub her back gently and let out a long breath. If he doesn't have any warrants, I'll make sure he gets some. Ones that will lock him up for good. "Where's Brent?" I ask. "Did he touch him too?"

She pulls away and wipes her eyes. "No. He's at the daycare. Randy was so pissed last night that he didn't even take him."

I nod. "I want you to hide out for a while."

"Grave, I can't afford to miss work."

I walk over behind my desk, open up the drawer and pull out some cash. Closing it, I walk back over to her. "This is five thousand."

Her eyes widen. "No ..."

"Yes." I remove the purse from her shoulder and throw the money in it. "I'm going to get you and Brent a room here. Go downstairs and Nigel will make sure you're checked in."

"He'll find me," she argues.

"No, he won't. The room will be under a false name. There will be no reason for him to look for you here."

Her shoulders fall. I know the look on her face and she's about to argue with me.

"This isn't about you. This is about Brent." I remind her.

"But you're going to take care of Randy?"

"I am." I assure her. "But that doesn't mean he won't be looking for you tomorrow. Or the next. I can't promise you that I'll have it taken care of right away."

She nods and chokes out. "You're right. Thank you, Grave."

"Call me if you need anything. Do you hear me?" Five thousand won't last her long, but it's a start.

She reaches up on her tiptoes and presses her lips to mine just as my door opens. "Meeting in five," my brother calls out.

Nat pulls away quickly and averts her eyes to the floor before I even had a chance to kiss her back. But I had no plan to do so.

I glare up at him. "I can fucking read a clock," I snap. His blue eyes drop to her legs and slowly look over the back of her as she presses her front into mine like a timid cat.

"Don't be late," he warns and then slams my door shut.

APRIL

I'm TIRED, AND I'm starving. I haven't eaten much. Don't really have the appetite after all the unanswered calls and ignored texts I've sent Ethan. He didn't even bother showing up at the shop today. Alexa sent me a text late last night inviting me out to the bar tonight, but I declined. I'm not in the mood to be around a crowd.

I stand in the cooler, searching on my phone. I can't find anything about what the fuck a Queen is or what connection it has to do with Kingdom. I did, however, find out that four Kings own it. Titan, Bones, Cross, and Grave.

He fucking owns a quarter of the hotel and casino, and I'm having a hard time processing that information. The answer has been in front of me the entire time. That's why Ethan asked if *he* had given me that card. He was talking about Grave. He knows who he is. Grave holds all the answers I need. I just need to get his cell number off his info that he left when he ordered the flowers for his mother.

I go back to the office and sit down at the desk. Going through the computer, I pull up his information and look at his number. What am

I going to say to him? Why would I be calling? Making up my mind, I let out a deep breath before I type in his number on my cell.

It rings a couple of times before I hear his voice. "Hello?" The single word comes out rough. I look at the clock and silently curse myself. It's still early. I haven't even opened the shop yet. "Hello?" he asks, sounding irritated this time.

"Hi," I say and flinch. *Way too chipper.*

"Who is this?" he growls, getting angrier by the second.

"It's April. From Roses," I clarify.

"Oh." His voice changes to surprised.

"I'm sorry if I woke you," I rush out.

"No, no. You're fine. What's up? Everything okay?"

I frown. *That's an odd question.* But I guess so is this unexpected phone call. "Yes, of course. I was just checking in to see what your mother thought of the flowers."

He's silent for a long second. So long that I pull my cell away from my ear to make sure the connection isn't lost. Finally, he speaks in a clipped voice. "Loved them."

"Great." I sigh in relief. "I'm glad to hear that."

He clears his throat. "Is that really why you called, April?"

He's caught me. I'm like a window, people can see right through my shit. I never was good at lying. Looking down at my black nails, I try a different approach. "I was actually wondering if you would like to grab a cup of coffee. There's a little shop just a couple of doors down." I bite my bottom lip to keep from rambling.

"Sure." He sighs heavily. "I can meet you there in an hour."

"Oh." I was not expecting that answer. "I can do that." I'll just have to close the shop since I know Ethan won't be showing up to help. "I'll meet you there."

I WALK INTO THE SMALL COFFEE SHOP AND PICK THE FIRST round table to my right. There's only one other person here at the moment in the corner booth, but they have their earbuds in while working on a laptop.

My knees bounce up and down as I try to think of an excuse to bring up Kingdom and ask how my brother fits into the situation. I don't think saying *hey, I googled you last night and saw you're part owner. Do you know why my brother has a key card to there? Oh, and hey is your brother connected with the mafia?* That would be a good conversation starter. *Not.*

I look up just as a sport bike pulls into the front row parking spot. It's a Yamaha R1, and Grave is driving. He turns it off, kicks the kickstand down, and gets off it. I watch him walk to the door dressed in a pair of dark wash jeans, black combat boots, and a black T-shirt that shows off his one sleeve and muscular arms. He wears a white hat backward that he takes off and spins around. It has that same black circle and K that sits in the middle. I now know that represents Kingdom.

He enters the coffee shop, and I stand from the table. "Hey," I say lamely, all of a sudden feeling uncomfortable. I'm not sure what the fuck I'm doing or why I'm doing it.

He turns to look at me and removes a pair of black Aviators from his face. His blue eyes meet mine, and he smiles. "Hey."

The guy is gorgeous. There's no question about that. There's just something about him that I like. Or maybe it's the fact that I haven't met someone new in a while. The last guy I crawled in bed with was Derek, and that was over a year ago. It was a random hookup because we were out and had some drinks. We'd had sex before, so it was familiar.

"Have you ordered yet?" he asks.

Right! We're here for coffee, not to fuck. "I have not," I answer.

He takes the few steps over to the counter, and asks, "What would you like?"

"Small coffee. Black, please."

He places our order and then waits for them to make it while I sit back down.

"Come here often?" he asks, sitting down across from me with our coffees.

"Yeah," I lie. I hardly ever come here. I'm not much of a coffee drinker. "How about you?" I ask and then inwardly curse myself.

"First time." He chuckles.

This is so fucking awkward. I'd rather be having one of those dreams where you're naked in front of a crowd instead of this. At least I know that wouldn't be as embarrassing.

ELEVEN

GRAVE

I FIND IT very off that April called me to meet her for coffee, but I didn't question it. The moment I answered the phone and she said her name, I knew it was about Ethan. But I'm not going to willingly give her any information about him. If she wants to know, she'll have to come out and ask.

She averts her eyes and blows on her coffee. I look her over. Her hair is up again today in that messy bun she seems to love. Her face is free of makeup. She looks gorgeous, but her ice blue eyes look tired, and I bet it has to do with Ethan.

"I like your bike," she says, looking out the window.

"Thank you," I say, taking a sip of my drink. I went out with Cross last night and got fucked up. I left my car at Kingdom and woke up at my house this morning, so I decided to drive my bike.

"So what is it you do for a living, Grave?" she asks, unable to look me in the eyes.

There it is. The million-dollar question. "I work at Kingdom," I say vaguely.

Her dark brows lift. "Oh really? How long have you worked there?"

"Going on four years now," I answer.

She nods her head.

"How long have you worked at Roses?" I counter.

She places her cup of coffee down. "I started working there when I was twelve."

"That's a long time."

"My mother opened it, and I helped her out. I took over when she passed away."

My chest tightens at her words. Her mother is dead. Just like mine. "That was nice of you to help her," I say before taking another sip.

"Yeah, well ..." She shrugs. "It was all she had, but she loved it."

A silence falls over us, and my cell vibrates in my pocket. I pull it out to see it's Lucy.

> Lucy: Where are you? I thought you were coming over this morning.

Ignoring the message, I lock my phone.

"What about your father?" I ask. "Does he help you with the shop?"

She shakes her head. "Left when Ethan and I were young."

Well, fuck! This is going worse than I thought it would, but at least I know who Ethan is to her—her brother. That's good to know.

My cell vibrates again but this time it's my brother calling. "One second," I tell her, then answer it. "Hello?"

"I need you to be in my office in an hour," he barks.

"I'll be there when I get there," I say and hang up on him.

Her ice blue eyes go from my cell to mine. "You can go if you need to," she says softly. Obviously, she's changed her mind about whatever she wanted to meet me about.

I want to tell her that it's fine, but I do need to get to Kingdom. I'm not in the mood to put up with my brother yelling at me all day, so I stand. "I'll walk you back to Roses," I say, tossing what's left of my coffee into the trash can by the door.

She stays silent as we walk down the sidewalk and into Roses. She turns to face me once we step inside. Her eyes run over my neck tattoo and then my sleeve. She's never treated me differently or looked at me any different than other customers, but I want to know what she's thinking. Do they turn her off? Disgust her?

I can see the question written all over her face. The one that everyone asks—why did you get those tattoos? Do they mean something? Do you think you'll regret them when you're older? It's always the same.

"I like art," I say. Her eyes find mine, but she doesn't say anything. "That's what you were thinking, right? Why I have so many?"

She averts her eyes to her black sneakers, and a blush covers her cheeks. *God, she's gorgeous.* In a dream sort of way. Like nothing I've ever seen in person.

"Can I show you something?" she asks shyly.

"Yes," I answer, stepping away from her to allow her space.

She walks toward the back. I follow her without being told. She pushes a back door that reads *exit only,* and we enter a narrow back alleyway. She takes a few steps away from the door and then turns to face me. I come to a stop and just stare down at her. It's a sunny day here in Vegas, and the sun hits her eyes just right. They look almost see-through. Hypnotic. "What did you want me to see?" I ask, clearing my throat.

Placing her hands on both of my shoulders, she spins me around to face the back of the building with her. "What the ...?" I trail off as my eyes look over the building. It's covered in various shades of blue, red, green, yellow, and purple.

I step up to it and run my fingers over the brick. Blue water plays its part of a river. Tips of white make it look like it has rolling waves. To the right are mountains with peaks covered in dark clouds. To the left are tall buildings at night. Silver makes up the windows as they shine from the moonlight. "Someone vandalized your building," I say. "It's beautiful."

"You think so?" she asks softly, still standing behind me.

I nod. "Absolutely." I take a step back, coming to stand beside her and place my hands in my front pockets, just taking it in. "Fuck, it must have taken them forever to do it." It spans the entire back of the building. There is no way this was done in one night. Well, that's not true. I guess it depends on how many people they had working on it at once. But it doesn't look like several people did it. It looks like one. Art is like anything else. Everyone's strokes are different. There is nothing in this pic that doesn't match. No. One person did this. And it took them more than one night. They used paintbrushes. Not like they threw some spray paint on it and ran. Maybe she didn't notice it at first. She doesn't come out here very often, and they came back multiple times to do it. "I can pick up some paint and cover it up," I tell her.

"What?" she asks, turning to face me.

I do the same and look down at her. "I can cover it up." I sigh. "Not gonna lie, I'd hate to do it, but they shouldn't have done that to your building."

She tilts her head to the side, looking up at me. "If you could erase any of your tattoos, would you?"

I frown but answer without hesitation. "No."

She looks over at the back of the building and smiles. "Me neither." She steps up to it and places her hands on the brick. "I did this."

My eyes widen. "What?"

She turns to look at me. "I painted this."

My mind is a little slow at the moment, so I point at it. "You did this?" I ask stupidly.

She looks down at her black Converse and bites her bottom lip. All of a sudden, she's nervous.

I step into her and place my hand under her chin, lifting it so she looks up at me. Her piercing blue eyes shine from the sun hitting them. Then she lifts her hands and runs her fingers softly over my neck tattoo. I can't help the shiver that runs through me at her softness.

"I like art too, Grave." She speaks quietly as though the world can't know our secret.

My hand drops from her chin to wrap around her waist, and I pull her body flush with mine. She doesn't fight me or push me away. "You're amazing," I say honestly. I've never met anyone like her before. She's the exact opposite of me. Full of life. Breath of fresh air. Talented.

She gives me a soft smile. Her eyes drop to my lips, and I try to think of anything else but her hands on me because I don't want to get hard and ruin the moment.

But when her hands cup my face, I lose the battle. Her eyes meet mine again, and she whispers, "Kiss me."

I begin to walk forward, forcing her to walk backward. Her back gently hits the building, and I bring my left hand up and cup the side of her face. She leans her head back, staring up at me with heavy eyes.

"Fuck, you're beautiful," I whisper.

"Grave ..." My nickname shakes on her lips. Her hands come up to my chest and grip my T-shirt.

"April," I whisper, and she whimpers.

Lowering my lips, I gently touch mine to hers. She parts her lips for me, and my tongue enters her mouth. She tastes like sugar. Addictive.

She moans into my mouth, and my other hand comes up to hold the other side of her face. I tilt her head and deepen the kiss, memorizing every stroke of her tongue on mine. The way she pushes her hips into my hard dick and grips my shirt, greedy and wanting.

I pull away and rest my forehead to hers. We're both panting. I open my eyes to look down at hers, and they're still closed. "Have dinner with me tonight," I say before she comes back to reality. Before she remembers who I really am and why she wanted to meet with me this morning, bursting this bubble she has built around me.

Her eyes open, and she looks up at me. "Okay."

APRIL

AFTER I WATCH Grave exit the shop, I pick up my cell to call Alexa but then pause, afraid of what she'll say about my date with him tonight after what her brother told us about the Kings. So instead, I dial up Jasmine. We traded numbers that first night when we went out after leaving her own party.

"Hey, doll." She answers on the first ring.

"I need to talk to you," I say in a rush. My heart's still pounding from our kiss. It was a mistake. I know it was. It was so unexpected, but again, it was what I wanted. When he asked me out on a date tonight, I didn't think twice about it.

"Everything okay?" she asks.

"I'm not sure." I bite my bottom lip.

"Tell me everything and we'll figure it out together," she assures me.

I like Jasmine. I don't know her all that well, but she seems to be a good kind of friend to have.

"You know the Kings, right?" I come right out and ask.

"Yeah ..." she trails off. "Why?"

"I have a date with Grave tonight." I close my eyes and bow my head in shame. Why did I say yes? Why did he have to kiss me like that? My heart still pounds. He looked at me like he was seeing something for the first time. My skin still tingles from where he touched me.

She whistles. "Oh, girl. What are you doing around noon today?"

I frown, but answer, "I'll be at the shop."

"Okay, I'll come pick you up then," she states.

"Why?" I ask.

"We're going to go have lunch with the girls."

Jasmine and I pull up to Kingdom. "What are we doing here?" I ask, getting out as the valet slides in the driver's seat of her car. I've never been here. But the hotel and casino dominate the Las Vegas Strip. It has four towers—one for each King—and is its own city.

"The girls and I have a tradition that we meet up for lunch at Empire."

We walk into Kingdom, and it's exactly as I expected. White marble floor with the same black circle with a golden K in the middle. We entered the hotel side. I can see off to the right where it opens into the casino.

She grabs my hand and pulls me to a bank of elevators. We make our way up to the twentieth floor, passing slot machines, and enter the restaurant. I see the girl from the other night; Emilee I think was her name. And another woman I don't know.

"Hey ladies, this is April." She introduces me before she slides into the booth. I sit down beside her since both women are on the other side, facing us.

"It's good to see you again." Emilee nods.

"I'm Haven." The brunette reaches out her hand to shake mine.

"Nice to meet you."

We all open our menus. "What's good here?" I ask.

"Everything," Jasmine answers, licking her lips. Then she lifts her eyes to look over at the entrance. "Haven, how long is Nite gonna be on babysitting duty?"

I follow her eyes over to a man I didn't see when we entered the place. He's standing with his arms over his chest and legs spread wide. His eyes are on our table, and he's dressed in a black three-piece suit with an earpiece in his ear. He looks like he belongs in the Secret Service. *Who is this Haven chick?*

Haven sighs. "I don't want to talk about it."

Emilee rolls her eyes, and Jasmine just laughs. Then a silence falls over them.

"So, uh, Jasmine mentioned you girls have lunch here often," I add, breaking the silence. I like Jasmine, but I'm confused as to why she brought me here.

"Yeah." Emilee nods and then it's quiet again.

I look over the menu trying to figure out what I want when I hear Haven speak. "Hey babe. That was fast."

I look up and meet a set of dark eyes that I know well.

"April," Luca says my name in surprise.

"You know her?" Jasmine is the one who asks.

"Yeah." He places his hands on Haven's shoulders "April is my favorite florist."

"Oh." Haven's eyes light up. "I love all of the flowers he brings home. And your vases, they are gorgeous."

"Thank you." I blush at her praise. But it's not hard to figure out who she is—his wife.

"You own a flower shop?" Emilee smiles at her own question.

I nod.

A man I remember seeing on my computer comes to stand next to Luca behind Emilee. His name is Weston Mathews—aka Titan—one of the owners of Kingdom. Now shit is starting to make sense. The dots connecting. "Do you do weddings?" he asks me.

"I do."

"Oh, my gosh. Will you do our wedding?" Emilee asks. "I've been looking for a florist."

"I'd love to but ..."

"Yay." She claps her hands excitedly. "I'll come by after lunch, and we can go over what I have in mind."

"Okay," I say smiling, happy to help them out. "How many people are you thinking of?" I ask. I'm not a baker, but the number of guests will give me an idea of how big it's going to be.

She looks up over her shoulder at Titan. "How many were on our final list, babe? I think it said two hundred and twenty."

If I was eating food, I'd choke on it. "That's a lot." I almost gasp.

"Yeah." He nods. "Something around that."

"There was more, but she started scratching names out." Titan adds.

"When is the wedding?" I ask.

"We're thinking November."

"That's in two months." My eyes bug out.

"What's the rush?" Jasmine asks.

"We just don't want to wait." Emilee shrugs. "And I put you down for a plus one." She winks at Jasmine. "Who are you bringing?"

She waves her off. "I'm riding solo."

"You'll be riding something." Emilee laughs.

"As long as it's not Trenton." Haven pulls her lip back with disgust at the name.

"Okay, ladies, we have to go. We just came by to say hello." Titan leans down and kisses Emilee on the forehead. "We have a meeting with the rest of the Kings in ten."

The couples say their goodbyes, and once we're alone, Jasmine speaks. "We need to go shopping after this."

"I'm down," Emilee says. "Then I'll come over to your shop?" she asks me.

"Of course," I answer.

"Sure." Haven nods. "Occasion?"

Jasmine elbows me. "April has a date with Grave tonight."

"No fucking way!" Emilee gasps.

"That's awesome." Haven tilts her head to the side, smiling. "This must mean he's done with Lucy." She shakes her head. "She's as bad as you are with Trenton." She points at Jasmine.

"Who is Lucy?" I ask. I know nothing about Grave except what I read on the internet. And all that told me was that he is the youngest heir to Kingdom and the most likely to end up in prison. He had a few mugshots. Mainly for DUIs and reckless behavior. It's no secret why Kyle Reed is known as Grave. The guy has a death wish. He's an adrenaline junkie.

"Lucy is a train wreck," Haven answers.

"They have a bad past," Emilee adds.

Haven snorts. "I was never friends with her. Hell, I didn't even know who she was until recently. But she's bad for Grave. Feeds into his addiction."

I go to ask what she means by that when the waitress walks up to our table and takes our orders.

TWELVE
GRAVE

I'M SITTING AT my desk when my office phone rings. "Hello?" I answer.

"Hey, babe," Lucy speaks.

I sigh. I've been ignoring her calls all week. "Hey."

"I've been calling you," she says, and I can practically hear her pouting.

"Been busy working," I say truthfully. We had meetings all day. My brother is up my ass, and Titan still looks at me like he wants to smash my face in for my comment about his fiancée sucking my dick. "What did you need?"

"I'm going to be at the Airport tonight. Want to go?"

"No. Not tonight," I answer as my door opens. "Hey, I gotta go."

"Wait—"

I hang up. "What do you want, Bones?" I ask, watching as my brother enters my office.

He comes to stand in front of my desk with his tatted arms crossed over his chest. "I'm leaving tonight for New York," he states.

"And?" I ask.

"I'll be gone for the weekend."

"I thought you broke up with Lola?" She was some supermodel he'd been fucking for a few months. She wanted to introduce him to her parents, and he dumped her ass.

"I did. I'm going for other reasons."

Ah, I bet it has to do with *Kink*. Some secret society sex club he joined. I heard him talking to Titan about it the other day in the conference room.

"Okay," I say, dismissing him by looking down at my computer.

He doesn't take the hint. Instead, he sits down. "Can you behave yourself while I'm gone?" he asks.

"Yes," I say through gritted teeth.

He sighs. "Kyle ..."

"Get the fuck out of my office, Dillan," I growl, glaring at him. "I have work to do."

He slaps his hands on his thighs and stands before leaving my office. Fuck, he's been on my ass more than usual lately.

I PULL UP TO A TWO-STORY HOUSE OUTSIDE OF LAS VEGAS. IT sits on the end of a street all by itself. April had messaged me earlier with her address. I place my car in park and get out. Walking to her door, I run a hand over my hair. Once I get to the porch, I ring the bell and rock back and forth on my heels, waiting for her to answer.

She opens the door dressed in a little black dress. It has a V neckline with long sleeves. It stops at her thighs, showing off her long, thin legs. She wears a deep purple choker that matches her hair that is down and in big curls. She has her makeup done how I like it. Her ice blue eyes lined in black with that deep purple lipstick. Her six-inch black heels give her extra height, but she's still shorter than me.

She averts her eyes, running her hands down her dress, and bites her lip nervously

"You look gorgeous," I say, stepping up to her.

Her head snaps up, and her eyes meet mine. She licks her lips, and I cup her face, feeling her out. This morning was not a mistake. It didn't go the way she wanted it to, but I can't deny I'm attracted to her. And the fact that I stand here on her porch to take her out means she is attracted to me as well.

"So do you," she whispers.

The corners of my lips curve into a smile before I press them to hers. I kiss her softly, just our lips when I really want to push her back into the house, tear off her dress and carry her to her bedroom.

"Come on," I say, pulling on her hand without even allowing her to give me that option.

APRIL

I sit in his passenger seat, trying to calm my racing heart. I don't know why he makes me so nervous. Maybe it's because he holds so much power over this town. He tried to downplay what he does with Kingdom this morning over coffee, but he knows that I know the truth. There's too much of him on the internet not to know.

"I love your dress," he comments while he drives down the highway toward The Strip.

"Thank you. I went shopping with the girls today. Jasmine said I had to get it."

"The girls? Jasmine? How do you know her?" he asks curiously.

"Met her through a mutual friend," I say.

He nods and shifts gears.

"She's really nice," I add, trying to rub my sweaty palms on my dress without looking obvious. It's been a long time since I've been on an actual date. Men these days would rather fuck you and then split than take the time to get to know you.

He nods. "She can be. She can also be crazy."

"You know her well?" I ask, wondering if they have a past. Haven is married to Luca, who seems to be good friends with Titan, who is engaged to Emilee, a best friend to Jasmine. So it wouldn't be farfetched to think he and Jasmine have been close at some point. They are all part of a very tight circle.

"Yep. Went to high school and college with her," he answers.

That's something I won't find on the internet. "What makes her so crazy?"

"She used to date this guy name Trenton." *That's who Haven mentioned when Emilee was talking about Jasmine's plus one.* "She would slash his tires. Got him kicked off the football team for drugs." My eyes widen. "Pretty sure she would have lit him on fire if it wouldn't have killed him." He laughs. "He was a prick, though. He would have deserved it."

I chuckle. "Now I know why she and Alexa are friends. She can be crazy too."

He laughs, and his cell starts to ring through the Bluetooth in his car. He picks it up from the cradle on his dash and pushes ignore, but not before I see **Lucy** light up the screen.

Interesting. "You can answer that," I tell him, and he gives me a side-eye. "You know, in case it's important. I understand," I add.

He shakes his head. "It can wait."

A silence falls over his car, and a thought hits me. *Lucy Mason.* After the conversation I had with the girls today, I did a little research before our date tonight. It wasn't hard to find. The girls hadn't mentioned her last name at lunch today, but all I had to do was search Grave and I noticed the same woman popped up in pictures with him. One was even a mug shot of her. She had been arrested for DUI. It had said she was driving a car when pulled over due to speeding. That was just a few months ago. I had read comments that stated she was with Grave, and he is friends with a judge and was released on a technicality. Something about the cops hadn't read them their Miranda rights. I'm not sure how true that is, and you can't believe everything you read on the internet, but I do believe that Grave has connections all over this state, if not even further.

WE PULL UP TO THE VALET AT THE MANDALAY BAY CASINO, AND a man opens my door for me. I thank him as Grave comes around the front of the car and takes my hand. We haven't spoken since Lucy called, and I didn't miss that he shut his cell completely off after that.

First red flag.

I stay silent as we walk through the casino, not knowing where we are going, but I never get out much.

We come up to a restaurant that reads Fleur in white letters across the top. A man greets us dressed in a black three-piece suit. "Hello, Grave." He nods and looks at me. "Ma'am."

"Hello." I smile at him.

He turns his attention back to Grave. "Your table is ready, sir. Please follow me."

They seat us in the back at a round table. Grave pulls my seat out, and I sit down, thanking him. He sits across from me, and I place my napkin in my lap. My knees start to bounce once again. "Do you know everyone in Vegas?" I come out and ask.

"Pretty much," he answers. "I've lived here all my life."

"Owning a quarter of the biggest hotel and casino doesn't hurt," I add.

He smirks. "I was wondering if you did your research."

I shrug. "A little."

He arches a brow, his eyes on mine daring me to say more. I want to but not about his business. I want to ask about Lucy. Haven didn't make it sound serious, but I'm betting she doesn't know the whole situation between them. I look down at the table, unable to go there just yet. We'll see how the date goes. Maybe tomorrow.

THIRTEEN
GRAVE

DINNER WENT BY fast. Before I knew it, she'd had a few glasses of wine. I had water. I didn't want to be drunk when I drove her home. I also haven't had a hit yet today. I'm not even craving one.

We didn't talk a whole lot. She was more focused on eating than digging for information, and I like that. Whatever she wants to know about me, she could read online, which she has obviously done. There are a few stories that the media have made up, but for the most part, I'm guilty for what they've accused me of.

"Oh, my gosh, that food was amazing." She sighs, leaning back in the passenger seat.

"I'm glad you liked it," I say, taking a quick look over at her. Her eyes are closed, and a smile tugs at her painted lips. "Just how drunk are you?" I ask with a laugh.

She opens her eyes and tilts her head to look at me. "I'm stuffed. Not drunk. It takes a lot to get me drunk."

"Not a lightweight, huh?"

She laughs. "No. I partied too much in high school for that."

"Not in college?"

"I dropped out of college freshman year." She sighs. "I had to help my mom with Roses."

"I'm sorry."

"It's fine." She waves me off, sitting up straighter. "I had no idea what I was going to do with my life anyway. I was just wasting money."

I exit the highway and pull down her street. I stop in her driveway and get out, opening her door for her and walking her to her house. She unlocks the door and pushes it open.

"I had a great time tonight," I tell her as she turns to face me.

She smiles and runs her hand down my shirt. "It doesn't have to be over."

My cock instantly hardens, and I swallow a growl. "April ..."

She steps into me. "I'm an adult, Kyle." She uses my real name, reminding me she's looked me up. No one ever calls me that except for Bones when he's pissed at me. "A woman. I know what I want. Do you?"

I reach out and cup her face, pulling her into me. "I do," I say before pressing my lips to hers. She moans into my mouth, and I shove her dress up her legs before lifting her off her feet.

She wraps her legs around my waist as I step inside with her and slam the front door shut with my shoe.

"Where to?" I ask, pulling from her mouth.

"Up the stairs. Last door on the right," she rushes out.

I make my way up the stairs and enter her bedroom. The lights are off, and she reaches over, flipping them on and I lick my lips. I like a woman who isn't shy. I've been dying to look at her body. To touch her skin.

She wiggles out of my hold and stands before me. I reach up and rip my shirt over my head and toss it to the floor.

Her hands go to my bare chest, and she runs her fingers down over my body until they reach my jeans. She's undoing my belt as I kick off my shoes.

I grab her dress and yank it off her. She stands before me in a black lace bralette and matching thong with her heels on. "You're perfect," I say, looking her over. She doesn't have any tattoos, but her belly button is pierced with a black bar and purple ball on the end.

She pushes my black boxer briefs down my thighs and licks her lips as she stares at my hard cock. A barbell is pierced through the end.

She wraps her hand around the base, and I hiss in a breath when she jerks on it, forcing me closer to her. My hands go to her hair, gripping it between my fingers to yank her head back. She whimpers, and I bury my face in her neck, sucking on her skin.

"God." She moans when her hand begins to slide up and down my cock. Pulling away all of a sudden, she slams her hands on my chest and pushes me onto her bed.

I didn't expect her to be aggressive like this. But I like it. I love a woman who knows what she wants and goes for it.

She crawls between my legs and leans forward, wrapping her lips around my cock while she looks up at me.

"Fuck, April." I slide my hand into her hair again. My eyes stare into hers as she swallows my cock like she's done it a million times.

My hips thrust upward while she opens her throat for me and lets me fuck it. I get more forceful. Tears start to fill her beautiful ice blue eyes and run down her gorgeous face, smearing her black eyeliner that I love so much.

I sit up, placing my left arm behind me on the bed to help prop me up while the right one stays in her hair. I use it to control her head. The sound of my cock sliding in and out of her mouth fills the room while she moans around it. "Fuuucckkk," I groan as my balls begin to tighten.

I yank her head off me and flip her onto her back. I don't want to come in her mouth. Not yet.

She opens her legs for me, and I feel her shaved pussy with two fingers, confirming what I already knew—she's soaked. I shove my arms underneath her knees, spreading her legs wide and slide my cock into her.

She cries out and slaps my chest. I grab the inside of her elbows and pin her arms down to her sides as I start to move. She looks up at me with heavy eyes, face smeared with makeup and parted lips. She's still gasping from my cock in her mouth.

Our bodies are slapping while her bed hits the wall, and our bodies are already covered in sweat. She throws her head back, crying out as her pussy tightens around me, and I realize this is the first time I've had sex in a long time when I wasn't high or wasted.

I almost forgot what it felt like not to be in a drug-induced haze. To actually feel a woman come undone.

She closes her eyes, and her body shakes under mine. I shove her arms above her head. Leaning down, I capture her lips with mine and kiss her deeply, swallowing her moans and cries of pleasure.

I pull back and flip her onto her stomach. Gripping her hips, I yank her ass up in the air. I look down and see her cum covering my cock. It jerks. I lean down and kiss her back, tasting the saltiness on her skin. I spread her legs with my knees and slide back into her. I lean forward, reach around her waist, and play with her clit while I kiss her neck.

"Oh, God ... Grave ..." Her hands slap the headboard as she presses her hips against me. "I'm gonna come again." She's gasping.

"Good," I growl, gripping her hair and pulling it off the back of her neck to give me better access. I bite down on it, and she shivers.

I pick up my pace, and her voice grows louder, filling the room. Her hands grip the sheets and her body tightens, then she does exactly what she said she was going to do and comes once again.

APRIL

I LIE ON my back. My entire body shaking and covered in sweat. Grave falls on his back next to me with his hand on his bare chest.

I look over at him. His eyes are closed, and his lips are parted as he tries to catch his breath. I slide my hand over his chest and run the tips of my fingers over his nipple piercing.

His eyes pop open, and his head falls to the side so he can look at me. "I didn't use protection," he says as if he just realized it.

I smile at him. "I'm on the pill."

He lets out a long breath.

I laugh and joke. "Caught up in the moment?"

"Yes." He nods once before licking his lips.

I get up and straddle him. I run my hands over his six-pack to his chest, exploring him. I sat across from him at dinner for a couple of hours, and all I could think of was this—us coming back to my place.

The more time I spent with him, the less I thought about Lucy and the more I thought about him and me. I wanted a taste. I was craving him.

He opens his eyes and grips my hips. His thumbs rub circles on my hip bones. His eyes on my chest.

"Stay the night," I say, not wanting him to leave just yet.

His eyes meet mine, and I have an instant of panic.

"I mean ... if you don't have anywhere else to be tonight." It's still early. Not even ten yet.

He sits up, placing both his hands on my face, and places his lips on mine. I open for him as his tongue enters my mouth. My eyes close, and his arms wrap around my waist, holding me in place, and he pulls away.

"I wasn't going to leave," he states, before shoving me back down onto my back.

FOURTEEN
GRAVE

MONDAY MORNING, I walk off the elevator at Kingdom onto the thirteenth floor. I take an immediate right and enter the conference room. The guys already sit around it.

I plop down in my seat, and my brother looks at his watch, then at me. "You're early."

I say nothing.

"Have you even been to bed yet?" he asks, looking me over.

"I got five hours of sleep, not that it's any of your business," I say with a smile. I spent the entire weekend at April's. I wouldn't say I got much sleep because neither one of us did, but I was sober the entire time. "How was New York?" I ask him to make conversation.

He eyes me skeptically and answers slowly. "Fine."

"I'm sure it was," I say, and his eyes narrow on me. "So what is this meeting about?" I question, getting down to it.

Bones goes to speak, but the doors open behind me and I hear Nigel. "Grave, you have a phone call on line one."

I get up from my seat and walk over to the far side of the room and pick up the phone, pressing one. "Hello?"

"Hey man, it's Mac."

"I'll call you back," I say, not even giving him a second to argue before I hang up on him. I exit the conference room and walk down to my office. Closing my door, I sit behind my desk and pull my cell out of my pocket and call him back. We have a jammer in the conference room. That way no cell phones can be recording of any kind. We do a lot of work in there with some very well-known Elite's. Never know who wants to get blackmail information to fuck you over. And I don't trust my brother to not pick up the office phone to listen to my conversation.

"Hello?" Mac answers.

"It's me. What do you have?"

He sighs and I know it's not going to be good. "Well, I ran the search through the database on the name you gave me ... Randy Smith."

"Yeah."

"And he's clean."

I run a hand down my face. "No way." That can't be true. "The fucker was just arrested last week at Glass."

"He was not."

I know I was pretty fucked up, but the cops were called. He threw my glass of liquor onto the fucking stage for Christ's sake. "What the fuck ...?"

"He was escorted from the premises and told not to return." He interrupts me.

They banned him? I need to talk to Luca about this shit. "Fuck!" Well ... this isn't going how I planned. "What if I talk her into pressing charges?" He beat her. I doubt the bruises have faded completely.

"You can, but it'll get him locked up for maybe twenty-four hours at best. He'll make bail and then it will just make things more difficult for her. You know how this shit goes. There's not much I can do. If he's been giving her hell for this long, he's not going to give up now. Next time she may not get the chance to come to you for help."

I throw my head back and close my eyes. Natalie and her son don't deserve this. No woman deserves to be treated like this. They need to feel safe. Protected, and I'm all they have. "What if I delivered him to you?" I offer, getting an idea.

He's silent for a long second before he finally sighs. "I don't want to know any part of your plan."

"What plan?"

"Fuck," he hisses. "I'll do this for you. But only because if someone would have helped my mother like you're trying to help Natalie, maybe she'd still be alive. Message me when you're ready." He hangs up and I place my cell on the desk.

Bowing my head, I place my hands over my face and close my eyes. I have to do something. Nothing good can come from Randy being able to touch them. And Natalie has nowhere to run. He'd find her no matter what. Men like that don't let their toys go. And that's all she is to him.

I could kill him. But I'd prefer the guy rot in a prison cell, knowing she's out there living her best life with his son. Someone else out there raising his son.

I pick up my cell, making up my mind and send a quick text to Luca.

> Me: I need some supplies.

> Luca: Whatever you need. I can meet you later on today.

APRIL

I'VE BEEN SMILING like a fool all day. I spent the entire weekend locked in my bedroom with Grave. I didn't expect him to stay that long, but I wasn't going to kick him out. He kissed me goodbye this morning and promised he would return tonight with dinner. I hope it's something we can eat off one another.

I open my cell to see I have a text from him.

> Grave: Still at Kingdom. Will be for a couple more hours.

I exit the cooler and walk up to the desk just as the front door opens. *Odd.* I thought I locked it. "I'm sorry, we're closed," I tell the man who enters.

He looks up at me with dark eyes, and my stomach drops when I see he has a crowbar in his hand. Three more guys enter behind him.

"May I help you?" I ask, and my voice shakes.

The last guy to enter turns and locks the door. *What the hell?* "Hey ..."

"We're here to see Ethan," the guy in the front says to me.

I frown. "He's not here." The truth is, I haven't seen him the past three days, but that's not uncommon since he's been avoiding me lately. He sent me one text on Friday that he was staying at a friend's house for the weekend. Otherwise, I wouldn't have allowed Grave to stay over.

"Ethan?" he calls out and goes to walk past the desk.

I step in front of him. "He's not here ..." He shoves me out of the way. "Hey!"

"Ethan?" He walks back into the office and kicks the door open.

"I'm calling the cops," I announce and grab for my cell on the countertop, but another guy snatches it before I can get it.

"No need," he says simply and throws it to the floor, crushing my screen. "We won't be here long."

Then the other guy returns and takes the crowbar, smashing it into the glass.

"Stop!" I scream and run over to him.

Someone grabs my hair and yanks me back. I cry out as my scalp burns. The first guy who entered comes to stand in front of me. He grips my face, cramming my cheeks into my teeth. My hands hit his chest, trying to shove him away. "Where is he?" he demands. His almost black eyes glare down at me. His thin lips in a flat line and his dark brows pulled together.

"I don't know," I growl. *What has my brother done?*

He lets go of me, and the guy releases my hair. I take a shaky step back from them. They turn and bust another glass door.

"Stop!" I shout.

I spot my phone on the floor, and I run over to it. A guy grabs me and throws me into a glass door. I bounce off it and land face-first on the floor. I hold my side as I groan at the impact. "How much?" I ask, trying not to cry. My worst fears have come to life. My brother is in deep trouble.

The one with the crowbar squats down next to me. He takes the claw-like end and slides it across my cheek, pushing my hair away from my face. I hold my breath, hoping he doesn't cut me with it. The metal cold against my skin. "You can't afford it, honey." Then he stands and kicks me in the side.

I immediately go into the fetal position to shield my body from another blow. My breath gets caught in my lungs due to the pain, and my teeth grind.

"Tell him we'll be back." Then I hear more glass shatter before the door dings, notifying me of their exit. I get up onto my hands and knees, breathing heavy, and look around. Tears sting my eyes as I look over what is left of my mother's flower shop. Even my vases that were on the shelf are now broken on the floor next to me. My hands shake as I reach out for them, the glass cutting me in the process.

I push myself up, grab my busted phone, and run to my car. I rush into our house and go straight to his room. I'm not an idiot. I know my brother isn't a saint. He's been caught stealing before. And last month, I found a gun under his bed. When I questioned him, he said he was holding it for a friend. I didn't believe that for a second.

I open his drawers and start throwing things around, not knowing what I'm looking for but needing to find something, anything to tell me how much he owes these guys and why.

Yanking open his closet, I pull things off his hangers and shelves.

A hat falls and another one of those key cards fall out of it. I reach down and pick it up. Turning it over, I see a skull in the middle of it with a tilted crown on top. Blood drips down over it. *Kingdom* is written across the bottom in black letters. I grip it in my hand and storm out of the door.

I PULL UP TO THE HOTEL AND CASINO, AND I JUMP OUT BEFORE the man can even open my door.

"Will you be staying the night in the hotel, ma'am?" he asks.

"No," I growl, running up the stairs to the entrance.

I make my way through the glass doors and come to a stop. The floor is black and white checker marble with flecks of gold thrown in like confetti. The walls are a dark gray, and the ceiling is black. The inside is just as dark as the outside.

"Welcome to Kingdom. How may I help you?" one of the ladies standing behind the front desk asks.

I walk over to her, then open my mouth, but pause, not sure what to say. Instead, I dig the hotel key card of my pocket and show it to her.

She looks over my wild hair and dried up blood on my hand, but smiles. "I will have Antonio show you to your room."

Thank God something is going my way tonight.

"Hello, Miss. Please follow me," a man says, coming up next to me, dressed in a suit and tie.

I follow him silently. My first thought was to call Grave, but my cell is busted, so I can't read my numbers, and I don't have his memorized. I doubt if I just ask for him, they'll call him. I bet my ass a lot of people do that and get nowhere. So I'm going to focus on my brother instead. Grave can't help me. He doesn't even know Ethan.

The man takes us over to a bank of elevators, and I take a deep breath. My brother forgets who I am sometimes. He doesn't remember when I beat his ass five years ago after he wrecked Mom's car. I took the fall for him and said it was me, but I made sure to kick his ass first.

Stepping in, he pushes a button, and my toes tap on the floor while it takes us up. My skin is on fire, my blood boiling. If those guys don't kill my brother, I'm going to.

The doors open, and there's a long hallway. The man takes us right, walking down the narrow hall to a door. He holds it open and enter an arena-like structure full of people. It's a fucking event center. They're shouting and clapping. I look ahead of me to see a ring in the center. Two men are inside it. Their hands are up, and they bounce from foot to foot. My eyes widen when I see one of them is my brother.

"Motherfucker!"

He's fighting again.

"You'll need your card to enter the room," the man tells me.

"Thank you," I growl, knowing I can take it from here. I storm down to the front, shoving people out of my way. I stand there with my arms crossed over my chest as he hits a guy so hard, he falls to his side. People cheer, and the ref holds up my brother's right arm. He's got a huge smile on his face and blood dripping down his chin.

He exits the ring and walks through the crowd. Guys slap him on his back, and women run their hands over his body. The kid is only nineteen. He can't even legally drink alcohol, much less fucking fight.

I storm after him. I call out his name, but he doesn't hear me.

"Excuse me, miss. You need a pass to access back here," a man says, wearing a black T-shirt with security written in yellow.

I let out a growl as I yank the card out of my back pocket. "Is this good enough?" I shove it in his face.

He steps to the side, allowing me by. I catch sight of the back of my brother before he enters a room to the left. I start to jog and shove the door open to follow him. "Just what in the fuck do you think you're doing?"

He spins around, and his eyes widen when he sees me. "April, what are you ...?"

I slap him across the face, cutting him off. "What the hell did you do?" I shout.

His wide eyes stare down at me, and fresh tears begin to sting mine. His eyes roam over my face, and he frowns. I know I look like shit. I didn't wipe off the makeup that's already been smeared before I left my house. "Fuck, Ethan! What did you do? Please? What have you done?"

FIFTEEN

GRAVE

I enter the room with Titan, about to beat the shit out of the kid myself. "I warned you," I growl.

He ignores me as he stares at a woman before him. My eyes start at her black high heel boots, that lace up her ankle. Then they travel up over her dark skinny jeans that fit her bubble ass perfectly. Dark purple hair falls over her back. It can only be one woman. "April?" I ask.

She spins around, and her eyes meet mine. Tears run down her perfect face, and her blue eyes widen when they see me. "What are you doing here?" *Why is she in this room?* How in the hell did she get back here? Did he bring her with him tonight? Thinking I wouldn't beat his ass if she was with him? The kid doesn't know me.

"Fuck!" Ethan hisses, turning his back to us.

She doesn't answer me. Instead, she turns to him. "Grab your shit, we're leaving!" she orders.

"What's going on?" I ask, coming up behind her. They ignore me. I grab her shoulder and spin her around to face me. She pushes me away. "What's going on?" I demand this time.

She huffs, crossing her arms over her chest. "Did you send them?" she demands.

I look at Titan. He shrugs, just as clueless as I am, and leans up against the wall. His eyes looking her up and down, wondering who the fuck she is. "Send who? Where?" *What is she talking about?*

She turns to her brother again. "How much do you owe him, Ethan?" she snaps.

His jaw tightens, and I frown.

"Fucking answer me!" she screams, fisting her hands down by her side.

When he looks away from her, she rounds on me. "How could you do this?" Fresh tears fill her eyes. "You should have just come to me."

"I don't know what you're talking about," I say honestly.

She begins to dig in her purse. She removes a checkbook before she lets her purse fall to her feet. "I'll pay you. Right now. If you promise to let it go." She licks her wet lips.

"April, I don't know ..."

"Fifty thousand," Ethan mumbles, interrupting me.

We both look at him. Her checkbook falls to her feet where her purse already sits, and she gasps. "You owe him fifty grand?" she asks, blinking in disbelief. Then her hands ball into fists. "They destroyed the shop. They broke everything, Ethan. What am I going to do now?"

"Wait. What?" I ask, looking at her.

She bites her bottom lip and bows her head, quietly crying. Her hands cover her face, and her shoulders begin to shake.

I cup her face and force her to look up at me. "Did they touch you?" I demand.

She pulls back and looks away from me. "They did whatever you told them to do."

Why does she think I did this?

"I'm sorry," he tells her softly. "I didn't know ..."

She runs for him. Her body throws them both into the wall before she takes him to the ground. He brings his hands up to shield his face while she balls her fists and starts punching the shit out of him. "They destroyed everything! They're going to kill you!" she cries, swinging her fists at him. She's kicking his ass more than his opponent was in the ring.

I wrap an arm around her waist and yank her off him. She kicks and screams as I toss her into Titan's arms. "Take her to the office. I'll be right there."

He drags her out, kicking and screaming. I turn on Ethan. He picks himself up off the floor and wipes the blood from his lips. "Fuck! She's crazy ..."

I punch him. He stumbles back into the table. "Who the fuck do you owe fifty thousand dollars to?"

He grinds his teeth and takes in a deep breath. "I got into some trouble ... had to borrow some money."

"For what?"

He reaches up and rubs blood off his chin. "I lost in a poker game. And I needed a loan. They said I had a month to pay it back. It's only been two weeks."

I run a hand through my hair. He's not old enough to gamble so it has to be somewhere that is under the table. I'm praying it's not where I think it is. "Who is *they*?"

He hangs his head. "The Mason brothers."

I lean my head back and take a deep breath. *Motherfucker!* "How do they know about the flower shop?"

He swallows. "I had Turner Mason meet me there the other day when he loaned me the money. In the alleyway."

I fist my hands, reminding myself I can't kill this kid. *Fuck!* "Was April there?" He nods and then looks away. "Get the fuck out of here!" I order, pointing at the door.

"I never meant for her to get hurt. Or the shop ..."

I grab him by the back of his neck since he's still shirtless and yank him to me. "I'm going to pay your debt." His eyes widen at that.

"But your ass is gonna pay me back every fucking cent. Do you understand that?"

He nods quickly. I shove him to the door. "Get the fuck out!"

Cross sighs, standing by the door. I never saw him enter. "Grave, man, I'm not sure this is a good idea."

"I didn't ask you!" I snap. Then I run a hand down my face. *Fuck.* I need a drink. Or to get high. Pulling out my cell, I make a call while exiting the room and head toward the thirteenth floor in tower one where our offices are.

GETTING OFF OUR PRIVATE ELEVATOR, I WALK PAST THE EMPTY reception desk and down the hallway, knowing she's in my brother's office. Titan would take her there.

I push open the door to find her sitting in a chair with her back to me. My brother sits behind the desk, as usual, with his eyes on her. Titan leans up against the wall, his arms crossed over his chest.

She spins around and jumps out of her seat when her watery eyes meet mine. I walk up to her and place both of my hands on her tear-streaked face. "I've taken care of it."

"Did you do this?" she asks, her ice blue eyes searching mine.

"No." I sigh. "I had nothing to do with it. But I'm gonna handle it."

She sniffs.

"How bad is the shop?" I ask.

"Destroyed."

My chest tightens. "Did they hurt you?"

She bites her bottom lip but stays quiet. There's a small bruise on her cheek. I remove my hands from her face and begin to run them over her shaking arms, looking for any sign of damage. Her hands have small cuts all over them, the blood now dried. I then run mine through her wild purple hair, and she hisses in a breath. I feel a cut, and my teeth clench. "How many were there?"

108

"Four," she whispers.

"When did it happen?" Titan asks, surprising me.

She stays looking at me but answers him. "Tonight. Maybe an hour ago."

My brother sits back in his seat, releasing a sigh. "Do we know who did it?"

"I don't know who they were," she answers him, but I nod.

I know them. Very well. "I'm gonna take you home," I tell her, and she doesn't argue.

SIXTEEN
GRAVE

WE EXIT THE front of the hotel, and my car is already waiting for us. "Here you go, Grave."

I help her into the passenger seat and then jump behind the wheel. Putting the car in gear, we take off.

She looks out the window, her head resting on it. "I don't wanna go home," she states softly.

"Roses?" I ask.

She just nods.

"Okay." I yank on the e-brake and turn the wheel, making a U-turn.

My phone begins to ring through the silent car, and I press ignore when I see **Lucy** light up.

Twenty minutes later, we pull up to the shop, and she doesn't wait for me to open her door. She enters, and I follow her. There's glass all over the place. The three glass doors to the left are all busted. Flowers and petals cover the floor along with water. The shelves to the right that held her vases are torn off and pieces of them are on the floor as well.

"I have someone coming," I tell her.

Her eyes meet mine. "What?"

"I made a call. A friend of mine is coming to stand guard at the door for the night. Then tomorrow morning, I have another friend coming to clean it up for you."

She looks away from me, tears building in her eyes. "You don't have to do that."

"I know."

She sniffs, and I walk over to her. Placing my fingers on her chin, I lift it so she looks up at me. The first tear runs down her face. "I'm ... I'm sorry for what I said before ..."

"Don't worry about it." The truth is, she wasn't far off. This is what I do. What the Kings do. I can't blame the Mason brothers for what they did. Or how they did it. But I can take care of this issue. I'll pay Ethan's debt, and it'll all go away. And I'll make sure her shop is better than it ever was.

I hear the bell go off, signaling someone entering, and I let go of her to turn and face my friend Lance. "Hey, man." I pull him in for a half man hug.

He whistles looking around. "Guessing you didn't do this?" he asks.

"No." Comes my clipped answer.

He nods, getting the point. "I'll stay as long as you need me to."

I turn around but don't see her. "April?" I call out, walking toward the back. I enter the office and see a door on the left open. I hear water running. Walking into it, I see it's a small bathroom, and she has her hands under the running faucet, washing them off.

I come up to her and see them shake. "Let me help you."

She sniffs as I pump some soap onto my hands and cover hers with mine. They begin to shake uncontrollably. "Hey." I grab them tightly. "You're okay," I assure her. "I'm going to take care of it."

She holds her head down, and I pull her hands from the water. "Look at me," I order.

She lifts her head, and my chest tightens at the look of defeat in her eyes. Everything this woman has gone through—her mother dying, having to quit college to take over her mom's shop, dealing with Ethan—is a lot. "I promise you. I'm going to take care of it."

She yanks her wet and soapy hands from mine and wraps them around my neck, burying her head into my chest. "Thank you," she sobs.

I let out a long breath, just thankful she's able to stand here in front of me. It could have been a lot worse. "Come on. Let's get you cleaned up and I'll take you home."

"I don't want to go home."

APRIL

WE WALK INTO Alexa's bar, and I sit at a booth in the corner. It's darker back here, and the music isn't as loud since there aren't speakers in this area. I'm not here to party or make friends. Just want a drink in quiet.

Grave sits down next to me. He remains silent. I hate that he's helping me after I accused him of sending them to the shop. I'll owe him big for this. But what am I supposed to do? The debt is too big for me to pay. I don't have that kind of money or resources, and I'm maxed out. The house Ethan and I live in isn't paid for. Business has been slow, and I didn't want to close, so selfishly, I took out a loan to keep it open. I thought I was doing the right thing. Now I realize that I was wrong. Is that why Ethan didn't come to me? Because he knew I couldn't afford to help him? He has to know I would have done anything to save him, even if that meant selling the shop. He is the most important person in my life. He's all I have left.

"April?" Derek comes up to our table with a big smile on his face, but it drops the moment he sees me. "What the hell happened to you?"

"I'm fine." I wave him off, not in the mood to talk about it. I washed off the dried blood and what little makeup I had left, but I have a bruised face and cuts on my hands.

"April—"

"Bourbon," I interrupt him, knowing a Corona isn't going to cut it tonight.

"I'll have what she's having," Grave speaks, and Derek looks over at him. His dark eyes narrow on him as if he just noticed I'm not alone.

Derek's eyes run over Grave's tatted up arm and neck. Then the piercings in his face. He is not impressed. "I thought I knew all of April's friends." He arches a dark brow.

"You do," I announce. My words don't offend Grave in the least. He leans back in the booth, places his arms out wide on the leather, and grins up at Derek.

"April, this is Grave," he growls, his eyes growing as he realizes who the guy is next to me. "He owns a quarter of Kingdom—"

"I know," I snap. Derek opens his mouth, but I speak first. "I came for a drink. Not a lecture."

He turns without saying another word.

"Ex?" Grave muses.

"Something like that." I place my elbows on the table and bow my head, trying hard not to think about what happened tonight but failing. Tears of anger threaten my eyes. I sniff.

"Hey." I feel his hand on my back, and I pull away from him.

"Don't," I warn. "Don't act like you care."

He sighs. "Of course I do, or I wouldn't have taken care of it."

"I didn't need you to do that," I snap, looking over at him.

His blue eyes roam my face before landing on mine. I plan on getting fucked up, and I know it won't take any convincing to get him there. "How were you going to pay them off?"

"I would have thought of something," I hiss, irritated with him. But not sure why. It's not his fault. I hate asking for help. And I hate it even more that he's the one who offered. He knows I can't afford to turn it down.

He leans forward, placing his forearms on the table, bringing his face in closer to mine. I refrain from pulling away. "What would you have done if they would have demanded payment from you?" He arches a pierced brow.

My stomach knots at his words. "What exactly are you implying?"

He reaches out, taking a few pieces of my purple hair between his fingers. His eyes watch the motion before running up my neck and over my face. "You're very beautiful, April." His eyes meet mine, and my breath picks up, remembering the weekend we just spent together and how it feels like it was a lifetime ago. "Men like the Mason brothers take whatever they want. So my question is, what would you have done if they wanted you?"

SEVENTEEN
GRAVE

THE MASON BROTHERS don't rape women, but that doesn't mean their thugs wouldn't. I have no doubt that if one of them wanted her, they would have done it. The only thing that kept her from being sexually assaulted was that they wanted money from her. If they would have forced themselves onto her, they would have killed her afterward. Then the Mason brothers would have killed them.

She looks away from me, dismissing the direction this conversation was going just as the punk returns with our drinks. "Here you go." He hands her hers and slams mine down on the table. Then he turns and walks back toward the bar.

I pick mine up and joke, trying to lighten the mood. "They don't keep rat poison in the back, do they?"

She snorts and places hers down and yanks mine from my hands. She tosses it back, hissing in a breath.

Two hours have gone by and I'm craving a hit. April is drunk. She can barely keep her eyes open. She hasn't said much. But Derek hasn't taken his eyes off us from his post behind the bar.

They have a past. I'm just not sure how far back it goes. The guy obviously has a thing for her, and it's not hard to tell they've fucked. He sees me as his competition, but I have news for him, there is nothing he could do to beat me. If I want it, I win.

April gets my attention when she slams her empty glass down on the table. "I'm ready ... to go." She hiccups.

"Okay." I pull a few hundred dollars from my wallet and throw them in the center of the table. Then I get out of the booth and reach out my hand to her. She's going to need help walking out of this place.

"April?" The douche comes up to the table. "You need to stay. Have some water ..."

"She'll be fine," I tell him, pushing him out of the way.

She takes my hand and scoots across the leather. Once she hits her feet, she stumbles into me. I wrap an arm around her small waist and throw hers over my shoulder.

"April." He steps into me. His chest pressed to mine. I have six inches on him, but I'm also holding a very drunk woman. Both of my hands are full.

"Step back," I warn.

"Or what?" He smirks. "Going to hit me?"

The fucker knows I can't hit him. If so, she'll fall. So I use the other option I have. My leg. I knee the motherfucker in the balls.

He falls to his knees, forcing him to the nasty ass bar floor when he doubles over. I readjust April, and we make our way out to my car.

APRIL

I know getting drunk was irresponsible. I'm drowning my problems for the time being, which I never really do. They're still going to be here tomorrow, but I'll deal with them then.

I fall into his passenger seat, and he shuts my door. My face falls into my hands, and I try my best to keep from crying. Yelling. If my brother were here, I'd punch him again just to get my point across.

"Hey." He rubs my back while we sit in the parking lot. I turn into him, letting him hug me.

"That was all she had." I sniff, inhaling his cologne as I bury my face into his shirt.

"Look at me." He places his fingers under my chin and lifts it, so I have to look up at him. "I'm going to take care of it. I promise. It's just a speed bump."

"I won't be able to repay you." That's the hardest pill to swallow. Our mother raised us to live within our means, but this is going too far. Maybe I should just sell the building as is and walk away.

"You won't owe me anything." He leans forward and kisses my forehead, and I sit back in his passenger seat as he fastens my seat belt, then starts the car before pulling out of the parking lot to take me home.

I lie my forehead against his cool window and my eyelids close on their own.

"April?" I hear his voice.

"Hmm?" I open my heavy eyes.

"We're here." He turns his car off.

I open the door and manage to climb out of his passenger seat. He's there the next moment to help me up the stairs and into the house. "Ethan?" I call out once we enter. "Ethan?" I get no response. "He better be here." I yawn.

"I'll check," he assures me.

He helps me up the stairs and into my room. I don't even care about showering right now. I grab my shirt and lift it up over my head before tossing it to the floor. Then I kick off my shoes and undo my jeans. I turn to see I'm alone in my room. "Grave?" I shove my jeans down my legs and fall into my bed. My sheets feel nice and cold. I close my heavy eyes but open them a second later.

"Here. Take this." He's standing next to my bed with a glass of water and two aspirin.

I toss them back and then take a sip of the water before handing it back to him. He places it on my nightstand and pulls the covers up to my neck. Then he runs his warm hand over my forehead.

"Thank you," I whisper. My eyes growing heavy again. It could be the loss of adrenaline or the drinks that I had. Possibly a combination of the two.

He smiles down at me, his perfectly straight teeth glowing in the soft light from my window. "I'm always here for you, April."

"I like you," I admit without shame. The sober me would have a red face but drunk April doesn't give a shit. It's why I don't drink very often; the truth will always bite you in the ass the next day. That's how I ended things with Derek. I was drunk and told him that although the sex was good, I didn't see us having a future. Thankfully, he was able to still be my friend.

He chuckles. "I'm glad to hear that because I like you too."

I sit up, placing my face right up against his. His panty-dropping smile disappears instantly. I reach out and run my hand down his shirt. I can feel his muscles tense underneath it. "April ..."

"Shh," I say against his lips. "I want you." And lean into him. My lips pressing against his as my heavy eyes close.

His hand cups my face, and he kisses me softly, delicately. I open my mouth for him to deepen the kiss, but he pulls away. I take a deep breath. "We shouldn't. Not tonight." He breathes, placing his forehead to mine.

"Grave ..."

My cell ringing in my purse on the floor interrupts me. He gets up from the bed, walking over to it, and I lie back down. My heart pounds, my mind foggy and pussy wet. This is not how I pictured my night going.

"Hello?" I hear him answer it. I don't even bother to ask who it is. "Yeah." He lowers his voice and turns his back to me, but I can still hear him. "Can you come over to April's and stay with her tonight?"

He pauses. "We went out, and she had a few drinks ..." I snort at that lie. "Thank you." He hangs up and walks over to the side of the bed again, placing my cell on my nightstand. The screen is busted, but it still works. I'll have to go buy a new one in the morning. "That was Jasmine. She's on her way to stay with you."

"Why can't you stay with me?" I ask through a yawn.

"I have somewhere to be."

EIGHTEEN
GRAVE

THE AIRPORT IS to the Mason brothers as Kingdom is to us Kings. They rule their domain. But the Kings run shit through a legit casino whereas the Mason boys run most of theirs illegally.

I pull up into the parking lot that back in the day was filled with rental cars.

The Mason brothers live like the Kings. Nothing is out of reach. They live like the billionaires they are. Running a multi-billion-dollar business has its perks.

Getting out, I walk through the parking lot and up to the double doors in the back like I own the place.

"Grave, didn't know you were fighting tonight," a man by the name of Miles says when I walk by.

"I'm not," I call out, walking over to the elevator. It takes me up to the fifth level, and when I get out, two men meet me with machine guns pointed right at me.

"Oh," Harry says. "Sorry, Grave."

"No worries," I say as they lower their weapons. The brothers keep this place highly guarded for many reasons. One is that there are always a few million dollars on-site. Cash that they keep in a safe room, but still. Over the years, men have tried to gain access to it. The place was even set on fire once, but not one penny was stolen. All four men were hung the following night.

The Mason brothers used them as an example.

I nod to the two guys and shoulder past them. Coming to the door at the end of the hall, I open it and enter. Four guys sitting at a round table. Trey Mason looks up at me. His dark eyes crinkle around the edges from his wide smile. He wears his shoulder holster with a Desert Eagle in each one. They look too big for his smaller build. Leaning back in his seat, he takes a drag from his cigarette before blowing it out. "Grave."

The man who stands at the table to the right, stuffing guns into cases, turns and looks at me. It's Tanner Mason. He's the eldest brother, and I thought he was in prison. Without another word, he goes back to packaging the weapons.

Trey stands and walks over to me, pulling me in for a manly handshake/hug. He slaps my back. "What's been going on?"

"Not much," I say, looking around the room. "Where's Turner?" He usually handles these types of situations. He's the middle brother. Trey, here, is the baby. They don't let him take care of much when it comes to business. And I really don't want to have to speak to Tanner. He hates me but has a legitimate reason to.

"He's loading the truck, preparing for a run to Phoenix tomorrow," he answers, checking his watch.

I nod. Among other things, the Mason brothers sell weapons and ammo to the Mexican Cartel. They are in as deep as you can get with them.

"Grave?" A guy who sits at the round table stares up at me. I can tell by the look in his eyes that he's high. Not to mention the lines of coke that sit before him on a small mirror. "I know you."

"I don't know you," I counter.

He smirks. "You won me twenty thousand last weekend."

Ahh, I see. *My fight.* "You're welcome."

"I told you," Trey adds. "The guy never loses a fight."

"Why are you here, Grave?" Tanner acknowledges me. His voice shows his irritation.

I square my shoulders. "May I speak to the two of you?" Might as well include him. If he's present, he's the boss. "Privately?"

Tanner's eyes drop to the duffel bag I'm carrying and nods. "In the office." He gestures his chin to the door at the back of the room.

Trey and I follow him and enter the room. On the wall behind the desk is a massive picture of a woman framed in black wood. The camera is above, looking down on her. She lies flat on her back in the middle of a king-size bed with her arms and legs spread wide open. Each limb is tied to each wooden corner post with rope. There's a black blindfold covering her eyes. Her fake tits stand straight up even though she's lying flat on her back. Both nipples pierced with spikes. Her mouth is held open with an O-ring open-mouth gag connected to a leather head harness. On her stomach is written *use me* in black magic marker.

Rumor is their father gave it to them when they took over his business. It's a reminder that men do as they please. They come as they please. Women are just toys to be used.

"What is it that you want, Grave?" Tanner asks, sitting at the desk, getting my attention. "Need some fire power?"

"Not today." I toss the bag onto the surface and unzip it. "It's fifty grand."

Tanner arches a brow, looking down at it, then back up at me. "If you want someone dead, you'll have to pay more than that."

Trey snorts.

I don't need a hitman. "I can do that on my own." We never use the Masons for help. My brother actually hates them. Titan has nothing to do with them. I don't mind them and neither does Cross. I used to spend a lot of time with Trey back in the day until we got fucked up together, and he did a job that led to Tanner going to jail. "This is about April."

His brows pull together. "Is that supposed to mean something?"

"Roses," I state.

"Ah, the little flower shop." He nods. "What about it?"

"Her brother owes you money. And this ..." I point at the money. "Is the payment."

Trey smiles. "So my goonies were able to make him pay up. Was he too afraid to come pay me himself?"

"No."

"Then what ...?"

"I'm doing this for his sister." Trey's brows rise at the declaration. "When your goonies showed up, she was the only one there."

He says nothing at that because he already knew. His guys would have reported that back to him. So he is also aware that they put their hands on her.

"So ... you're paying the kid's debt." Tanner speaks. "How generous of you."

My teeth grind. Showing concern for a woman shows weakness. And I've been fucking his little sister for years with no care in the world. "I told him he will be paying me back."

"I'm listening." Tanner leans forward at the desk.

"His ass will be in your ring. Fighting. Until I'm paid in full with interest."

He nods. "I'll put him on the roster."

Knew he wouldn't mind. "One more thing."

"What is it?" He sighs, looking at his watch as though I'm keeping him from something important.

"Promise me that you won't return to Roses."

"Grave ..."

I wasn't done. "And you won't touch April."

He stands, his shoulders squaring. The Mason brothers don't like being told what to do. The Kings don't necessarily work with them. We each stay in our own corners, per se. But I need his word because I'll hold him to it.

He begins to walk around the desk, leaning up against it, and places his hands in the front pockets of his black jeans. "And you?"

126

"What about me?" I ask, already knowing exactly where this is headed. I expected it.

"I want you on that roster. You fight. Here."

I haven't fought here in years. Growing up, this is where I came. Back then, you were limited on where you could beat the shit out of someone. Now that I own Kingdom, I can walk into that ring whenever the fuck I want. I'm not an MMA fighter or a boxer. I don't do it for the money. I do it because I literally want to beat the shit out of someone. But I knew coming in that the money wasn't going to be enough. Not when they're presented with an opportunity to make more. I'd do the same thing. "I'll fight."

Finally, he nods. "Then you have my word. We won't touch Roses or April. But I can't make any promises on the kid. He's here a lot. This isn't the first time he's owed us money."

"I'll handle him," I state. I'll wrap a fucking shock collar around his neck, if need be.

"Then it's settled." He picks up the bag and walks out. Probably to go put it in the safe room.

Trey comes over to me and slaps me on the shoulder. "Let's have some fun."

I want to say no, but instead, I find him leading me out of the office and back to the table that sits in the center of the room. I plop down in a seat just as the door opens. In walks Lucy and I inwardly sigh. I've been ignoring her

She wears a black leather miniskirt with heels that lace up her calves and a white see-through shirt with a black bra. Her bleach blond hair up in a high ponytail and looks like her leftover makeup is still on from yesterday.

"Hey, babe." She walks over to me. "I didn't know you were going to be here." She pushes my chair back and straddles my legs before I have a chance to avoid the situation. Her skirt riding up in the process.

My eyes drop to her black lace covered pussy and then back up to hers. I instantly think of April, and my lips on hers in her room an

127

hour ago. She wanted me. I wanted her. Fuck, how I wanted her. But she was drunk and had been attacked. She needed to rest and heal. I needed to get the fuck out of there and take care of business before the Masons sent their bitches back to do more damage. I'm just thankful that Jasmine had called her. Ethan wasn't at the house, so there's no telling where that punk ass kid is. I needed someone there watching her. For her safety and my sanity.

"Hey." Lucy gets my attention, wrapping her arms around my neck and whispering in my ear. "I've missed you." She starts rubbing her hips into mine.

I see Trey watching me out of the corner of my eye. He's taking it in. Seeing how I react to her. I just paid fifty grand and made them swear not to touch April. They know there's something going on there. I need to play up my role with Lucy for now. Since she is the one half naked on my lap and I've never turned her down before.

My hands grip her thighs and I lick my lips. "I tried calling you earlier." Lie. "It went straight to voicemail."

The door opens and Tanner re-enters, followed by Turner. "Jesus Christ, Lucy. Have some fucking respect for yourself!" he hisses.

Turner Mason is the middle child. He does runs for the Cartel and takes out their competition. He's their own personal hitman. He and Tanner are all business, but Tanner doesn't mind getting his dick wet, no matter the situation. Turner's dick is a little more complicated than that. He used to be obsessed with a girl. I don't know the whole situation, but I wouldn't be surprised if he kidnapped her and has her tied to a bed, mimicking the girl in the picture that hangs in their office.

Her head snaps over to glare up at him. "Fuck you, Turner!"

Tanner tosses my now empty duffel bag by my chair. Turner just shakes his head in disappointment at his sister.

Lucy grew up without a mother. She had her brothers and a dad, so all she knows is men. I'm not saying it's an excuse. I'm just saying that I understand where she thinks she has to be half naked and high for attention. Her father raised her to be like the woman in the picture hanging on the office wall. And if I told her I wanted to do the same thing to her right now on this table while everyone watched, she would say yes in a heartbeat.

I'm not into that—bondage, BDSM—*crawl to me on all fours and lick my shoes while you call me daddy* type of shit. Bones is, though. Bones has to be in control in every aspect of his life. That's why he stays sober, and I'm always high. I like the out-of-control experience.

Can I be aggressive in bed? Absolutely. But I'm not into degrading women.

"He's such an ass," she growls, watching Turner over my shoulder while she still straddles my hips.

"When did Tanner get out?" I whisper in her ear so no one can hear us.

"Last week. Wish he'd go back."

My brows arch. They used to be close since he was the one who ended up raising her. Their dad passed when she was thirteen, and Tanner took over the father role, but it was too late. She had already been groomed to be a whore and needed acceptance from any man she could get her hands on. But I don't think any less of her. I've never been one to judge someone, and I'm not going to start now.

"Let's go back to my place," she offers, kissing my neck.

Fuck! I'm not sleeping with her now. Not after I slept with April. That's who I want. That's why I've been avoiding Lucy.

"No, he's here to hang out with us." Trey saves me. "So get off his cock and go do some work." He slides the mirror covered in cocaine, razor blade and hundred-dollar bill over to me.

"Trey ..." She starts to whine.

"You heard him," Tanner barks at her. "Go get to work, Lucy."

She glares at him over my shoulder, and that right there is why she wants him to go back to prison—he's making her work. Probably serving drinks or taking bets down in the pit for the fights.

"Fucking bastard," she hisses, getting off my lap and shoving her skirt down her thighs. Trey laughs at her as she storms out.

APRIL

I WAKE UP with a pounding headache. Rolling over onto my side, I bury my face into my pillow and groan.

"That rough, huh?"

I sit up with a scream at the sound of another's voice.

"Whoa." Jasmine holds up her hands with her back resting against my headboard.

"What are you doing here?" I ask, placing my hand to my pounding chest.

She tilts her head to the side and frowns. "Damn. You were really drunk last night."

I fall back onto the bed.

"I called you, and Grave answered, asking me to come stay with you. Something about you were drunk. He had something to go do, and he didn't want to leave you alone."

"Grave asked you to come over?" I look up at her.

She nods, shoving a flaming hot Cheeto in her mouth. "He waited for me to get here before he left."

I smile and pull the covers up to my neck before I roll over onto my side to face her.

"Oh God." She laughs.

"What?" I ask.

"I know that look. You like him," she states matter-of-factly.

"I ..."

"Like really, really like him." She wiggles her dark brows.

I pull the covers over my head so she can't see my cheeks turn the color of her Cheetos.

She rips them off and smiles down at me. "He needs someone like you."

"What does that mean?" I ask, sitting up and pulling the covers with me. I dig my hand into her bag and take a chip.

"Grave can be a good guy. He just needs someone who is willing to straighten him out."

That didn't help me understand one bit. "Either I'm still asleep or I'm too drunk to make sense of your words."

She sighs. "Grave isn't one of those guys who hides his feelings. He feels more than anyone I know, and when I got here last night, I could tell he cares about you."

My heart starts to race at her words. "Why? What did he do?"

"The fact that he didn't leave until I arrived tells me all I need to know."

"How well do you know him?" I don't get to spend time alone with Jasmine, but I remember Grave talking about knowing her really well.

"I've known him all my life." She eats another Cheeto. "After his mom passed, he ..."

"Wait." I place my hand up. "His mom died? When?" That was how I met him. He ordered flowers for his mother's birthday.

"Uh, let me think." She holds up her right hand. "I think he was eighteen when she died. May have been seventeen. We were in high school."

I tune her out as I look at my wall, trying to figure out why he ordered her flowers if she's dead. I mean, I know that people place flowers on graves of loved ones they've lost, but he never once mentioned that. He made it sound like she was alive. He even told me she loved them. Why would he ...?

I close my eyes. I had written on the card. He left it blank, and I thought it had been a mistake. I was wrong. *Shit!* "Fuck!" I growl.

"What?" she asks.

I open my eyes and scrunch up my face. "I think I did something bad."

"Oh." Her green eyes get big with excitement. "Tell me. Tell me. I'm awesome at keeping secrets."

NINETEEN

GRAVE

I KNOCK ON the hotel suite door at Kingdom.

"Coming." I hear the woman's voice. Seconds later it opens. "Grave, hi."

"May I come in?" I ask her.

"Of course." She steps to the side and I walk into the suite, looking around.

"Everything okay?" she asks from behind me.

I turn to face her. "Yeah, I just wanted to come and give you this." I reach into my back pocket and pull out the envelope full of cash.

"Grave." Natalie raises her hands, shaking her head. "I can't take that ..."

"I need you to hide here for a few more weeks."

Her eyes widen. "Grave ..."

"I've got it handled." I promise her. "I just need you to promise me."

She nods, biting her bottom lip.

"Has he tried to contact you?"

"Yeah." She sighs. "I called my provider and had him blocked."

"Good. That's good." I start to walk back toward the door. "I have

133

to go, I just wanted to come by and let you know that everything is going to be okay." I hand her the envelope again and this time she takes it.

Exiting her suite, I make my way down to the parking garage to get my car. Making my way to Roses.

"THANKS, MAN," I TELL LANCE.

"No problem. Let me know if you need me again," he says, exiting the front door of Roses.

I turn to a good friend of mine who owns Landing Construction. I sent him a message last night to meet me here first thing this morning. "How long do you think it'll take?" I ask him.

He's walking around, his cell in his hand, taking notes. "Honestly?" He sighs. "Maybe a week." He shrugs. "But that's once the parts come in." He makes his way over to where the three glass doors once were. "I got the measurements for the glass and the shelves." He looks over across the room where the vases sat. "Getting them installed won't take much time, though. My crew could have it done within a couple of days."

I nod. "Just let me know what I owe you."

He locks his phone and places it in his back pocket. "I'll have it ordered by lunch and will let you know."

I look up when the bell rings and see April enter. She has a white baseball hat on with her hair up in a ponytail that's popping out through the back. She wears a black T-shirt with cutoff denim shorts and a pair of black Superstars. A coffee in her right hand and sunglasses shielding her eyes.

I slap him on the back, dismissing him. "Sounds good."

"Miss." He nods to her as he exits Roses.

"Who was that?" she asks, coming over to me.

"That was the man who is going to make this place look like new," I answer, letting my eyes run over her bare legs. My cock reminds me that I turned her down last night. My mind reminds me it was the right thing to do. "How do you feel?" I clear my throat and try to think of anything but me and her naked in her bed.

"Like run over dog shit."

I frown. "Why aren't you at home in bed?"

She removes her glasses and throws them down on the front counter and starts to walk toward the back. "Because my brother never came home last night so I figured he'd be here."

I follow her to the back office. She shoves the door open, and it's empty. "I've been here for an hour, and I haven't seen him."

She sighs, running a hand down her face before she looks up at me. She's washed her face clean of the makeup from last night. Falling down into the chair behind the desk, she rips her hat off her head. "Who did this?" she asks.

"The Mason brothers," I answer.

She hangs her head but doesn't say anything to that. I highly doubt she knows who they are. "You need to go home," I tell her.

Her eyes narrow up at me. "I need to be here."

"There's nothing you can do right now. I've had the place cleaned, and the contractor was just here. It could take a couple of weeks before it's ready to re-open."

She slams her fists down on the desk. "I'm going to fucking kill him."

"I've taken care of it."

"I wouldn't need your help if he hadn't gone and fucked someone over!" she yells.

I change the subject. "How did you even get here?" Her car was at Kingdom last night when we left in mine.

"Jasmine took me to get a new phone since my screen was shattered. Then to Kingdom to get my car," she growls. "And why did you have her stay with me?" She arches a dark brow. "I didn't need a babysitter, Grave."

She did. But I'm not telling her that. I watched her deck her brother like he was nothing, so I don't want her jumping over that desk and coming at me. One, she'd hurt herself, and two, I was raised that you don't hit women, even if they punch you.

Thankfully, the sound of the bell ringing gets me out of having to lie to her. She gets up from the desk and runs out of the office.

"Where the fuck have you been?" I hear her demand before I even make it back to the front of the shop.

Ethan stands there with a black eye and busted lip. He looks around and sighs. "Did I tell you I was sorry?"

"Your words don't mean shit!" she snaps at him.

I walk up behind her and place my hands on her shoulders. She shrugs me off and steps into him. "You will pay Grave back for every penny."

"Yes, ma'am." He nods.

I cross my arms over my chest, expecting him to tell her that I already told him that, but he doesn't.

"And you will be here at Roses working every day the moment we open back up," she adds.

He nods. "Yes, ma'am."

"Your ass will be home by nine o'clock every night, and you will always inform me where you're at!" He opens his mouth, but she goes on. "And you're no longer allowed at Kingdom. You're too goddamn young to be there anyway!"

He nods once again. "Yes, ma'am."

With that, she spins around and heads back to the office, slamming the door shut.

APRIL

It's been a week since I found out my brother owed the Mason brothers. I feel bad about how I yelled at Ethan the morning after. I had become a mom to him, no longer a sister, but I feel like he's making poor life choices that are going to get him killed. If that means being his enemy, I can live with myself.

So far, he's held up to his word. He's at the shop helping me get it back up and running. And home every night. He doesn't speak much to me, but he can hate me all he wants as long as he follows the rules.

I exit my shower and wrap a towel around my chest, tucking it into itself and see Grave at my sink brushing his teeth. I don't get to see him very much. Kingdom takes up most of his time. At least, I hope that's where he is and not with Lucy. The question is always there on the tip of my tongue, but I'm too chicken to ask. I lean up against the counter and look at him. "This is my fault," I admit. Shame washes over me. It reminds me that I've failed Ethan. I could have been better. It's my fault that we're in the mess we're in anyway.

He rinses out his mouth and sets the toothbrush down. "Well, if you weren't so tempting, I could get to work on time." He yanks the towel free of my body. His blue eyes instantly dropping to my legs.

"No." I slap his chest. "The fact that Ethan is in trouble."

He sighs, running a hand through his dark hair. He doesn't like to talk about it. Every time I bring it up, he changes the subject. As if he's taken care of it, and it's over. But it's not.

"He wanted to move back home when our mother passed, but I wanted to stay. I shouldn't have been so selfish." There was nothing there for us. Seattle was depressing. I thought a life in Vegas would be better, but I was wrong. "Too many things are readily available, making it easy for him to get in trouble. They don't call it Sin City for nothing." And he's still two years away from being twenty-one. What will happen in years to come when he realizes he doesn't need me and my strict rules?

"Listen." He grips my hips, then spins us around to where he's leaning up against the countertop, and I'm standing between his legs. "I have it under control. He's not going to get into any more trouble. Not while I'm around," he adds with a smirk.

I've noticed that Grave doesn't take much seriously. When the situation starts to head that way, he makes jokes. "And how long is that for?" I ask, biting my lip nervously. I owe him so much already. How can I ask him for more? He's quickly becoming someone that I like having around.

His eyes scan my face as he reaches up and places a few strands of wet hair behind my ear. "However long you want me to be."

I wrap my arms around his neck and lean up on my tiptoes to press my lips to his. He's right about one thing—I'm always making him late. It has been so long since I've had any sexual release that I crave it from him. Need it. He's so fucking good at it.

"Are you coming back over tonight?" I ask when I pull away.

"No. I'll be at the Airport tonight." He frowns at that thought, running his finger down my chest bone.

Why would he be there? "Doing what?"

His cell starts to vibrate next to him where it sits on the counter-top. **Bones** flashes across his screen, and I step back so he can walk out of the bathroom to answer it.

I haven't brought up his mother or the fact that he ordered her flowers. His reasons aren't any of my business. I just hope that what-ever he needed from those flowers, he got. Everyone grieves differently. And there is no timeframe on how long you can mourn a loved one.

I start my morning after-shower ritual when he comes back into the bathroom.

"What were we talking about?" he asks, walking up behind me.

"You blowing me off tonight."

He pulls my wet hair off my shoulder, and his eyes meet mine in the mirror. "It'll be late."

"You can wake me up." I offer.

He spins me around, grips my hips, and sets my ass on the cold counter. "How would you like me to do that?" he asks.

"Surprise me."

He steps between my legs, pressing mine apart, and grips my wet hair, pulling my head back. Then his lips are on mine, letting me know we're both going to be late today. The only difference is he has a job to get to and all I have is an empty shop.

TWENTY

GRAVE

"WHAT CAN I get you?" I ask the guy who stands at the bar inside of Crown. I run it most of the time. Bones didn't want it. Titan was too busy running the Queens and Cross wanted to open up his own tattoo parlor, so I took our exclusive night club at Kingdom.

"Two shots of Patron and two Miller Lites," he answers, pulling his card out of his wallet.

I turn my back to him and start to pop the tops on the beers when I feel my cell vibrate in my back pocket.

"Hey, get him two shots of Patron," I holler at one of my bartenders as I step away to answer my phone in the office. "What's up?"

"Hey, man. Just wanted to let you know that Randy has been booked."

Fucking finally. "What are the charges?"

"Well, your plan worked. Not only did the bastard decide to fuck up, he did a royal job at it." I smile. "He ran his car right into a tree. He was drunk and had pills on him. When we went to arrest him, he punched my partner in the face."

"Yes." I chuckle.

"Yep, it definitely worked in our favor," he adds. "But it gets better."

"Go on."

"Found out that he did have a warrant. But it's out of Florida. And they want to extradite him. He's looking at fifteen to twenty years there."

"That's good enough for me. Thanks, man." I hang up the phone and walk back out into the club. First thing in the morning I'll go and tell Natalie the good news.

APRIL

I WALK INTO Roses, and people are already here working on the shop. This week has been intense, to say the least. I accepted Grave's money to fix the shop, not like he was going to give me an option. And I hate to admit it, but it looks better than it did before.

Workers have been in and out every day doing the finishing touches so I can open Monday. I just set my purse on the counter when I see the front door open. "Hey."

"What's up, ho?" Jasmine asks, removing her sunglasses and eyeing the guy's ass bent over cleaning up his mess off the floor. She winks and gives me a smile.

"What are you girls doing here?" I ask.

Haven places her Louis Vuitton on the counter next to my fifteen-dollar purse. I have a feeling these women grew up with money. "We wanted to stop by and see the shop."

I haven't told them about what happened. I'm too ashamed and afraid they will judge Ethan. He's really a good kid who just made some bad choices. Haven't we all done that at some point? "Thanks. It should be ready for business on Monday." As far as they know, I'm remodeling, and they have no clue that Grave is footing the bill.

"I saw the boutique next door to you is for sale," Jasmine adds. "Have you thought about buying it? Expanding?"

"No. But that would be a good idea." If that was an option. I don't get enough business to justify that kind of expansion, but a girl can dream.

The door opens, and Emilee walks in followed by Titan. I swallow nervously. He knows what happened here and that the Mason brothers are responsible for the destruction. I'm praying he doesn't say anything.

"You look like you just rolled out of bed," Jasmine says to Emilee.

Her dark hair is up in a messy bun, and she's wearing one of Titan's T-shirts that's hanging off one shoulder with a pair of gray yoga pants and tennis shoes.

Emilee waves her off. "We just had a couples massage. Dear Lord, it was amazing!" She sighs, rubbing her neck.

Titan walks up to the counter and pulls an envelope out of his back pocket, sliding it toward me.

"What's this?" I ask, picking it up.

"That is your deposit for our wedding," he answers.

I open it up. "Deposit ....?" I trail off as I pull the check out. It's written out to me for twenty-five thousand dollars. "What?" I breathe.

"I figured that would be enough to get started." He knocks his knuckles on the counter, then turns, giving Emilee a kiss. "You ladies have fun today," he calls out before he leaves.

"Emilee?" I cough out her name. "This is ..."

"Not enough?" she asks, tilting her head. "I can write you another one for the difference."

Is she joking? "...insane."

She waves me off as though she just bought me a five dollar lunch.

"No. Seriously." I put it down and walk over to her. "I don't even have the ability to produce that much. It's just me ..."

"You have us." Jasmine throws her arm over my shoulders, pulling me into her side. "We will help make it happen."

"What?" I look up at her in a daze. The shop has been down for a week, so I'm already behind. I would love nothing more than to do this for Emilee and Titan, but it's just not possible.

"We're the kind of girls who have your back. No matter what," Jasmine adds with a wink.

Haven nods. "We got it."

Emilee smiles. "Just let me know when and where you need me."

Jasmine pulls away from me and places her eyes back on the guy who is now on his knees, back to setting the tile. "I know where I wanna be." She whistles.

I SIT AT THE TABLE EATING LUNCH WITH THE GIRLS. THEY talked me into walking down the street to a sub shop. My mind is still reeling from the check Titan wrote out to me and trying to figure out how I can give Emilee what she wants. My biggest fear has always been failure. Having to close the shop that my mother loved so much. And if it wasn't for Grave, I would have had to do that a week ago when it got destroyed.

Jasmine starts digging through her Saint Laurent purse next to me. Emilee and Haven sit across from us in our booth next to the window.

"What are you girls doing tonight?" I ask, trying to get my mind off it.

"Titan is getting off early today and we're leaving town. Flying to New York for the weekend." Emilee answers first.

"What are you doing there?" Haven asks, taking a sip of her water.

"Are you going to that sex club?" Jasmine asks excitedly. "If so, I want to come."

"No." Emilee laughs. "One of Titan's friends is opening his restaurant tonight, and he invited us."

"Sex club?" I ask Jasmine.

She nods quickly, pulling a lip balm container out of her purse.

"It is cool as fuck. Membership only. Like a secret society, BDSM style."

Haven rolls her eyes, and Emilee chuckles.

"Interesting," I mumble, taking a sip of my diet Coke.

"I so want to open one here," Jasmine goes on.

"Grave said he was going to the Airport tonight. I wanted to go," I say. Obviously, it's not McCarran or he would have said that. I can't see the guy having a second job. Kingdom already takes up too much of his time. But what the fuck else would he be doing there? He didn't say *hey I'm going out of town for the night, be back tomorrow.* So he can't be flying somewhere.

"Oh, there's no way Luca would let me go there." Haven shakes her head. "I'm not even going to ask."

"I would if we were in town." Emilee frowns. "I can go with you girls next weekend for sure, though."

"I'll go with you," Jasmine says, unscrewing the lid. "What about Alexa?"

"She can't. She has to work the bar at night until she can hire more help." I don't get to see her all that much unless I go up there to hang out. The woman is a hustler. Owning two businesses doesn't allow much time to play.

Jasmine runs her fingers through the lip balm and goes to put the lid back on. "Anyone want some?"

"Sure." I reach out and dig my finger into it before smearing it across my lips. Then I rub them together. "Mmm, tastes like watermelon."

"So good." She agrees.

My lips start to tingle immediately. "What is this?" I lick them. The tingle intensifies to a burning sensation. "My lips are stinging."

She looks at the container. "It's actually nipple enhancer."

"What?" I squeak, dipping my napkin in Emilee's water and placing it on my lips.

"It makes them tingle," she explains as if I don't understand. "Enhances them for nipple play."

"Shit. They're on fire, Jasmine." I hiss in a breath. I can feel them expanding like a balloon.

"I know." She smiles. "I like it."

"I wanna try." Emilee reaches across the table and puts some on her lips.

"Why are you using that?" Haven asks.

"It makes your lips plump," Jasmine answers in a duh voice.

"Why don't you just get your lips done?" Haven offers.

"I'm not quite ready for that commitment," she replies.

"Hmm." Emilee nods. "I like it too."

"What even made you think to put it on your lips?" I ask, holding the soaked napkin to my mouth.

"I tried it on my nipples one night. A guy was sucking on them, then kissed me. Boom! It's my newest lip balm."

Note to self: never use anything that Jasmine has on her. It's like just say no when a stranger offers you candy. "What time are we going to the Airport tonight?" I manage to mumble, running an ice cube over my swollen lips. It reminds me of going to the dentist and your mouth going numb from the injections.

"I'll pick you up around ten, and we'll get ready at my house," Jasmine answers.

"Isn't that late?" I ask, the ice melting and running down my chin.

"If Grave is at the Airport, then he's there to fight. And he'll be the main event. That doesn't happen until two or three a.m."

"Fight?" My brows rise.

Emilee nods. "Oh, yeah. Grave kicks ass at fighting. The guy can't lose."

"He's never mentioned it," I mumble, wondering just how much I don't know about him. We don't have heart-to-heart conversations. I've never been the type of woman to push a guy to give me details about their life. Maybe because I'm not one for sharing either. But my life is pretty boring.

TWENTY-ONE
APRIL

I STAND IN Jasmine's bathroom, curling my hair. The room is bigger than my master bedroom. It has heated floors and a marble counter. His and her sinks. She stands in front of one while I'm in front of the other. The whirlpool bathtub sits off to the right of us with the large shower behind it that you can enter from either side. I looked inside, and there are five showerheads. There's a fireplace in the corner that is see-through into her master suite. I'd never leave this bathroom.

"Can I ask you something personal?" I turn to face her.

"Sure. I'm an open book." She pops the lid off her lipstick.

"What did Haven mean by Luca would never allow her to go to the Airport? Is he really controlling? I remember that there was a guy who you mentioned was her *babysitter* when we were at lunch that first time I met her." I think they said his name was Nite.

"Luca runs the Las Vegas American-Italian mafia."

I gasp. *Holy shit!* Derek was right! "You're serious?" He had said that Bones had an in with the mafia. And Luca was on the phone talking about going to Kingdom. Could that be the connection? If so, then that means he's got to be close to Grave as well.

"Yep." She nods. "Don't you ever watch the news? Their engagement was a big deal."

"No," I say honestly, going back to my hair somewhat in a daze.

"Well, a lot of people would love to get their hands on Haven to get to Luca. So although to some, he may appear controlling or possessive, he's really just keeping her safe."

"I can see that." I can't imagine the kind of life where you're always having to look over your shoulder or never knowing who is after your husband. Or yourself. Wanting a family but afraid to bring a child into that world.

"Are you ready for that kind of life?"

I set the curling iron down and look over at her. "What do you mean by that?"

"I mean ..." She pops her nude-colored lips. "That being with a King could have the same ramifications. They're powerful but also hated by many. Being with one could make things difficult. For you. For him."

"Are you asking me if I'm in love with Grave and willing to risk my life for that?" That's what I take from her cryptic words.

She gives me a quick side-eye. "Are you?"

"No," I answer, shaking my head.

She sets down her lipstick and turns to face me, a smirk on her face as if she knows some secret. "So you're willing to walk away from him?"

I go to say yes but shut my mouth. "I mean ... I like him."

She places her hand on my shoulder. "Do you like him enough to fight for him?"

My mother raised my brother and me to fight for what you want, but you also can't make someone love you. They either want you in their life or they don't. You can't keep what doesn't belong to you. "What exactly am I fighting?" I ask confused.

"Lucy. I know she would do anything to have him, however she could have him. Even if that meant being a side piece."

"You're saying he's not the type to be faithful?" *Is anyone?* I'm not going to put Grave in a category with just men. Women cheat too. I've never done it because I've had it happen to me, and it hurt. I don't understand why a man or woman can't just be honest with the person they're with and say *I don't want to be with you anymore.*

"No, you're putting words in my mouth." She sighs. "I'm just saying that you need to decide what you want. Either take it or let her have it." She shrugs. "Because honey, that choice is a hundred percent yours."

She walks off to enter her closet. Grave doesn't make me feel like I have to compete or there is a race I'm desperately trying to win. But that doesn't mean it doesn't exist. I know Lucy still calls him. The question is, does he call her after he leaves me? And if he does, how would that make me feel? Pretty fucking pissed if I'm being honest with myself!

He's supposed to be mine, right? We've only had one official date, but who the fuck has time to date anymore? I don't need to get dressed up and go to an expensive dinner for someone to prove they like me. I just need quality time with them, and we've done that. Every chance we've gotten. I feel comfortable around him and can be myself. He's saved me. He's saved my dream. That means more than lobster and steak. The way his lips kiss mine make me melt. The way he touches me sets me on fire. And I know I do the same to him. He can't stop because he keeps coming back for more.

Is it just sex for him? I can't answer that. Only he can. But he did say he was staying around as long as I wanted him to.

I look at myself in the mirror and take a deep breath. I don't want to share him. I want to be selfish.

Making up my mind, I pull my eyeliner out of my makeup bag and put on a couple more layers top and bottom before grabbing my hair and teasing the crown to give it a little more volume.

"How's this look?"

I turn to see Jasmine wearing a black crop top, hanging off one shoulder, revealing a black lace bra strap in a pair of denim shorts and fishnet tights. "Dammmmnn." I approve. The woman is hot.

"You think?"

My eyes drop to her legs. "What happened to your knees?" I ask.

She growls. "I gave head last night. Fucked my knees all up."

"On what? Gravel?"

She lets out a sigh. "That's why I wore the fishnets. To try to hide them better. Are they that bad?"

I shake my head. "No. I just noticed the right one ..." The left isn't as bad. But you can see they're bruised, and one has a pretty good cut. "I hope you got yours too," I add.

She gives me a smile. "Oh, he delivered." The smile drops off her face. "Then he went and fucked it all up."

She drives us about thirty minutes outside of Vegas. All I see is desert for most of it, but then sure enough, there's an airport in the middle of nowhere. It looks like McCarran on Thanksgiving break. Cars and trucks fill a large parking lot on the side. She pulls into a parking garage and takes us up to the sixth level. People walk around, getting on and off the elevators.

She finds a spot and pulls into it, shutting off the car. "Stay close to me," she says.

"Is this place dangerous?" I suppose that's a question I should have asked before we came. I would have packed Mace in my bag.

"It can get rowdy." She nods, reaching in front of me and pops open her glove box. She grabs a knife, before slamming it shut. Then reaches into the back seat and grabs her purse, shoving the knife inside of it.

"Hey, ladies." A guy whistles at us as we walk by his truck. He has the tailgate down and sits on it with two of his friends. You can smell the weed they're smoking. "Wanna ride?" He grabs his crotch.

"Sorry, boys." She reaches out, throwing her arm over my shoulders, pulling me into her side. "The only thing she'll be riding is my face later."

His eyes widen and one of his friends spits out his drink. "Can we watch?" he asks, hopeful.

I laugh at the fact he thought she was being serious.

"They're all the same," she whispers, shaking her head.

We walk across a sky bridge and enter the building. It looks exactly like an airport would. There are conveyor belts where luggage would ride, waiting for passengers to pick them up, but they look like they haven't been used in years.

We step onto a moving sidewalk and come up to the terminals. I stop and walk over to one, looking out the floor-to-ceiling windows to the runway. People crowd around while cars are lined up at the end. A woman stands before them with a green flag in her hands. "What are they doing?" I ask as Jasmine comes to stand next to me.

"Racing. They do it every night." She turns and walks off, and I follow her.

We go down an escalator and walk through the building, passing more gates until we come up to what appears to have once been a food court. Looking down over a railing, I see an arena-like structure. A makeshift bar sits off to the right, and people are crowded around it.

Two men stand in the middle of the arena, fighting. It's not like a UFC fight. This is more of a backyard kind of fight. One guy wears a hoodie and jeans while the other is in shorts and a wifebeater. No gloves or mouth guards.

We make our way downstairs and to the bar, ordering some drinks.

"Jasmine?"

She stiffens beside me as someone from behind us calls out her name. Turning around, she leans her back against the bar. "What are you doing here?" she asks.

I look over my shoulder to see a guy walk up to her with a smile covering his handsome face. Brown eyes look her up and down while he licks his lips, like he's thinking of the past. "Oh, my God, babe." He reaches out to hug her.

She places her hands up, stopping him. "Go away, Trenton." She dismisses him and turns back to the bar just as the bartender sets two drinks down in front of us.

I reach into my purse to grab a twenty, but she sets a card down. "I want to start a tab," she tells the guy.

He nods and takes it.

"Babe?" The guy behind us continues. "I've been calling you."

"Yeah? How's your wife feel about that?" she asks, not looking back at him.

My brows rise.

He makes his way next to her, placing his forearm on the bar. "I told you we're getting a divorce."

She laughs. "You always were a liar."

He looks at me. Nodding his head, he winks. What the fuck, dude? "Hey, baby ..."

"She's dating Grave," she informs him.

His eyes widen for a split second and then go back at her. "Jas, come on ..."

"Go away, Trenton!" she snaps at him. "Or I'll send screenshots of those pics of your cock that you keep sending me to your wife with the time stamp and dates."

His jaw tightens, but that's enough to make him storm off back into the crowd. "Divorcing his wife, my ass," she hisses, then lifts her hand for the bartender.

"I'm guessing that wasn't the guy from last night?" I ask.

She snorts. "No. The guy from last night isn't married, but I'm not sure he's any better." She slaps the bar. "Fuck this drink. We need shots."

APRIL

An hour and countless shots later, we remain close to the bar when I look to the right and see Grave standing about twenty feet away talking to a man who is with a woman. He's shirtless, wearing nothing but a pair of black basketball shorts and tennis shoes, and his hair is wet like he just showered. My eyes run over his tatted and muscular body. My thighs tighten. Grave is by far the sexiest man I've ever seen. He has that unobtainable air about him. Like he's the type of guy you want but know you can't keep. The one who would give you a night of endless orgasms and never call you back. An absolute fuckboy. Yet he keeps coming back. And I keep letting him in. I'm going to ride that train until it runs off the tracks.

"Who is Grave talking to?" I ask, placing my attention on someone else. I'm drunk and horny. "That woman looks familiar." She has dark brown hair pulled up in a high ponytail. She wears a simple white sundress with black Superstars. She looks cute yet comfortable but totally out of place here with this crowd.

Jasmine follows my line of sight. "That is Lovely Mathers."

"I know that name …"

"Judge Mathers' daughter." She fills in the blank.

"Right." I nod. "Didn't she have a drug problem and went to rehab?" I remember reading something like that about her.

"Rumor is her father put her in a psych ward but told everyone she went to rehab."

"Is she crazy?" I ask.

Jasmine throws her head back, laughing. "Girl, the right man can make any sane woman crazy."

"True."

"But no, she wasn't. She went to school with us. She made straight A's and was never in trouble. Her younger brother went missing, and Judge Mathers announced her stay in rehab. Said that after the disappearance she turned to drugs and alcohol abuse."

"But you don't believe that?"

"Nope." She shakes her head. "My ex Trenton…" She growls the words. "At the time said that his mother saw her being brought into the psych ward of the hospital by her father. That she was screaming and crying. He took her into a room, then came out alone."

"He just left her there?" I ask in shock.

"I've heard she was put in a straitjacket and remained in it for two weeks while locked in a padded room."

"Jesus." I hiss.

"I've also been told that she was restrained to a hospital bed for two weeks with a catheter and fed through a feeding tube down her nose. Either one could be true. Or it could be worse. Who knows?"

"Why would her father do that to her?" What has happened to that poor girl?

"Look around." She lifts her hands to gesture to the crowd. "How do you think the Kings and the Mason brothers run this town? It's because they pay someone higher up a cut."

I swallow at the mention of the Mason brothers. "So he's just a twisted fuck."

"Yep, and he won't let anyone stand in his way. Not even his daughter."

"Poor thing." She just stands there, her eyes straight ahead. Like a doll. Or someone who has been trained to be ignored. But I see her. She stands out and it's not because of how she chose to dress. "Why is Grave ignoring her? He's only talking to the guy. Acts like she's not even there."

"Maybe she prefers it that way," she guesses. "Some people choose to wear blinders, so they don't have to face what's right in front of them. Turner Mason—he's the middle child—used to be obsessed with her."

There's that name again. "Did they date?"

"No." She laughs. "She was too good for him. He knew it. The whole town knew it. Except for her. She had no clue he was into her." She looks up at the high ceilings. I do the same and see the little black domes all over the place. I know what they are. Cameras. "If he finds out she's here, he'll jack off later tonight while watching the surveillance video."

"Gross," I say. "Wait?" My mind a little slow from the alcohol. "What?" I ask. "Why would he be watching the surveillance tapes?"

"The Mason brothers own this place," she states.

My palms begin to sweat. My eyes start looking around frantically. I don't know what they look like. Would they recognize me? My eyes land back on Grave, and I watch a blonde walk up to him. "That's ..."

"Lucy Mason," Jasmine finishes for me.

She's a fucking Mason as well? My hands clench as she runs hers down his bare arm.

"I'm usually the first one to jump in and cut a bitch, but if you want to stay and watch him fight, I'd suggest we do it some other time," Jasmine says, taking a sip of her drink.

I look over at her.

"Her brothers own the place," she reminds me. "We'll be thrown out in two point five seconds if we jump on her. Although, I must admit, I can do a lot of damage in that short of time. So if that's the commitment you want to make, I'm in."

I look back over at them. He's still talking to the guy and doesn't acknowledge Lucy, but that doesn't offend her in the least. She's still touching him. Her body now pressed into the side of his.

A new guy walks up to them and grabs her upper arm, jerking Lucy away from them.

"Who's that?" I ask like she knows. Jasmine seems to know everyone.

"That is Trey Mason. The baby."

I take a step back, my heart racing at her words. "I shouldn't have come here."

"What? You wanted to see Grave ..."

"Yes, but I didn't know the Mason brothers owned the place," I snap, and she frowns. "They had someone break into my shop," I blurt out. The alcohol has my mouth running. "Who knows what they'll do if they knew I was here."

"They what?" She gasps.

"Let's go." I turn and start walking, not wanting to explain it right now. But a hand grips my arm and I'm spun back around. My heart pounds in my chest when I look up into a set of blue eyes.

"Hey," Grave says. "I knew that was you. What are you doing here?" he asks, looking from me to Jasmine.

I lick my numb lips. "I wanted to come see you. But ..."

"But what?" He frowns.

I step into him and stand on my tiptoes to whisper in his ear. "I didn't know that this place belonged to the Mason brothers."

He cups my face when I pull back. "They won't touch you. I promise. But ..." Letting me go, he digs his cell out of his pocket and begins to type away. "Doesn't mean I want you here without protection."

"Are you afraid I'm going to get pregnant?" Jasmine jokes.

Grave snorts. "Your chance of reproduction does not concern me," he replies, typing away on his phone. Then he looks at me. "Nite will stay with you girls."

Jasmine throws her head back with a sigh. "You're giving us the babysitter? I come here all the time."

"Yeah, and so do I. I know what happens to women here when no one is watching."

The hairs on the back of my neck stand, but he leans into me, cups my face, and kisses me. I wrap my arms around his neck and open for him, kissing him back. His hands slide down my back and grip my ass. He lifts me up effortlessly, and I wrap my legs around his narrow hips.

I pull away, panting and whisper against his lips. "Be careful."

"Don't worry about me, baby." He slaps my ass, and I jump down, laughing just as Nite shows up.

"Watch them," Grave orders him, and Nite nods once.

Grave gives me one more kiss and then walks off.

"Hi, we haven't officially met. I'm April." I hold out my right hand, and he shakes it firmly. He then starts to look around the crowded place. I wait for him to say hello or introduce himself. But he completely ignores me.

"He doesn't speak," Jasmine offers, glaring up at him.

Oh. "At all?"

She shakes her head. "He took a vow of silence back in college. He's a mute," she snaps, "and we're not staying here with him." She goes to walk off, but he reaches out, grabs ahold of her hair, and spins her around to face him.

Her hands go to his broad chest as she glares up at him. And before she can argue with him, he slams his lips down on hers. I watch her body melt for him as he openly kisses her. Wrapping my lips around my straw, I drink while she opens her mouth for him, and he deepens the kiss, pulling her neck back even farther and devouring her. I swear I hear her moan.

Then, just like it didn't happen, he yanks away. "Fuck you, Nite!" she shouts and then slaps him across the face. She jerks out of his grip and storms off.

"I have a feeling you're the guy from last night." I laugh, taking another sip of my drink. So she's got something going on with Nite. I never saw that coming.

He lets out a huff, grabs my hand, and drags me through the crowd to catch up with her.

TWENTY-TWO

LUCY

I STAND BEHIND the bar with my fingers curled tightly around the tray. I watch the girl with the purple hair walk through the crowd, wearing a smile on her face and carrying a drink in her hand.

She was kissing Grave. I saw it. *Twice.* Is she the reason he's been ignoring me? For her?

"Hey!" I yell over at Trey, who's standing next to me going through his phone. "Who the fuck is that woman?" I snap.

"You'll have to be more specific," he calls back, not even bothering to look up at me.

I slap his phone out of his hand, and it falls to his feet. "What the fuck, Lucy?" he shouts.

"Her." I point at her before she disappears into the crowd with Nite.

"April." He looks down at me and starts to laugh. "Oh, you don't know about her?"

"What about her?" I growl.

"She's Grave's new fuck buddy."

"No ..."

"Yep. Her brother owed us money. He paid us fifty grand for him and made Tanner agree we wouldn't touch her. Or her shop."

"What shop?" I demand.

"She's a florist. Has a place called Roses."

A fucking florist? Who the fuck was he buying flowers for in the first place? They sure as hell weren't for me. I did see her with Jasmine. I guess he could have met April through her. But she must be using Grave, right? Fifty grand is a lot of money. I can't even get him to commit to a dinner. But he will pay fifty grand and make my brother promise to stay away? Why? What does she have that I don't?

"Let it go, Lucy," he warns, reading my face.

I go to storm off, but he grips my upper arm, keeping me in place. "Don't. Tanner made a deal with him. It's settled. Find a new fuck buddy." He looks me up and down. "The way you throw your pussy around, it won't be hard to do." He lets go of me, picks up his phone, and walks off.

I slam my tray down.

"Bad day?"

I look over to see Jimmy Trust. He always races Grave out on the tarmac and loses. The guy blows Daddy's money all the time. "What do you want?" I growl.

He smiles at me. "Are you pissed because Grave got a new toy?"

Motherfucker! Everyone is going to know about him and this April chick by morning after that display they just put on. Why did he bring her here of all places? Everyone knows we fuck. We've been hooking up for years. "Grave can fuck whoever he wants." The lie burns my mouth. I mean, we're not exclusive, but he's never shoved another woman in my face before like he just did.

"Sure. That's why you were watching him like a hawk." He looks out across the bar, and she stands there next to the makeshift ring, waiting for Grave to go on. Jasmine on one side and Nite on the other.

"She's hot." He nods to himself. "I like the whole purple hair and piercing thing."

"What the fuck do you want, Jimmy?" I snap. "A drink?"

He turns to face me, placing his forearm on the bar. "How about we even the scoreboard?"

"What the fuck are you talking about?"

"You want Grave to remember you, right?" He steps into me. "Then you make him jealous."

I pull my lip back with disgust. "Are you suggesting I fuck you?"

He licks his lips, placing a hand on my hip. "Or I fuck you." He shrugs. "However you prefer."

GRAVE

I STAND NEXT to the ring with my eyes on April. She's laughing. Her head thrown back as Jasmine leans in, holding onto her. They're both drunk. I can still taste the liquor on my tongue from our kiss.

I meant it when I told her the Mason brothers wouldn't touch her. Not here. Not ever. Tanner won't go back on his word, and that's why I made him promise. It's also why I'm standing here shirtless about to beat the fuck out of some unlucky kid. He leaves her alone, and I fight. I bring in money for them.

She's worth that.

Nite stands next to them, his eyes always scanning the crowd. No man allows their girlfriend to come here alone. Too many empty rooms and dark corners for them to be raped or beaten. The Airport doesn't have hours. They're open twenty-four hours three hundred sixty-five days a year. Sometimes, even the homeless will find a corner to sleep in just to get off the streets for a night.

The Mason brothers don't give a fuck. They're protected and so is their money. That's all that matters.

"Ready?" A hand slaps my bare shoulder.

Colt Tinsley stands next to me. He helps run this place. Either he's taking money out on the tarmac before races or he's overlooking the fights—he's their go-to man. "Yep," I answer, pulling my cell from my pocket and handing it to him.

He smiles. "Okay, then. Go knock someone out."

I enter the ring, and the crowd starts to scream out my name. I smile, lifting my hands to protect my face. The thing about fighting in the pit at the Airport is that there are no rules. It's a free-for-all. You fight until someone is on the floor unconscious, and however you accomplish that is up to you.

The man who stands across from me has every bit of six inches in height on me and probably five in reach. I've seen him fight before. There's a reason they call him thunder and not lightning. He's a big guy, which limits his movements. He hits hard but moves slow.

I step into him and swing. My right fist makes contact with the side of his head. He immediately swings back, and I duck, throwing another punch to his ribs. He bends forward, giving me an opportunity to grab his head and lift my knee.

He takes a step backward, dazed.

"Come on, fucker," I taunt. *My girl is here.* I gotta show off for her, show her what I'm made of, so she knows I can protect her if she ever needs me.

He charges me, wrapping his arms around me and picking my feet up off the floor. I'm body slammed down onto my back, the concrete momentarily taking my breath away.

I slam my elbow into his jaw, knocking him off me. I roll over onto my side as he starts to get up on his hands and knees. I throw my legs around his neck and squeeze, dragging his ass back down to the floor. And I hold him there. He fights me—his legs kick the floor and his nails dig into my thighs, but I hold on.

He starts tapping my leg as if he expects me to let go. I guess he didn't get the memo on how these fights work.

The crowd is chanting my name and slapping the railing. I feel him start to loosen his grip on my thighs. His body relaxing. Seconds later, he goes completely limp, and I let go of him, jumping to my feet.

Everyone is jumping up and down and hollering as I exit the pit. Colt hands me my phone and a wad of cash. "Here you go."

"Thanks." I breathe and make my way over to the bar, dying for a drink.

Tanner Mason waits there for me with a bottle of water in his hands. The guy looks like he owns a Fortune 500 company with his black three-piece suit. He always dresses up with his highlighted hair combed back. If you didn't know him, you'd think he was a stuck-up rich kid. But I know him and he's nothing close to that. He's a killer in a five-thousand-dollar suit that you don't want as an enemy. Too bad he hates me for putting his ass in jail. "Good job, Grave."

I nod and unscrew the lid, throwing it back. Some of it dribbles down my chin and onto my bare chest. He places another one on the bar. I suck in air, tossing the now empty one away.

"Oh, my God. That was awesome!" April comes up next to me, shouting.

I watch Tanner look her over. Her black skinny jeans and white sheer top that shows off her black bra leaves nothing to the imagination. His eyes lingering on her tits and ass longer than I like. He finally pulls his eyes from her body to me. "I see now why you made the deal."

My hand tightens, squeezing the full water bottle.

"I'll see you next weekend." Then he turns and walks to the other end of the bar.

I finish the water and turn to face her. She has a big smile on her face. Her eyes are lit up by the bright lights, and she looks gorgeous as always. But the way she's looking at me is with pride. I've never seen someone feel that toward me. It feels better than any fight I've ever won and any high I've ever had.

If she wasn't here, I'd go to a side room and snort some cocaine with Trey. But she is, and I don't want to do anything other than take her home and bury myself in her. She's become my new addiction. I've never restricted myself when it came to drugs and alcohol, so why would I do that with her?

I reach down, wrap my arm around her waist, and pick her up, planting her ass on the bar. Burying my hands in her thick, purple hair, I kiss her.

She digs her nails into my ribs, pulling me closer. I rub my hard cock into her stomach, and she moans into my mouth. Pulling away, she pants, "Take me home."

APRIL

I'M STANDING AT the bar between Nite and Jasmine. They're not speaking to one another. Obviously, Nite doesn't speak at all, but she hasn't said one word to him since he kissed her, and she slapped him.

"Are you sure you can drive home?" I ask her.

She opens her purse and yanks her keys out. "Positive."

Nite reaches around me and snatches them from her hand.

"Hey ..."

"Nite will drive you home," Grave states, walking back up to us.

I asked him to take me home, and he said to give him fifteen minutes. He's now dressed in a pair of dark jeans and a white T-shirt that reads Kingdom across the back. He has a black hat on backward, and it makes my already shaky knees wobble and my mouth water. I take another sip of my drink.

"Grave ..."

"He's driving you home, Jasmine," he states, and she lets out a huff. "Be careful," he tells Nite and then holds out his fist. Nite bumps his into it and nods his head. "Let's go." Grave grabs my free hand in his and starts pulling me into the crowd.

"We came in the other way," I say, looking over my shoulder, watching Nite grab Jasmine by the arm and dragging her away.

"I'm not parked in the parking garage." He stares, looking down at me. "You need to finish that before we leave or get rid of it." He stops at a trash can.

I suck what's left of it down and then toss it into the trash, making him laugh. He walks us down a dark tunnel and out a set of double doors—where two men stand with machine guns—into a parking lot.

He's parked right up front. Throwing a duffel bag in the trunk, he opens my door for me, and I fall in.

He gets in and starts it up before backing out. I've never been one for violence, but watching his fight turned me on. My underwear is already soaked, and my thighs tighten, knowing what's to come when we get back to my place. But I can't wait that long.

I bend down, digging through my purse and find a hair tie. I quickly place my hair up in a messy bun as he gets on the highway. I have about twenty minutes before we reach my exit.

I reach over and go for his belt. He looks down and grabs my hand. "April ..."

I lean over and kiss his neck, and he releases a growl. My lips move to his ear, and I nibble on it. His hand lets go of my hand, and he helps me out by undoing his jeans for me. I smile, lowering my lips back to his neck and kiss him. He took a shower at the Airport. That's why he needed fifteen minutes. He smells like his spicy cologne.

Pulling away, I look down and see he's pulled his cock out for me as well. He's hard. His free hand wraps around it and slowly strokes it. His thumb running over the piercing at the end.

I shove his hand away and lean down, opening my mouth to take him in.

TWENTY-THREE
GRAVE

HER LIPS WRAP around my cock as I fill her mouth. "Fuck," I hiss.

She pushes down, the tip touching the back of her throat, and I pump my hips, pushing farther and needing more. She sucks up my shaft, and I wrap my free hand in her messy bun and shove her face down.

She moans around my cock and readjusts her knees in the passenger seat. Her ass is up in the air. Thank God my windows are blacked out or we'd be giving everyone I pass a show. One hand wrapped around my cock while the other is on my thigh, holding herself up. I press on the gas, needing to get to her house sooner than I had planned.

I pick up my pace. My hand in her hair controlling her movements. Her saliva runs down my cock and coats my balls, and I wish I could remove my jeans completely. But that will have to wait.

My cell starts to ring through my speakers, and **Lucy** flashes across the screen on my dash. I let go of April's hair long enough to push decline.

She lifts her head. "Who ...?"

I grip her hair and shove her face back down. "Don't worry about it," I growl, not wanting her to stop. Lucy is no way a threat to April. My actions prove that. Even if April wouldn't have shown up tonight, I wouldn't be going home with Lucy.

April takes me back in, and this time, she doesn't stop until after I'm done coming in her mouth.

APRIL

WE PULL INTO my driveway and exit his car. I'm trying to put my key in the front door when he comes up behind me, wraps his arm around my stomach and pulls my back into his front. Gripping my hair, he yanks my head back and lowers his lips to my neck. He sucks on the sensitive skin, making my body break out in goosebumps.

"Grave," I whimper. "I have to unlock the door." My other hand is holding his duffel bag.

Letting go of my hair, his now free hand comes up and skates under my shirt and over my stomach to my chest. He squeezes my boob over my bra. "Think anyone will see if I fuck you right here on your porch?" He growls.

I suck in a breath and jiggle my keys, trying to get the door unlocked once again. "Probably."

"Then let them watch." His hand moves downward this time and shoves its way into my jeans.

I manage to get my key in the door and push it open, pulling away from him. I spin around, reach out and grip his shirt, yanking him into the house and dropping his bag at our feet.

He shoves my back into the wall, grips my hair and yanks my head back, lowering his lips to mine. He devours them, not even giving me the chance to take a breath.

"Grave ..." I pant, pulling away. "We have to go upstairs ..."

He rips my shirt up and over my head, picks me up and carries me to my room with my lips on his. He slams the door shut with his shoe, then tosses me onto my bed. He doesn't even give me a chance to catch my breath before he's naked and ripping my jeans down my legs.

His hands grab my thighs and opens them up for him. He slows down, lying between them. His lips gently kissing my inner thigh.

I arch my back, panting. I cry out when his teeth bite into my sensitive flesh.

He kisses his way to my pussy before pushing in a finger.

I'm already soaking wet. I've been wet for him. My hands make their way to his head. I knock his hat to the floor and grip his hair.

He enters a second finger, and I pump my hips. "Oh, God." I yank on his head.

Removing his fingers, he reaches up and grabs my wrists, pinning them down to my sides while his tongue enters me.

TWENTY-FOUR
GRAVE

I LIE IN April's bed. She's passed out facing me. An arm across my chest and a leg across both of mine.

I kiss her forehead and close my eyes just as I hear my cell vibrate.

Sliding out from underneath her, I crawl off the bed. I grab my jeans off the floor and remove my cell from my pocket. I see it's a video from Lucy.

Deciding to watch it, I walk into her bathroom and flip on the light but turn the volume all the way down. I don't want it to wake up April.

It shows Lucy still at the Airport. She's in the private room sitting at the round table. A mirror in the middle with a razor blade and a bag of cocaine. She then flips the camera to herself and blows me a kiss. Her mouth is moving, but I can't hear what she is saying or make out the words. Ending it before it's done, I delete it and place my cell on the counter. Turning on the faucet, I splash my face with some water. The need that I would normally have for the drugs not really there.

I turn off the water, grab my cell, and flip off the light. Walking back into her bedroom, I pull my jeans on and make my way downstairs to get a glass of milk. It just sounds good right now, but I stop when I get to the last step. I see a figure in the entryway, so I reach over and flip on the light.

"Shit!" Ethan all but shouts, jumping back from the front door.

"Keep it down. Your sister is asleep," I tell him.

He runs a hand over his mop of hair. I swear the kid never brushes it.

"About time you two stopped fucking," he says with disgust.

I take a step toward him and he throws up his hands like I'm about to punch his lights out. He's not far off.

"I'm leaving," he rushes out. "I was on my way out."

"Where the fuck you going this late?" I ask.

He squares his shoulders, shoving his hands in the front pocket of his hoodie. Why the fuck is he wearing that? It's not even cold outside. "Just because you're fucking my sister, doesn't mean I have to tell you shit." He spins around, yanks open the front door and slams it shut.

"Babe?" I say, running my knuckles down the side of her face.

"Hmm?" she mumbles, her eyes opening and then closing again.

"I'm leaving," I say, straightening and placing my watch on my wrist. I'm already fucking late for work. Like I am every fucking day. I didn't set my alarm last night.

"It's Saturday." She stretches under the covers.

"I know." *Kingdom never sleeps.* It's why we choose to live there rather than our homes that we built.

"Stay with me." Her eyes open fully, and she reaches out to me.

"I can't." Even though I want nothing more in this world than to crawl back in bed with her.

She sits up, the covers falling to her waist, exposing her bare chest

170

to me. She arches a brow and licks her lips. "Are you sure?" Her hands reach out and grab my dick through my jeans.

I growl and jump onto the bed, pinning her down to it as I hover above. "I have to go, but I'm free tonight."

"Early enough to do dinner?"

I lower my head and kiss her neck. "As long as you promise to be my dessert."

"Promise?" She pants, arching her hips to meet mine.

I groan and push mine into hers so she can feel how hard I am. I've never known what struggle was until I met her. "Promise." I pull away and crawl off her. "Now go back to sleep." I kiss her forehead, and she rolls over, giving me her back with a sigh.

I grab my cell off her nightstand and exit her room, closing the door behind me. I make my way down the steps and to the front door. I see my bag still lying in the entryway where April dropped it last night. I pick it up and walk out to my car. Throwing it into my passenger seat, I pause before I start my car and look over at it.

This is the first time in a long time that I haven't woken up feeling like shit. Hungover or still high. I unzip the side pocket of the bag and reach inside to remove the pill bottle.

"What the ...?" I bring it onto my lap and look inside it. It's empty. I had a pill bottle there last night, and it was full. Where the fuck did it go?

I had it upstairs at the Airport, and then when I showered ... someone was in my bag. The question is, who the fuck was it? It was there when I left. I had checked it. Then I came to April's. She never got into it. We had sex, and her drunk ass passed out. Then Lucy messaged me. I went downstairs ... Ethan. It had to have been him. He was standing in the entryway and was spooked when I turned on the lights. His hands in the pockets of his hoodie. He was hiding my pills from me so I wouldn't catch him. He was leaving so he could go take them.

Motherfucker!

APRIL

I stand behind the counter, going through emails on my phone. Roses opens in two days but after Grave left my house this morning, I decided to get up and do a few last-minute things up here. The bell rings, signaling a customer has entered, and I look up in a panic that I forget to lock the door behind me.

"We're closed." I exit out of my email and open my call history, my finger hovering over Grave's name.

"Hi." The man waves as he steps inside, letting the door shut behind him.

"I'm sorry, but we're closed," I repeat, my thumb ready to call him. The guy is dressed in a pair of dark jeans and a white T-shirt that has a red Corvette on the front. His dark eyes look around, and he nods in approval when he gets to the vases on the shelves.

"I saw you at the Airport last night." His dark eyes meet mine.

My body tenses. I knew I should have left after what Jasmine told me. "Who are you?" I ask.

He gives me a warm smile. "I'm Jimmy. Jimmy Trust. I'm good friends with Grave."

"Oh." My shoulders relax a bit. "Are you looking for him? Because he's not here."

He shakes his head. "No. I just wanted to come by and place an order for someone." Ducking his head, he looks up at me shyly through his lashes. "For a special someone."

I set my cell down. "Well, as long as you don't need it today or tomorrow, I can help you out with that."

"I won't need them until next week."

Opening the top drawer, I pull out my pad and a pen and slide it across the counter. "Just fill this out for me."

He comes up to the counter, closing the distance between us, and starts writing down all the info. When he's finished, he places the pen down. "Thanks so much. I want my girl to know just how special she is." Then he exits without another word.

I look down at the paper and frown when I see Lucy Mason written out.

Picking up my cell, I call up Grave.

"Hey, babe," he answers immediately.

I bite my lip to hide my smile as if he can see me. "Hey."

"Everything okay?" he asks.

I love that he asks me that. "Yeah." My eyes drop to the piece of paper on the counter and I chicken out. "I know you said we could do dinner tonight, but I was just wondering if you'd like me to bring you lunch today." I'll ask him tonight about Lucy. Obviously, they're not exclusive. Or if they were, they're not now. I saw how he avoided her last night and he didn't even know I was watching him at that point.

"Why don't you come up here for lunch and we'll eat here together," he offers.

"Sounds good."

"Pull around the back of Kingdom and enter the private entrance. A man by the name of Nigel will be at the desk and will escort you up to my office."

I remember that guy. I saw him when Titan took me kicking and screaming to Bones's office after my shop was destroyed because of the money my brother owed. "Any particular time?"

"I'll clear my schedule whenever you arrive."

I smile at that. "See you soon."

———

"Here you are." Nigel says, opening the glass door for me to enter the Kings office.

"Thank you."

"Of course, ma'am." He nods. "His office is the last one on the left."

I walk down the dark gray hallway and pass the first door on the left; Cross is in gold letters. I take a look in to see he's not in there. The next door on the left reads Titan. He too isn't in there. But I didn't expect him to be. Emilee told us that they were going to be in New York for the weekend. I come up to the end of the hall. The door on the left has Grave on it. I know the one on the right is Bones.

I softly knock on Grave's door. "Come in," he calls out.

I enter and come to a stop when I see him sitting at his desk with a phone to his ear. Cross sits in the chair across from it. He turns to look at me over his shoulder, flipping a Zippo in his right hand. "Hey," I say lamely.

"I have to go ..." Grave says into the phone. "Yeah, yeah. I'll get it done." Then he hangs up. "Even when he's in New York, he's up my ass." He growls, standing and walking around his desk over to me.

My heart picks up. I'm not sure why I'm so nervous about being here. Maybe because this is his element. This is his domain. I'm used to being in my bed with him naked.

He wraps his arms around me and pulls me in for a hug. When he pulls away, he gives me a gentle kiss on my forehead that causes butterflies in my stomach. "How's your day?"

"Good." I walk over and sit down next to Cross and push my hair behind my ear. "Yours?"

He sighs and sits down at his desk. "The usual."

I'm not sure what that means because we never talk about King-dom. I don't push him to share information regarding him and the Kings. What they do here is none of my business. And after what Derek told me, I think I'd rather not know. I don't expect Grave to be a saint. All I expect from a guy is that he treats me right and respects me. The rest can always be worked on.

A cell phone rings and Grave picks his up from his desk. He lets out a growl and looks at me. "Give me a second."

"Yes, of course." I say stupidly like he asked for permission. I sit up straighter in the comfortable black leather chair. My ass sinks into it. It's exactly what I would expect for a King.

Grave exits the room and a silence falls over it. I don't know Cross very well. I don't know any of the Kings actually. I've only ever met them once and I was having a bad day. I did see Cross once before in Roses, but there was very minimal interaction between the two of us.

His green eyes meet mine. He flips the Zippo open. The flame burns before he slams it shut. "It's a reminder." He says when he catches me staring.

I could lie. Pretend I wasn't wondering what the fuck he's doing. But instead I ask, "Of what?"

He flips it open again, tilts his head to the side, and watches the flame dance at the tip of his tatted fingers. Then his eyes slide to mine, the green darkening to black and sending a chill down my spine. "That if I wanted to, I could burn the motherfucking world down."

He takes a cigarette from behind his ear and places it between his lips, then raises the lighter. But I speak, making him pause, "You know smoking will kill you." My grandfather died of lung cancer. Smoked his entire life. My mother begged me and Ethan not to ever smoke. That it wasn't worth it in the end.

He removes the unlit cigarette from his lips and smirks at me. "So will falling in love with a man who has a death wish." My eyes widen. "And I don't see you putting an end to that." He replaces it between his lips and lights the cigarette then flips the Zippo shut. "Guess we'll both die due to our own stupidity." He blows the smoke out.

The door opens, and Grave re-enters. Cross stands and exits without another word. "Sorry, I'm ready for lunch now." He drops into his desk chair.

Cross thinks I love him. Jasmine thinks I love him. Do I? Am I doing something that everyone else sees but me? Am I being too clingy? Too obvious? Do I need to take a step back and look at it from a different angle? What if Grave thinks this too? Will it push him away?

"April?"

"Hmm?" My eyes snap up to Grave's. He gives me that smile that makes my heart pick up. "You okay?" he asks.

"Yeah, just been a long week," I lie, not wanting to make him question anything. I came here to see him and I'm not going to let Cross's words fuck that up. I get up and walk around. Pushing his chair back, I climb into his lap, straddling him.

He leans back, placing his hands behind his head, showing off his muscular arms with a cocky smile.

"A friend of yours stopped by Roses today." I do have feelings for Grave, but I need to know where I stand before I allow myself to feel anymore.

The smile drops off his face, and he tilts his head to the side. "Who?"

"He said his name was Jimmy. Think the last name was Trust?"

He snorts. "He's not a friend." He drops his arms and grips my hips.

I frown. "I told him we were closed twice, but he insisted on ordering flowers."

His jaw sharpens. "I'm installing a security camera system at the shop this week."

"You don't have to ..."

"I've already ordered the equipment. It'll be here tomorrow."

I arch a brow. "Wanna keep an eye on me?"

"Always." He winks.

Shit, this guy makes my underwear soaked in the worst way. But I have to know. "Well, Jimmy was there to send flowers to Lucy. Lucy Mason." I watch his facial expression to see if he gets jealous, but nothing changes. "Don't you find that odd?" I dig.

"Why would I find that odd? I told you he's not my friend."

I take in a deep breath and let it out slowly, dropping my eyes to his black Kingdom shirt to stare at his chest and try to keep my voice even. "She's your ex."

He lifts his hands and tangles them in my hair, lifting my face so I have to stare down at him. "Lucy Mason is not my ex."

"Fuck buddy." I correct my previous statement.

"Did Jimmy tell you that?" he asks.

"He didn't have to." I pull away from him and get up off his lap. I'm not going to rat the girls out.

"We were, yes. But I haven't ..."

"I've seen her call you several times when we're together," I interrupt him.

He snorts. "I can't help when she calls me, but I promise you that I ignore them every time."

"Maybe that's the problem, you haven't told her that you're with me." He may ignore her while he's with me but what happens after he leaves?

"It's complicated."

I give a rough laugh. "How is your ex, fuck buddy, whatever a complication? You either still want to fuck her or you don't."

His jaw sharpens and he runs a hand through his hair.

I go on, "Plus, I saw her last night at the Airport. She was all over you." Okay, so maybe that's an exaggeration but the bitch was thirsty. And she would have jumped his bones if he would have let her. Even Jasmine said that Lucy would take him however she could have him.

He stands from his chair. "Did you see me blow her off too?" he asks, walking over to me and pushing my ass up against the side of his desk. He reaches out and gently pushes my hair off my shoulders and runs his knuckles up my neck, pushing my head back in the process.

"She wants you." I fill the silence, my breathing picking up. Not wanting to let him distract me from the conversation. "And if that's what you want, tell me now. Don't string me along."

Gripping my hair, I cry out when he jerks my head to where I'm forced to look up at him. "Let's clear something up then." He licks his lips. "You're fucking mine, April. I don't want Lucy. Not anymore." His blue eyes roam my face. "I haven't touched her nor anyone else since I've been with you."

I swallow at his confession.

"All I think about is you." He lowers his lips to my neck and kisses his way up to my ear. "I only want to fuck you." My breath hitches when he begins to nibble on my ear. "The only woman I want to be with is you."

My arms wrap around his neck. "Be with?" *As in girlfriend?* We haven't said it out loud just yet.

"The question is, am I the only one you want?" He presses his hips into mine, pinning me to the desk and I can feel how hard he is.

"Yes," I breathe.

He pulls away and my heavy eyes look up at him. "I promise that I'm all yours, April. Are you all mine?"

I nod my head, licking my lips. "Of course, ..."

His lips land on mine and he lifts me off my feet, slamming my ass down on the desk before he rips my shirt up and over my head.

TWENTY-FIVE
GRAVE

"**Y**OU LOST THEM again?" Cross asks me as he stands in my bedroom at the Royal Suite in Kingdom.

"I had them in my bag," I growl, shuffling through my closet. I don't plan on coming back here tonight before me and April go to dinner, so I needed to grab some clothes.

He sits down on the edge of my bed. "And you didn't take them?"

I snort. "I would know if I had taken an entire bottle of pills last night."

He shrugs, flipping his Zippo open and closed. "Maybe April took them out."

I shake my head. "One, she didn't know they were there, and two, she wouldn't have had the chance. She sucked my dick on the way to her house, and the moment we arrived, we went straight upstairs to her room. After we were done, she passed out and never left. It had to have been her brother."

"But why would he steal from you?" he asks. "He has to know that you'd find them missing, put two and two together and then beat his ass."

"Yeah, well I think we've established that he doesn't think most of the time."

"True."

"I'm going over to the Airport to talk to him before I go to April's."

"Want me to go with you?" he asks, standing.

"Nah. I won't be there long."

I sit at the round table inside the Airport, having a conversation with Trey when my cell vibrates. I remove it from my pocket and put in my code. It's a text from April.

> April: Red or black?

> Me: Do I get pictures to choose from?

> April: Nope. Choose. Red or black.

> Me: Black.

She reads it but doesn't reply, so I lock my screen and place it back in my pocket when the door opens and Lucy walks in. I never did reply to that video she sent me. I deleted it, and that was that. She tried to confront me before I fought last night, but I ignored her then too. Lucy is a smart woman, and I thought she would catch on, but obviously, I was wrong.

Trey's cell rings, and he pushes away from the table to answer it in the office, leaving us alone.

Lucy stands there with her hands on her hips and a smile on her face. She licks her lips as they travel down to my jeans. "Well, hello, sexy."

"What are you doing here?" I ask her. "Working tonight?"

"Nope. Came by to get my check."

Lie. She gets paid in cash. Nightly. But whatever. I'm not going to call her out on it.

"Going out tonight?" she asks, plopping down beside me, looking over my button-down shirt and jeans.

"Yes." No reason to lie to her. *I promised April dinner.*

I watch her stick her bottom lip out. "I was hoping we could hang out."

"I have plans," I state, reaching out and taking a drink of my water. It's amazing that I haven't had an alcoholic drink in over a week.

"With who?"

"Since when do you care who I spend my time with?" I ask. April mentioned Jimmy coming into Roses today and ordering her flowers. I was hopeful that meant they were fucking, and she'd get off my back, but that doesn't seem to be the case.

She averts her eyes to the table. "Well, I was talking to Trey, and he said that you paid off a debt for a guy. And that you asked Tanner to leave his sister alone."

I roll my eyes. *Fucking Trey.* He can't keep a secret to save his life. That's another reason I quit hanging out with him. "That doesn't concern you," I state.

Instead of getting mad, she reaches out and touches my arm.

I pull away. "I need to get going."

She reaches into her shorts pocket and pulls out a pill bottle that I know contains ecstasy. The same one from the night in her penthouse after we gambled here. "I wanted to party with you tonight."

I shake my head. "Can't." I pull out my cell when I feel it vibrate again.

It's a picture from April. Opening it up, I see her standing in front of a full-length mirror in a little black dress with black heels on. She has the front of her hair up in a high ponytail the rest is down and curled. Her makeup's done heavy with the black liner just how I love it and her lips painted dark.

"Do you love her?" Lucy asks.

I remove my eyes from the picture to meet hers. Lucy looks like she hasn't been to bed yet. She probably hasn't. Her dark eyes are cloudy, her makeup messy, and I know she's high. Lucy never goes a day without a fix. Sometimes, it's just weed, and others, it's something more.

— "I don't know her." *I lie.* I've never hid things from Lucy because we both understand what we are—fuck buddies, and that's it. So for her to be this concerned about where I'm going tonight and who with is a big red flag. I won't give her any reason to confront April. Because that's exactly what she would do. And April already questioned my involvement with Lucy earlier in my office today. I don't want Lucy going to her and saying anything that can get me in hot water with April.

"Have you fucked her?"

"Jesus, Lucy." I push my chair back from the table. "That is none of your business."

She doesn't look the least bit angry. Drugs will do that to you. Numb you to everything. I know. That's why I did it. I stand and reach out to the glass of water on the table and down what's left of it, needing to get the fuck out of here.

"Hey, man." Trey re-enters the room, pocketing his cell. "The kid is fighting here tonight."

I grind my teeth and look at my watch. "What time?" I have an hour before I have to pick up April.

"Seven."

I nod and sit back down in the seat. "I want his ass in here the moment he arrives," I snap. I'm going to beat his ass before he even enters the ring. He's not going to take drugs from me. He's not going to be doing drugs at all. I won't allow him to do that to April. She already has enough going on.

"So ... you're staying?" Lucy asks, her voice full of excitement.

"Not for you," I growl, my good mood gone to shit.

APRIL

I PACE MY living room, my eyes on the clock hanging on the wall. He's two hours late. I haven't called his cell once. He never responded to my picture. He was talking to me and then just vanished. I've never been ghosted before, but I'm pretty sure this is what it's like.

I'm furious. So fucking pissed that he stood me up.

And that I fell for it in the first place. Things were going well, right? Did I say or do something that made me look desperate? Or in love? What could have scared him off? He's been just as clingy as I have and seemed generally interested. I've been blown off before, and he never once made me feel unwanted or that he needed space. I would have backed off and given it to him.

Did I say something last night while I was drunk? Honestly, the night is kind of blurry. I remember his fight. Me being turned on. The drinks. Then I went home with him. Gave him head. After that, shit gets foggy. So I could have said something to him but wouldn't he have mentioned that to me this morning when he woke me up and kissed me goodbye? Why make plans if he wasn't going to show?

That can't be it. He seemed fine at lunch today. I did bring up Lucy, though. So fucking stupid of me! I should have just let it go. But, again, he seemed fine. He fucked me right there on his desk, we had lunch and then he walked me down to my car. Kissed me goodbye with a promise to see me tonight for dinner.

My cell rings, and I run to it. I see its Jasmine. "Hello?" I snap.

"Hey, where are you?" she demands. I can hear the sound of her car in the background, letting me know she's driving.

"At home."

"I'm coming to get you. Get dressed."

I look over my black dress and sigh. "Unfortunately, I am. Where are we going?"

"Well, I just got a text from my ex. Remember him? Trenton? He said that he thought Grave was dating my friend, you, and I said yes. He proceeded to tell me that Grave is at the Airport ..."

I fist my hands. "Fighting?"

She ignores my question. "Didn't you guys have a date tonight?"

"Yes." Alexa had tonight off, and we were going to go have a girls' night, but Grave wanted to take me to dinner, so I dropped them for him. Big fucking mistake on my part. "I've been waiting two hours for him. He blew me off for the fucking Airport?" My next thought is he did it to spend time with Lucy. She works there.

"Yeah, Trenton said he's fucked up. Bad. I tried calling Cross, but he didn't answer. Bones's phone went straight to voicemail, and I don't want to bother Titan. I spoke to Emilee earlier and they were coming back early."

I bow my head, running my free hand through my hair. "What are you saying?"

She lets out a long breath. "I'm saying that this is the time you choose, April."

"Choose what?" I ask, but I'm already throwing my purse over my shoulder.

"If you're going to fight for him or not." She pauses. "I was told he was seen with Lucy."

I swallow the knot that forms in my throat. My heart beating faster at her statement. I was right. He's with her. But ... we had agreed we were exclusive, right? That was what he established at lunch today. This is my fault. I expected too much from him. A guy like Grave doesn't settle down. He's been fucking Lucy for years now. Isn't that what the girls had said? If he won't commit to her, then he won't commit to me.

He stood me up to be with her. Why not just tell me he couldn't make it? Or be honest and say hey, I don't want to go out with you tonight, someone better came up?

Making up my mind, I decide that I'm going to tell him in person to go to hell. "I'll be waiting for you outside."

TWENTY-SIX

GRAVE

I WAKE UP with a pounding headache. A ringing in my ears and sensitive eyes. I realize I'm in a bed. *It's not mine.* But I've been here before. I remember the purple accents.

I roll over to see April lying next to me. Sound asleep. "What …?" I trail off, lifting the covers to see she is on her left side, facing me. And she wears a shirt from Kingdom. It's a men's shirt, swallowing her up. And that's it.

Then I look at myself. I'm completely naked.

Fuck!

I lie back and run a hand down over my face. How did I end up with her last night? I look back over her, and she still wears her makeup. Black streaks that I know have to be from tears are now dry on her cheeks.

What did I do to her?

Fuck, we were supposed to have a date. Right? Why can't I remember it?

Did I physically hurt her? I lift the sheets once again and run my eyes over her exposed skin but see no physical signs.

I crawl out of bed and stumble to the en suite bathroom. I wash my face with cold water and brush my teeth with a random toothbrush. I'll use anything to get this awful taste out of my mouth. Then I use the mouthwash. The taste no longer lingers, but my mouth feels like fucking sandpaper.

What the hell did I do last night? And how did April end up here? Did I fuck her? I don't remember shit!

I run a hand through my hair. It's standing every which way. There are dark circles under my bloodshot eyes. And a cut in the corner of my upper lip. Not the first time I've woken up in this situation, just wondering how she got involved in it.

The bathroom door opens, and Titan enters. He takes one look at me naked and shakes his head, looking away. He tosses me a pair of gray sweatpants that are in his hand, and I sit my ass on the side of the tub to put them on, not trusting my balance to stand.

Once on, I stay sitting and place my elbows on my knees and lean forward. My face falls into my hands. "What happened?" I clear my throat at my rough voice and rub my throbbing temples.

"You got fucked up," he answers simply.

"No." I shake my head. "We had plans ..."

"She found you at the Airport. On drugs and with Lucy."

"Fuck!" *How did I end up with Lucy?* I can't remember. And what the fuck was I on? "What all did I do?" I ask roughly. "With ... Lucy?" I hate having to ask that question, but it's a possibility. The drugs and women run hand-in-hand. I get high, and get my dick sucked. Then I pass out and wake up alone. And I've always been okay with that.

"That's something that you need to discuss with April," he answers.

That doesn't make me feel any better. I drop my hands and lift my head to look up at him.

He leans up against the closed bathroom door with his arms crossed over his chest wearing a scowl on his face. "She and Jasmine found you passed out in a room on the floor." I swallow. "Jasmine called me. April was crying." I close my eyes. "Said they couldn't get you to wake up, but you had vomited on her."

"Fuck! Fuck!"

He sighs. "Emilee and I came back from New York early and went and picked you guys up. Brought you both back to our place. I had some Kingdom shirts in my car, so Emilee helped her clean up and change. I put you in the shower and cleaned you off."

I stand, and the room sways, so I place my hand on the wall to stabilize myself. And Titan steps into me. "She didn't want to stay with you."

Then why did I wake up with her? "But she ..."

"She stayed 'cause she didn't want you to die in your own vomit while you slept off whatever the fuck you had taken." His voice rises. "She didn't want that on her conscience. Whatever the hell you're doing, you need to stop."

My eyes narrow on him. "What does that mean?" My drugs and drinking aren't new to them.

"Whatever fascination you have with April. Cut it off now."

"Fuck you, Titan!" I push off the wall.

He shoves me back. He comes to stand against me, pinning my back to the wall next to the tub. "I've never told you what to do, Grave. It's not my place. But whatever you're doing with her. Call it off! Now!"

"Fucking move ..." I go to shove him away, but he doesn't budge. He's too strong, and I'm too weak at the moment. A night of endless drugs will do that to you.

He leans down, his lips by my ear. "She's better than you. Deserves better than you." I stiffen at his words. "She cares too much for someone who has a death wish. Stick with fucking Lucy. She's more your speed." Then he steps back, digs his hand into his pocket, and pulls out a bottle of pills. "April found these in your jeans." He throws them at my chest before exiting.

I spin around and punch the fucking wall, putting a hole in the sheetrock. Leaning my head against it, I close my eyes as I try to calm my breathing.

He's right!

April doesn't belong in my world. My mess. Lucy reveled in it. Begged for another hit. Begged for me to bring another girl into our bed. She likes her life dirty. Just like me. But I've been clean. For April. So why did I fuck it up?

I push off the wall and yank the bathroom door open and go to storm out of the bedroom but come to a halt when I see April standing by the bed. Her ice blue eyes red and swollen.

APRIL

HE STANDS THERE staring at me with hard eyes as though last night was my fault. They fall to my legs, and I push the oversized shirt down, trying to cover myself.

He notices and looks away from me, his jaw sharpening in the process.

I take in his body. He only wears a pair of sweatpants. They sit low on his narrow hips. His defined V fully on display. I can make out the softness of his dick behind them. Normally, I would blush at what we've done in bed, but all I can think of is what he did with Lucy last night.

"Grave!" I fall to his side in the center of the room. His eyes are closed, and his lips parted. "Grave, wake up!" I shout, tears burning my eyes.

Jasmine falls down next to me and pulls her cell out of her pocket.

I cry as I touch his neck with shaky hands. His skin is clammy and pale. Please don't be dead. "What did you do, baby? What did you take?"

I wanted to wake him up. Scream at him. Pound on his chest and ask *what the hell do you think you're doing?* Why do you waste your life? But I didn't. I learned a very important lesson last night.

They don't call him Grave for nothing.

"Are you even sorry?" I ask, breaking the awkward silence.

His eyes come back to mine, but he doesn't answer.

I nod, getting my answer. I reach down and grab my phone off the floor and turn to walk toward the door. I'm pulled to a stop with a hand on my upper arm. I almost cry out from his touch alone. I put my head down, staring at the floor as tears begin to burn my eyes.

He gently turns me around and lifts my chin for me to look at him. My eyes shoot to the left, staring at a speck on the wall, not wanting to make eye contact.

"Did I hurt you?" he questions roughly.

Just my pride. "No," I growl, mad at myself. That first tear runs down my cheek, and I bite my bottom lip in shame that I let him affect me this much. That I actually care that he stood me up to get high and fuck his fuck buddy. The one that he blatantly lied about not fucking anymore.

He lets go of my arm, cups my face with one hand, and wipes it away with his thumb.

My eyes finally meet his, and he stares down at me, giving nothing away. He's hiding behind a wall a mile high. I look down and see a bottle of pills in his other hand. The same ones I found on him last night when I tried to shake him awake. When I screamed his name in the middle of the room, and no one helped me. No one seemed to care he wasn't responding except for Jasmine. She was just as frantic as I was.

"Why do you do it?" I ask, my voice shaking. I feel like I was blinded to who he really is. To what he wants. It was all a lie, and I believed it. Last night opened my eyes. It's not hard to figure out this is his lifestyle. Last night wasn't just a one-time night with friends. How many times have I been with him, and he was high that I didn't know about? Is he just that good at hiding it? Or am I just that blind?

He shatters my heart with three words. "To feel alive."

There was no confusion. He knew exactly what I meant. And that scares me more than his answer. Anger takes over my heartache.

What he's done. To me. To himself. I slap him across the face. The sound bouncing off the walls in the quiet room.

His head snaps to the side. "April ..."

I slap him again. Harder. His eyes close tightly. "Did you feel that?"

He straightens, running a hand down his face while his breathing picks up. His bare chest rising and falling fast.

My hand stings, and his face now shows two handprints of mine. I slap him again.

"Stop!" he shouts, gripping my wrists and slamming my back into the door, making it rattle. His drug-hazed eyes glare down at mine. "I don't expect you to understand."

"I don't." The words get caught in my throat, and my bottom lip begins to tremble, trying to keep it together. "I kneeled on a floor last night, Grave. And I begged you to open your eyes. I cried for you not to be dead." I choke out. "Do you know what that feels like?" I yank my wrists free of his hold. He's weak. His body tired. Drugs will do that to you. Drain you of everything you have. I shove at his chest.

He takes a step back from me. "I don't remember anything from last night."

That makes me even more pissed. "You forgot we had a date? That you stood me up?"

"No," he barks. "I remember the date. I just don't remember how I ended up with Lucy."

There she is again. She just stood there like a deer in headlights.

"Lucy, what did he take?" Jasmine demands, still kneeling next to me. I've sat down on my ass in my dress and pulled his body into my lap. His head in my hands.

I cry, shaking him. "Please wake up..."

"Lucy!" Jasmine shouts, jumping to her feet. She holds her phone in one hand with Titan on speakerphone. "What in the fuck did he take?"

"He ... he ... a pill bottle ..." She sobs. Like she cares that he's dying

before our eyes. She was literally snorting a line of coke off a compact mirror when we burst into the room.

"Fuck!" Titan hisses through the phone. "We're almost there."

I start to dig through his jeans pocket. That's when his body jerks, and he begins to vomit.

"Did you fuck her?" I ask. Jasmine said that Trenton had went up to the office to speak to Trey and that was when he saw Lucy and Grave all over each other sitting at the table, but no one mentioned sex.

His jaw sharpens. "I don't know."

My chest tightens at his answer, and those tears return to my eyes.

He sighs and steps toward me. "April ..."

"Don't." I throw my hands up. I'm disgusted with him and with myself. I think I'm going to get sick at the thought of him with her. When he was supposed to have been with me.

"I was fucked up," he growls.

I gasp. "That doesn't make it okay, Grave."

"I'm sorry ..."

"Don't fucking lie to me!" I shout. Jasmine was right. I wanted him to want me. I wanted him to love me like I do him, but I can't compete with someone like Lucy. She gives him something I never will. Acceptance. "I can't be with someone who chooses to do drugs and fuck around on me. I refuse to lower myself to that level. I respect myself too much for that."

With that, I turn, yank the door open, and then slam it shut. I look over my shoulder to see he didn't follow me.

I didn't expect him to.

I walk down the hallway and enter the spare laundry room that Emilee showed me last night. I open the dryer to see if my dress is clean. Emilee was kind enough to bring us back here last night and help me out of my soiled clothes. I shut it when I see it's empty. "Shit." I hope it's still not in the washer. I open it up, and that too is empty. I go to leave but see my dress folded on top of the dryer.

Thank you, Emilee.

I quickly get dressed and drop the T-shirt in the small dirty clothes hamper. I hear voices downstairs in the kitchen, and I make my way down to them, carrying my heels in my hand from last night. Titan stands at the kitchen island with his back leaning against it and his arms crossed over his chest. Memories of last night come back to me.

The door busts open, and Titan enters with Emilee.

"I don't know what happened," I cry. My hands covered in vomit. "He just started getting sick."

"Grave?" Titan slaps his face. He doesn't move. "Grave, wake the fuck up, man!" he shouts, snapping his fingers in front of his face.

Still nothing.

"Get the door," he orders to Emilee before he picks Grave up.

Emilee stands at the oven, pulling muffins out of it.

"Thank you for everything," I say, getting their attention.

They both look up at me. She gives me a sad smile. "Of course. I'm glad we could help."

Titan says nothing.

"I'm going to get going," I say awkwardly, pulling my dress down. It's not short by any means, but I just feel vulnerable.

"Titan can give you a ride home," Emilee offers.

"No." I shake my head. "I'm gonna call an Uber."

"Nonsense." She waves me off.

Without another word, he pushes off the kitchen island, gives her a long kiss, and then walks toward me. I follow him silently into the garage. We get into a candy apple red Maserati and then he pulls out of the garage. I give him my address and then go silent again.

Twenty minutes later, he pulls up to my house, and I thank him. As I go to get out of the car, he finally speaks. "Grave isn't like the rest of us."

It makes me pause. I turn to look at him, waiting for him to elaborate.

He runs a hand down his face before releasing a sigh. "I told him to back away from you." His eyes burn into mine at his words. "That whatever is going on between you two, to call it off. And I stand by that decision." My heart pounds at his confession. "He's not someone you can change, April. And you're not the type of woman to accept what he has to offer." Then he turns to look straight ahead, dismissing me.

Numbly, I open the door and get out. I'm still standing there in complete shock at his words when he drives out of sight. He just said what I already told Grave, but that doesn't make the pain in my chest hurt any less.

TWENTY-SEVEN
GRAVE

I RIDE THE elevator up to the fifteenth floor in the South Mason Towers. I still feel like fucking shit. My mouth dry and my head pounds. Chest so tight it's hard to breathe. I feel like someone is sitting on it. I should be in bed, passed the fuck out, but this couldn't wait. I have something to say.

She's not expecting me. I didn't want to give away the surprise. I come to a stop, and the door slides open. I storm down the hallway and knock on the only door to the right. And wait.

Getting impatient, I go to do it again, but it opens.

"You fucking drugged me!" I shout in Lucy's face.

Her dark eyes are red and heavy. Her bleach blond hair a tangled mess and all she wears is a tight tank top with a thong while standing at the front door.

She blinks, her eyes trying to focus. "Grave ..."

I wrap my hand around her throat and shove her into her penthouse. I slam her back into the wall of the foyer and cut off her air.

I glare down at her. "It took hours for any memories to come back. And you know what I remembered once they did?" I growl in her face.

Tears fill her eyes and her lips are parted. I shake her viciously. "The water I had on the table. You did something to it while I was looking at the picture April sent me." I let go, and she falls to her knees coughing.

It's the only logical explanation. I didn't have those pills on me when I arrived at the Airport to speak with Trey while waiting for Ethan. I didn't have them when I was texting April. But I remember Lucy did.

"What did you give me?" I shout. I don't know what's worse. The fact she gave them to me without my knowledge or that she wanted to sabotage my date with April.

"How many, Lucy?" I demand, slamming my fist into the wall.

"I don't ... know." She whimpers. "I just dumped some in it."

"Jesus!" She thought she had to give me a high dosage due to my tolerance. It obviously wasn't my first time, so she wanted to make sure she gave me enough not to question what was going on.

"I'm sorry, Grave. I ..."

I reach down, grip her hair, and yank her to her feet. She cries out as I shove her into the glass table, knocking over a bowl that falls to the floor and shatters. "What the fuck were you thinking?"

"I'm sorry." She sobs. "I'm so sorry."

I sit at the table all of a sudden tired. My eyes heavy. I lick my lips.

"How do you feel?" Lucy asks, getting up from her seat.

"Pretty ... pretty good," I answer. Leaning back in the chair, I feel my legs falling open.

The side door to the office opens, and Trey walks out. Didn't he say that Ethan would be here soon? How long ago was that? He looks at me and then at Lucy. "You kids have fun." Then exits the room, leaving us alone.

She walks over to me. I try to sit up, but my body won't work.

"I can make you feel better." She pushes my chair back from the table and falls to her knees.

I close my heavy eyes and run my hand down over my face. "Fuck,"

I breathe. Did Trey give me something? Why am I here to begin with? I feel like I had something to do but ... April. That's it. We have dinner plans. She had sent me a picture ... Black dress with black heels. My cock starts to get hard. Yes, that's what I wanted to do—fuck her.

She unzips my jeans and pulls them down enough to take my cock in her hand. "That's it, April." *I moan her name.*

"You just sit back, baby. I'm going to make you feel so good." *She licks up my shaft.* "I always make you feel good, right?"

"Fuck, yeah!" *I agree, keeping my eyes shut.*

I let go of her, and she falls to the floor once again. "I fucking called you April!" *I shout.* I really thought it was her. "Are you that fucked up that you didn't mind?"

She looks up at me from her knees. Her makeup smeared with tears and snot. "I love you, Grave ..."

I let out a rough laugh.

"I'll be whoever you want me to be." *She sniffs.* "You thought it was her, but it was me. I did that ... I'm who you want!"

Fuck, she's clearly hallucinating. "Well, let me make this very clear for you." *I kneel to her level.* "Stay the fuck away from me, *Lucy*! You're right, it was your mouth I fucked last night, but you were not the one I wanted." *Then I storm out, slamming the door behind me.*

LUCY

I WATCH HIM *stare down at his cell, and I quickly pop open the lid to the pill bottle and dump it over his water. They quickly dissolve. They don't call it a date rape drug for nothing. But it's not rape when they want it. He wants me. Always has. Always will. We do this all the time—pop some pills and fuck.*

I'm his ride or die. I'm his meant to be.

Grave loves me. He just doesn't know how to show it.

"Do you love her?" *I ask.*

His blue eyes find their way to mine, and he lies to my face. "I don't know her."

I almost regretted what I was about to do. Now I feel like I should have added more.

He picks up his water and downs it. "I need to go."

He stands, and my heart races that he may leave. No. I haven't had my chance yet. She gets to show him how she cares about him, so I should get mine. It's only fair.

Just then, the door to the office opens, and Trey enters the room once again. "Hey, man, the kid is fighting here tonight."

Grave looks down at his watch. Probably wondering if the bitch will wait for him. "What time?"

"Seven."

He plops back down in his seat, snapping, "I want his ass in here the moment he arrives."

"So ... you're staying?" I ask, trying to hide my smile. It won't take long before those pills kick in. I'm already feeling mine.

"Not for you," he growls.

Oh, but you are staying for me.

I sob on my entryway floor as Grave storms out of my penthouse. I fucked up! I thought if I could show him how much I love him, that he would do the same.

He loves her. I know it, and he knows it. He was lying to me at the Airport last night when I asked him. I pretended that it didn't bother me, but it broke my heart. For six years, I've been there for him. I've crawled on my hands and knees to make him happy.

I would give him anything he asked for.

I run the back of my hand under my runny nose and crawl over to the open living room. My chest is tight, and I can't seem to swallow the lump in my throat. I make it to my cell, and with blurry eyes, I dial the only number I can think of.

TWENTY-EIGHT
GRAVE

Monday morning, I stand in my brother's office at Kingdom with my back resting up against the wall while he sits behind the desk. He silently glares up at me. His eyes burning fucking holes in me.

"Save it," I warn him. I'm not in the mood to be fucked with.

His jaw tightens, but he doesn't say anything.

The door opens, and I look over to see Cross enter and plop down in one of the chairs in front of the desk. He leans back and props his feet up on the desk. My brother puts his eyes on him. "May I help you?" he snaps.

Cross just snaps his Zippo open and closed.

My brother sighs, running a hand over his hair. His irritation showing. He wants to beat the shit out of me. *Bring it.* I'm in a fighting mood.

"Titan told me he took your girl home. She was pretty upset with you," Cross finally speaks.

"What girl?" my brother asks.

"No one," I answer, and my chest tightens. I need to go see her. Apologize. *But for what?* I'm not going to tell her what happened. I'm not going to tell *anyone* what fucking happened. This is what they expect from me. Drugs, women, and disappointments. No one would believe that Lucy drugged me, and I'm sure as hell not going to admit that I willingly let her suck my dick. The fact that I thought it was April won't matter.

The door opens again. This time, it's Titan. "Are we having another fucking meeting?" I growl.

Titan closes the door behind him and sits down next to Cross in the other chair.

"So, Grave is denying April," Cross says to Titan.

Titan doesn't even look at me. "Good."

Cross arches a brow at his words. "What ...?"

"He needs to stay the hell away from her." His eyes finally slide to mine. "She's too good for him."

"Is that what this is?" I demand. "Going to warn me to stay away from her? Well, don't worry about it. I'm done. It's over." I feel sick admitting that. Knowing that I fucked up the best thing that I will ever have.

"No." My brother sighs. "We want you to check yourself into rehab."

I snort. *Fuck that!* "No." I turn and walk toward the door.

"Grave, if you don't check yourself in today, then don't come back to Kingdom tomorrow."

I turn around and glare at him. "You can't fire me. I own a part of this business."

He shakes his head. "It's not about the business. Don't you understand? You are going to die!"

"I'm not afraid of death," I say simply just to piss him off more.

"Goddammit, Kyle!" he shouts.

His voice is making my head pound—intensifying my already unbearable headache. I reach out for the door handle.

"Don't you dare walk out of my office!" A glass paperweight flies next to me, hitting the wall so hard it puts a dent in it. "I'm talking to you!"

I open the door and walk right out, jumping on the elevator and getting the fuck out of this place with no intention of returning for the day.

APRIL

I SIT AT the bar, a bowl of peanuts in front of me, their shells covering the floor.

Alexa stands across from me, silently judging me. "Would you like another?" she asks.

I slide my empty glass across the bar, and she refills my water. I'm not in the mood to drink. I just want to stuff my face full of peanuts and wallow in my own pity.

"What's wrong with her?" Derek asks, coming up next to her.

"Grave cheated on her." She sighs.

"What? You were dating that asshole?" He snorts. "What did you expect?"

"Derek!" She shoves him away. "That's a shitty thing to say."

"I told her the Kings were not people to fuck with."

"Go fucking work," she snaps at him.

"He's right," I mumble. "I should have never fucked him."

"Jesus," he hisses.

A figure plops down beside me. "If sex is all you need, I can hook you up." Jasmine bumps her shoulder into mine playfully, trying to lighten the mood.

I don't laugh.

"Speaking of sex ..." Derek goes on. "You free tomorrow night?" he asks her.

Jasmine snorts. "I'm never free. Always top dollar."

He smirks, his eyes running over her chest. "How much will a hundred get me?"

"My foot up your ass."

He wiggles his eyebrows. "I could get into that."

"Oh, you'll love it," she answers.

"You two are disgusting." Alexa shakes her head.

I grab another peanut shell and break it before tossing the peanut in my mouth.

"I have a solution," Jasmine offers.

"What is it?" I ask, not really caring.

I miss him. That's the worst part. I fell for a cheater, and my dumb ass misses him. Telling yourself you're too good for them is easier said than done.

"This." She starts gathering her red hair in her hands.

"What are you doing?" Alexa asks.

"I'm putting my hair up. We're gonna turn on some gangster rap, and we're gonna cut a bitch." She pulls a knife out of her Louis Vuitton bag.

"You can't have that in here." Alexa gasps.

Jasmine ignores her and looks at me. Her green eyes wide with excitement. "I've found if you lick the blood off it, it's quite effective. Shows them you don't give a fuck. Most people frown on cannibalism."

"Give me that." Alexa reaches across the bar and yanks it from her hand.

Jasmine shrugs. "I tried. I'm not tequila. I can't make everyone happy."

"Tequila makes me want to fight," I say.

"Then tequila it is." Jasmine claps her hands.

"No!" Alexa shakes her head. "Water and peanuts only."

Jasmine pouts. "You're no fun." Then she gets serious and places her hand on my shoulder. "You know this isn't your fault, right?"

"It is." It's all my fault. My brother getting in trouble. Falling for Grave. I could have prevented it all. "I knew better."

TWENTY-NINE
GRAVE

I SIT IN the dark hotel room with the black shades pulled closed. I've become my brother. Is this why he's always such a dick? Because he loved someone and lost them?

"Numb" by 8 Graves blares through the speakers on my phone.

Cross stands next to the couch, getting his shit ready. He's the only one I'm talking to at the moment. I threatened him with his life not to tell the others where I'm at. I've had my cell off for a few days and cut all outside communication off until today when I messaged him to come see me.

He removes his gloves from his bag and pauses, looking down at me. "Sure you want to do this?"

"Yes." I've always been impulsive. April makes me think, and I fucking hate it. I was fucking drowning, and she was my last attempt at living. She saw my struggle and pulled me out of the water. She gave me life, and I gave her nothing. "Do it."

"I can't work in the dark ..." He trails off, walking over to the wall and turning on the bright lights.

I lie down on the couch with a growl and rip the blanket off the back, throwing it over my face. Maybe I'll get lucky and suffocate.

APRIL STRADDLES MY HIPS, HER PURPLE HAIR FALLING OVER HER shoulders. *She reaches up, running her hands through it and pushing it off her face, flipping it to the side.*

We've been in her bed all weekend. I've ignored every call and text from my brother and the other Kings. I want to spend every second I have with this woman. I haven't even thought about a hit or a drink.

I run my palm down her chest bone still feeling her heart pound, her skin slick with sweat. It travels lower until gripping her hip bone. She bites her bottom lip while her eyes run over the ink on my chest. They follow the lines of my skull with the tilted crown on my left pec. Then the crossbones underneath. All the Kings have them. "How old were you when you got your first tattoo?"

"Eighteen."

"I've always wanted to get a tattoo."

"Really? What do you want?" *My eyes run over her perfect tits and the curves of her hips, imagining them covered in ink.*

"I almost went through with it once." *She laughs.* "My best friend, Alexa, and I went out and got drunk. She was dating this musician at the time, and we had gone to their show. Anyway, afterward all the members of his band got matching tattoos. I wanted to get a petal on my arm."

"So why didn't you?"

"Because I know I wouldn't stop."

I reach up and run my hands through her tangled hair. "And why is that?"

"Because they're addicting."

"They are," *I agree.*

She runs her hand up my right arm, her fingers following the ink. "I've always wanted a sleeve. I love art. I just ..."

"Go on," *I urge her.*

"I don't trust anyone to draw on me. I'd want to do it, and well, I'm not a tattoo artist."

"You could be."

She laughs.

"Cross is a tattoo artist."

"He is?" Her ice blue eyes widen.

I nod. "Yep. He has a shop inside of Kingdom. If you were to draw him what you want, he'll do it for you."

"Grave?" I feel a hand on my chest.

"Hmm?" I sit up and look at Cross standing next to me.

The glass coffee table is littered with Red Bull cans and room service that we haven't finished. "We're done," he tells me.

"How long was I asleep?" I ask, feeling my arm tingle. He's been drinking sugar and I've had a few Lortabs to help with the pain and to get some rest.

"A little over two hours this time."

I place my face in my hands. Every time I sleep, I see her. She's like a recurring nightmare that I can't escape no matter how hard I try.

"I'm finished," he states.

"Completely?" I ask, looking up at him.

He takes the Zippo from his pocket and lights up a cigarette. "Yep. Take a look." He reaches out his hand to help me up off the couch in my hotel suite. He picks up the piece of paper on the floor and places it on the coffee table, so I don't step on it.

A total of a week, thirty-five hours and my other sleeve is complete.

APRIL

I STAND IN the middle of Roses with Alexa, Haven, and Emilee. Jasmine is over in the cooler on her phone. I went back in there a minute ago and she was cussing someone out about payment for a Queen. I was confused and ran out of there as fast as I could to give her privacy.

Emilee keeps staring at me. Every time I look at her, she averts her eyes. It's starting to make me paranoid. This is the first chance I've had to hang out with them since everything went down with Grave last week. The shop re-opened earlier this week and I've been slammed just trying to get back to where I was with orders. "Do I have something on my face?" I come out and ask her, patting down my cheeks.

"No." She sighs. "I just ... never mind." She waves me off.

Alexa pops a piece of popcorn in her mouth as she leans over the front counter. Like a crazy neighbor eavesdropping. She has her bleach blond hair up in a messy bun and zero makeup on her face. She closed down her bar last night and called me first thing this morning. Said she had the day off at the studio and didn't want to waste it sleeping. So, she showed up with an energy drink in each hand. She raided the small kitchen I have in the back and found some expired popcorn, but that doesn't seem to bother her.

"What is it?" I ask.

"It's just ... have you tried calling him?" Emilee rushes out.

"Not this again." Haven shakes her head. "He cheated on her. With Lucy!"

"But are you sure he did that? Did he admit to sleeping with her?" Emilee looks from Haven to me for verification.

"He couldn't remember," Haven snaps. "That's enough to kick his ass to the curb."

"Well, me and Titan ..."

"We all know that you and Titan allow other cocks into your bed, Emilee." She waves her off. "It's not even close to the same."

Alexa begins to choke, and pieces of popcorn go flying.

"What?" I ask shocked. "You guys have an open relationship?" I would have never guessed that about Titan. He just seems all possessive. And Emilee seems so in love with him. Why would they want to bring someone into their relationship? To each their own I guess. Since I've never done it, I have a hard time understanding it.

"It's not like that," Emilee answers me, narrowing her eyes on Haven for a split second. "We have an understanding. I love Titan. I do. With everything I have. He's going to be my husband. We don't allow all cocks into our bed. But sometimes, Bones joins us."

Holy shit! I think my mouth drops open. "As in Bones? Grave's brother?" No fucking way. I look over at Alexa, and now she's shoving handfuls in her mouth. Most are falling onto the counter.

"We dated in high school and throughout college." She shrugs. "It's no big deal."

"It's not the same," Haven repeats. "He fucked Lucy without April's permission."

I hang my head. That's the hardest part of all this. I haven't spoken to him in five days. I didn't expect him to chase me, and in all honestly, I wouldn't have given him the time of day even if he had. But I hate the loneliness of his absence. I hate not being able to call him and hear his voice. And of course, I miss him when it's late at night and I wish he was lying next to me in my bed.

Just then, Jasmine joins our conversation, exiting the cooler. "Oh, stop harping on that, Haven. You're just mad because you hate Lucy."

"Of course, I do." She lifts her nose up in the air.

I frown. "Did she and Luca date?" Maybe they were once fuck buddies too.

"Hell no," Haven snaps. "I thought ... There was a setup. What I thought happened, didn't. But it was meant to look like it did."

I'm confused.

"Exactly." Emilee walks over to me and places her hand on my shoulders. "Take what happened to Haven as an example."

"But I don't understand what happened ..." I try to argue.

"There's nothing wrong with talking it out." Emilee goes on, interrupting me. "I've learned that you need to communicate. And if you miss him half as bad as you act, then it doesn't hurt to try."

"Like I said ..." Jasmine comes to stand in front of me as Haven and Emilee walk over to the flowers on the shelves. Alexa turns her attention to me and Jasmine. "You have to decide. Fight for it, or let it go." She smiles. "And all I see is you holding on."

THREE HOURS LATER, THEY'RE ALL STILL HERE. WE'RE GETTING things in order for Titan and Emilee's wedding. It was something I didn't think I'd be able to pull off, but just like Jasmine had said—these girls are ride or die bitches.

It reminds me of how grateful I am to have had Alexa there for me for all those years and me for her. We've been through a lot of shit together. And although I'm no longer with Grave, I hope that these women stay my friends too.

I look up when the bell rings on the door. "Hello. I'm looking for a Miss April Davis."

"That's me." I lift my hand.

She hands me a rectangular box, it's longer in height then it is in width. But not very thick. "Whoa. It's heavy."

"You have a great day, miss," she calls out, exiting.

"Who is it from?" Alexa asks, already picking up the scissors on the counter.

"It doesn't say," I answer, setting it down and taking them from her. I cut the places that are taped and open the top. Reaching in, I grab the contents and pull it out.

Alexa gasps.

"Wow!" Jasmine states.

"That's gorgeous," Haven adds.

"Who drew that for you?" Emilee asks, taking the framed 20x30 picture from my hands.

I stare off at the front door where the lady walked out. My heart beating wildly in my chest. "I did."

"*Cross is a tattoo artist,*" *Grave tells me.*

"*He is?*" *My eyes widen while I straddle him naked. We haven't left my house all weekend. After our dinner, we came back here. You know when you sleep with a guy for the first time, and it can be awkward afterward? Like is he going to leave on his own? Or am I going to have to go crazy on his ass, so I don't have to put up with him again? It's not like that with Grave. Not only is the guy hot and great in bed, he has this relaxed vibe about him. Just a go with the flow type of personality. And I like it. He's easy to talk to and he seems truly interested in what I have to say.*

He nods. *"Yep. He has a shop inside of Kingdom. If you were to draw him what you want, he'll do it for you."*

"That would be so cool."

His hand goes behind my neck and pulls my chest down to his. "It would be," he whispers against my lips.

"Will you help me?" I ask, lifting my hips to reach between our bodies.

He groans when my hand wraps around the base of his cock. "Whatever you need," he promises. His right hand finds its way into my already tangled hair.

"Help me decide what tattoo to put where?" I arch a brow. I wasn't lying to him. I've always wanted a tattoo. But you hear how addictive they are, and I was afraid that once I started, I'd never stop. I love all of his. How free he must feel to express himself with such beautiful art.

That's why I paint on vases—to express feelings. Wants. Needs. My thoughts. It's like cleansing the soul. I want to know that feeling.

"Absolutely." He licks his lips.

I sit up and release his dick.

His arms fall to his sides, and he lets out a growl of frustration.

"Let's do it. Right now." I go to jump off the bed, but he grabs my arm and yanks me down onto my back. His hands push mine above my head while he straddles me.

"First, I'm going to fuck you." He gives me a grin, and his eyes drop to my chest. "I need to learn your body before we draw it."

"You should know it by now." I laugh.

I blink. It's my drawing. I took a white canvas I had in my spare art room at my house and painted myself on it. It's got my purple hair, with a full face of makeup. It's how I always wear it, black eyeliner, my lips match my hair and I have my septum piercing in. Ink covers my neck, multiple colors of pink, blue, and purple petals. I drew myself topless, but have my arms crossed over my chest to cover up my breasts, pushing them up in the process. Vines the color of night wrap around and up my arms to my shoulders. Red roses cover my upper chest that look like they're floating on top of a crystal blue lake.

"I love that," Grave *says standing behind me, wrapping his arms around my chest.*

I tilt my head, looking at the canvas. I just started drawing random things on my skin since I had my portrait painted. "I think it's too much. The water looks out of place."

"No," he disagrees. "They match your eyes perfectly."

The water fades at the end of the canvas. I chose to only paint from my crossed arms over my chest and up. But every inch of the skin I show is covered in something. "He kept it," I whisper, my throat closing. I hadn't looked at it since I drew it over a month ago. "How did he ...?"

"Who?" Jasmine asks.

I would have never had the balls to go through with them. That's why we did this.

"So you know what you'd look like if you ever decided to wear your own art." He had said.

Tears sting my eyes. "Grave." I swallow. "I drew this with Grave. He must have taken it with him and framed it."

"It's gorgeous," Alexa tells me. "That was very nice of him."

It was. "I don't know if I should shatter it or hang it." I sniff.

"Definitely hang it." Emilee shrieks as she rips it from my hands.

THIRTY

GRAVE

NOTHER NIGHT IN my hotel room. Cross sits over on the couch across from me. "Let's go out tonight," he offers.

"Not in the mood." I shake my head.

"I'm bored." He stands

"Then leave." I wave goodbye.

"I don't agree with Titan and Bones, but this isn't good for you either, Grave. It's been over a week. You need to get out."

No, I don't. Too much temptation. Drugs, women. I don't want either of them at the moment.

"What if I called some girls and had them come here?" He pulls his cell out of his pocket.

"Then you better get your own hotel room."

He sighs and falls back down onto his ass.

A cell starts vibrating, and I look at the coffee table. *It's mine.* I look at Cross. He looks at me, and after a second, he growls, reaching forward and picking it up.

"It's a message," he states.

"Yeah? Tell them to fuck off."

His eyes meet mine. "That's not the response you're going to want to give."

"Why's that?" I can only imagine my brother texting me to get my ass to Kingdom. Again. He only sends me about five a day. For someone who gave me an ultimatum, he sure does want me back at Kingdom awfully bad.

"Because it's April. And she received her drawing."

"What?" I jump up off the couch and snatch my cell from his hand.

> April: I got the drawing. Thank you. That was very sweet of you to frame it. I have plans tonight, but I was wondering if we could have dinner this weekend? If you're not busy, I'd like to talk.

THIRTY-ONE
GRAVE

WHEN I WAS in high school, I stole a motorcycle off the showroom floor and took it for a joyride. I lost control going into a sharp turn and ended up driving it right off a bridge into the lake. I managed to crawl out and make it home. My father just happened to have been home at the time. He beat the shit out of me. I was in a coma for a week due to his hands. I'm not sure if the fractured femur and broken arm were due to him or my wreck.

But by the time I was released from the hospital, my father had pulled some strings and got me cleared. No arrest. I should have just done the time. He never let me forget what he did for me. Then he beat me some more. Said that I deserved to know what hell felt like. What he didn't know was that I was already living in hell. And that's why I did what I did, to feel alive.

That's what April is to me. My hell. I knew all along it would end just like that day I stole the motorcycle. It was going to ruin me when she realized who I was and that she'd be better off without me.

I bring my car to a stop in her driveway and let out a long breath. I accepted her offer to dinner. I wasn't going to pass up any chance of seeing her, even if it makes it harder to go without her tomorrow.

I exit my car and walk up to her door. Knocking twice, I wait for her to answer. I'm nervous. For once in my life I'm ashamed of who I am. But I know I can be better. For her. For us. I just need the chance to prove that to her.

The door opens, and she stands before me, her purple hair down and straight. Her makeup done how I like it with black lining her eyes and dark lips. She wears a pair of denim shorts and a black T-shirt that reads *Always and forever* across the chest.

It feels like it's been years since I've seen her. It hasn't even been a full two weeks.

"Hey." She gives me a soft smile, and my knees almost buckle at the sound of her voice. She's the best drug I've ever tasted. The best high I've ever reached.

"Ready?" I ask, unable to get out a full sentence.

"Yeah." She steps forward, and I match it, taking one back to allow her space. She turns and locks her front door. The simple movement has the smell of her vanilla shampoo filling my nose.

I have to close my eyes and think of anything but her to try not to get hard.

Walking her over to my passenger side, I open the door for her, and she falls inside.

I go to the driver side door and remind myself. This is like that motorcycle I crashed. When I go down, it's going to fucking hurt like hell and leave scars as reminders, but I'd do it again in a heartbeat.

APRIL

He's acting different, and I hate it. I wish we could go back to that first day when I didn't know who he was, and he didn't care who I was. This is why I don't date. Why I don't allow anyone to help me or get close.

My mother always told me—you will get your heart broken, baby. It is inevitable. Part of life. It's how you handle it that either makes you a woman or a child. I didn't want to be the bigger person. I didn't want to put myself out there again to him. But he did something that no one has ever done before—listened to me. And it felt good. So here we are.

I look out his passenger side window, avoiding eye contact with him. It hurts. There's so much that I want to say but can't get the words out. Emilee hung that picture I drew up in the shop, and I find myself just staring at it. Wondering if I was that April, would I be stronger? Would he love me covered in ink like him? He'd see me differently.

"I have to run by my house," he speaks, and I jump in surprise.

"Oh, okay."

"I need to grab something," he goes on.

I nod, looking over at him. He has his left hand on the steering wheel of his Zenvo STI. The car starts at a little over one million. I Googled it after I first saw it. I had never even heard of this kind of car before. His black leather with gold stitching interior tells me he had it custom made just for him to match Kingdom. His right hand on the shifter. He wears a white long-sleeve shirt with holey jeans and black Chuck Taylor high tops. His face is freshly shaven. His long hair is slicked back away from his face. At first glance, he looks relaxed, but I see the tic in his jaw. His tight shoulders and the lack of his carefree laughter further proves my suspicion.

I hate that he's hurting. And I hate that I care.

All I keep thinking is when was he high last? Or has he been with Lucy since I walked away from him? Of course he has. What man would pass on a sure thing?

I turn, looking back out the window, and let out a long breath. *This was a mistake.* Because it's going to hurt even worse when the night ends and I have to walk away from him all over again.

We pull through the gate at the Kings compound. It's black iron with a gold K in the middle of it. The place is just as extravagant as their hotel and casino. Four houses sit in a cul-de-sac like structure. But they're not close enough that you could throw a rock at each one. A huge clubhouse sits in the center with a state-of-the-art outside kitchen, bar, fireplace with outdoor furniture and hot tub. I have a feeling that no one ever uses it.

He comes to stop in his driveway and parks in front of his four-car garage. Lifting his right hand, he presses the button and opens up one of the garage doors. "I'll only be a minute." He doesn't wait for a response and exits the car.

I lean my head against the headrest and close my eyes. They sting. "Don't do it," I growl, trying to keep the tears from falling.

I open them up and let out a little scream of frustration. This is crazy. I should just get out and start walking back home. I look over at Titan and Emilee's house. I can see the lights on through the front of their floor-to-ceiling windows. Maybe he'll take me home. He's done it before. Maybe …

A phone vibrates in the cup holder. My eyes drop to look down at it. It's Grave's.

It vibrates again.

Giving a quick look at the house, I see he's still inside. I pick it up and go to open the screen, but it's locked.

I know the code. I've seen him open it a hundred times whenever he gets a text.

It vibrates in my hand again, and I make up my mind. I punch in the four-digit code, and the screen pops up. His background picture is of his Charger sitting out on the tarmac at the Airport.

I click on the text message icon and open it up.

Lucy: I miss you, baby. I'm sorry for what I did.

My eyes shoot to the house again to check on him. Still no sign. *What did she do?* Is that why he's mad? At her?

My hand tightens on the phone. Is that why he agreed to this date? Because she stood him up this time? I'm just a backup plan? That's why it took him so long to say yes to me.

"That motherfucker ..."

It vibrates in my hand again, and this time it's a video. I hit play.

THIRTY-TWO
GRAVE

"WHERE THE FUCK is it?" I growl, while on my hands and knees checking under my bed for my extra phone charger. The one I have at the hotel isn't working properly, and my phone keeps dying. And I haven't felt like going to buy a new one. My house just happened to be on the way to dinner, and I thought I'd stop by and get it.

Standing up, I open my nightstand again. Shoving shit around, I dig for it but no luck. Where did I have it last ...?

"Grave?" I hear April scream bloody murder.

I run out of my bedroom and to the banister just in time to see her charging up the stairs. "What the fuck, April?" I snap, trying to calm my racing heart. I thought she was dying, for fuck's sake.

"Grave." She comes up to me, crying.

"What the fuck happened?" I demand, looking over her. We're in a gated community. No one can get in and out except for us Kings. She'd only been alone for about five minutes.

"We have to help her," she says, tears running down her face.

"Who?" I ask, looking around the second story of my house. "We're the only ones here."

"She messaged you." She shoves my cell into my chest. "A text and … video." She sniffs.

I take my cell from her hand and look down at it. Whatever she was watching was paused. I press play.

It's Lucy. My jaw tightens. She's standing in her penthouse apartment in the middle of the bathroom. Naked from the waist up. Someone is filming her. She's crying. Her makeup from days ago runs down her face. Her hair a bleached, tangled mess. "I'm sorry, Grave. Please forgive me. I love you. I miss you …" She hiccups. "I want you. Come and save me." She reaches out, grabs a bottle of pills and pops the lid. Opens her mouth and tips it back, swallowing a countless number of pills.

"Fuck!" I hiss.

"We have to go." April grabs my arm. "Grave, we have to."

I look up at her, and she sniffs. Her ice blue eyes are red, and her lips wet. "April, this is a trick," I tell her. This is what Lucy does. She needs attention. She needs to be seen and heard. Lucy knows I'm pissed off at her and want nothing to do with her right now. Possibly ever. This is her crying wolf.

Her brows scrunch as if I'm a heartless bastard. "What? No … the video …"

"Do you know how many times she's sent me videos like this?" I demand, shaking my phone. "This is what she does."

"Grave." She steps into me. "We have to help her. She's obviously crying out for help. Please," she begs.

"No," I say and place my phone in my pocket and start down the staircase.

"I thought you were dead," she says, stopping my feet. "I thought you died, Grave. And you know what?" I turn to face her. "I wouldn't have been able to live with myself if I hadn't done everything in my power to save you. Would you be able to live with yourself if she dies when you had a chance to help her?"

"Fine." I growl. "We'll stop by and check on her if that will make you happy." Then I turn and finish walking down the stairs.

Now April's back to not speaking to me again, but this time, at least I know why. *Lucy!* Because April thinks I'm a fucking jackass who doesn't care about others. And normally, that is me. I just refuse to tell her that. Lucy is trying to fuck shit up between me and April. Hell, she already has. But I can't tell her that. So I'll keep my mouth shut and let her see for herself. Last time Lucy did this to me was two years ago. Instead of coming over to see her, I took a trip to LA with Cross. She called me and said she took a bottle of pills and was lying in her kitchen naked with a steak knife. She wanted to end her life. I dropped everything, and Cross and I came running back to find her at a house party drunk off her ass. The pills she supposedly took were in her purse. I didn't talk to her for a month. Ignored all her calls and texts until I was ready to speak to her. Then, like always, I crawled back into bed with her because she pretended to understand me and care about me. She proved otherwise when she drugged my ass.

We pull into the parking garage of the South Mason Towers. We step into the elevator and take it up to the penthouse.

I knock on her door. "Lucy, open up!" I call out.

Nothing.

"Lucy?" I shout, pounding on it. "Open the fuck up." I turn to face April. "She's not going to answer. Let's go."

"No." She grips my arm before I can head back to the elevator. "We came here to check on her, Grave. I'm not leaving until I make sure she's okay." She crosses her arms over her chest. "Knock on it again."

Sighing, I pull out my keys to her place. I don't miss the snort that April gives me. This is what she wants and I'm tired of waiting. I want to spend my evening with April, so I'm going to move it along.

"Lucy!" I shout, entering with April right behind me.

The place looks trashed. Glass knocked over on the floor. Pictures hanging crooked on the walls. She's obviously had one of her parties,

221

and the maids haven't cleaned it up yet. I storm back in the bedroom and go to open it, but it's locked. "Open this door, Lucy!" I shout.

She doesn't say anything.

I take a step back, then ram my shoulder into it, knocking it open.

"Oh my God." April gasps.

Lucy is lying on her bed in nothing but a pair of underwear. She's on her stomach, her arms and head hang off the edge. "Lucy." I run over to her and flip her over, feeling her neck.

"Oh my God. Oh my God." April's voice grows frantic.

"She's got a pulse," I say, removing my cell from my pocket and tossing it to April. It falls to her feet. "Go to my contacts and call Dr. Lane." He's a doctor that Titan uses at Kingdom for his Queens—the secret call girl service we run. He'll get here the fastest. "Now!" I bark when she just stands there.

She jumps and picks up the phone as I lift Lucy off the bed and into my arms, carrying her into the master bathroom.

"Come on, Lucy." I bring her over to the toilet and shove my finger down her throat, trying to get whatever she swallowed out of her system.

I can hear April crying behind me while she rambles on to Dr. Lane about our location.

"Lucy?" I shout her name. Her head falls back, and I shove her matted hair out of her slick face to see she's really pale. I can hear the death rattle coming from her chest. "You're not doing this!" I growl. "Not fucking like this!"

APRIL

I STAND WITH my back plastered to Lucy's bedroom wall with a clear view into her bathroom. Both French doors are wide open. Grave sits on the bathroom floor with her in his lap. Just like that night I found him; she threw up on him. He shoved his fingers down her throat to make it happen. Never thought I'd be so happy to see someone vomit.

But she's awake. I can hear her softly crying. She trembles in his arms.

"Grave?" I hear a man call out from the front door.

"In here." My voice shakes.

An older man enters the bedroom dressed in a button-down shirt and pair of black slacks. He carries a suitcase in his right hand, but he's not alone. A man wearing a Kingdom T-shirt and jeans is right behind him. I remember him from the night the Mason brothers sent men to Roses looking for Ethan. It's Grave's brother, Bones. His angry blue eyes look me up and down before he dismisses me and makes his way into the bathroom.

"She's coherent." Grave starts talking to the doctor. "But she's ingested too much."

"What was it?" he asks Grave.

"I don't know," he growls.

My eyes start darting around the room, and I see the bottle on her nightstand. I pick it up and run into the bathroom. "Whatever was in here," I rush out, holding it out to anyone who will take it. I recognize it from the video she sent Grave.

Bones yanks it from my hands and reads off the bottle. I've never heard of it before.

"Okay, Lucy," the doctor begins, opening up the case he brought with him. "We're gonna pump your stomach, sweetheart."

"No," she softly cries out and my chest tightens. "No ... please ..."

"Grave, I want you to sit with her back to your chest." Bones helps Grave position the poor girl in his lap. "Good," the doctor says once they're situated. "Now reach around and hold her arms against her chest. Tightly," he orders.

My hands come up to my face so they can't hear me cry. They're going to hold her down and ram a tube down her nose.

"Grave ..." Her voice breaks. "Please don't ..."

He doesn't speak to her, and I hate that he's mad at her. This woman is in need of help. Has she always been suicidal? How many times have they had to do this to her? How many ...?

"Bones?" I hear someone shout out his name.

"In the bathroom," Bones answers.

Moments later, Titan enters the bedroom, and I see Emilee. Her eyes are red and puffy. She's been crying too. She runs to me and wraps her arms around my shoulders. "Are you okay?" she asks softly.

I nod and sniff.

"Okay, Lucy. You're going to feel a little pressure ..." He looks over at Bones. "I need you to hold her head back for me."

Bones grips her chin and tilts her head back where it rests on Grave's chest.

"Noooo," she cries out, fighting them as the doctor begins to feed the tube down her nose. She starts choking, and her body jerks.

Titan looks up at us, walks over to the bathroom door, and shuts them both in our faces, but that doesn't block out her cries.

THIRTY-THREE

GRAVE

I SIT IN the waiting room at the hospital with April on my right and Emilee on my left. By the time Dr. Lane finished pumping her stomach, the ambulance arrived.

Lucy is going to be admitted and kept for a seventy-two-hour hold.

No one has spoken. I was surprised to see my brother show up at Lucy's penthouse. I had April call Dr. Lane. He probably immediately called Titan who then called Bones. I know what they thought. April calling them crying about a girl named Lucy ... They thought I was fucked up with her.

It's happened before—other than the time April found me passed out on the floor at the Airport. I've never done drugs wanting to commit suicide, though. April was right—Lucy was crying out for help. And I'm thankful she wanted to go and check on her. Otherwise, she would have died there in her bed alone.

April lays her head on my shoulder, and I pull away from her. She looks up at me, those ice blue eyes no longer red from tears, but they look tired. I wrap my arm over her shoulders and pull her into me.

"Is she going to be okay?" she asks softly.

"Yeah," I say, but honestly, I don't know. Lucy has a long road with recovery. But my main concern is will she want to get the help she needs?

The emergency doors open, and I pull away from April to stand when I see Trey and Tanner enter. "Where is she?" Tanner asks the moment he spots me.

"She's been admitted ..."

"What the fuck happened?" Trey demands.

I run a hand over my hair. "She overdosed."

"What the fuck were you doing with her?" He bumps his chest into mine.

I take a step back, lifting my hands. It's been one hell of a day, and I'm not in the mood to fight. Not like this. Not here.

"He wasn't with her." I hear April snap from behind me. "She sent him a video ..."

"April." I shake my head, my way of telling her to sit down and shut the fuck up

"He saved her life!" she yells, not listening.

"April!" I shout.

"Sit your ass down, bitch!" Trey yells at her.

I turn back to face him, fist my hand, and punch him in his fucking face. So hard it shoves him back through the sliding glass doors. I walk outside but am shoved to the side. Bones comes to stand beside me and pulls his gun out of the back of his jeans

Trey steps up to the barrel. "Are you going to start a war over a whore?" he asks.

My brother cocks the gun. "Are you?"

Trey pulls his shoulders back and looks at me. Then at April. His dark eyes run up and down her body, lingering on her chest. It makes my blood boil knowing he's thinking of her the way he was taught. Like the woman in the photo hanging in their office. He raises his right hand and rubs his chin, his lips turning up at the corner. "Did

Grave tell you that my sister sucked his dick that night? Right before you found him unconscious on the floor."

My body tenses. They know exactly what we did because there are cameras in there. I'm sure the fucker watched it.

April doesn't say anything, but I can feel her anger instantly. Like a fire at my back, heating my skin. I stay facing Trey. As long as she's behind me, they'll have to go through me first.

He takes a step toward me. Bones keeps the gun pointed at him, ready to fire if need be. "And did he tell you that she drugged his drink?"

"Trey!" I snap.

"Is that true?"

I expected that question from April, but it came from my brother. I ignore him.

Trey laughs as his eyes land back on mine. "They expected you to be fucked up, so they never even questioned it." He looks at April. "But you? You, of all people, I thought you'd give him the benefit of the doubt." He looks her up and down again, this time licking his lips. "You were the name he called out while she was on her knees. And I'd like to know why."

I lunge at him. My body hits his so hard that it knocks the wind out of me. We hit the concrete sidewalk, and I don't even think. I just start pounding on his face. No way in hell will I let him touch her. He's already sent his men after her once. It won't happen again.

My fist hits the side of his face, and blood splatters the sidewalk. "Fucking touch her and I'll saw your fucking hands off!" I warn.

I go to hit him again, but I'm yanked back by Titan. He shoves me to the side. I wipe the sweat off my forehead with the back of my bloody hand.

Tanner leans down and picks up his dazed brother. "Get the fuck out of here," he growls.

"We have a deal!" I shout at him, and I want to know that he's going to honor it.

He nods. "We have a deal." Then he drags his brother back through the double glass doors into the hospital.

I'm gasping for breaths. My hand hurts, and I'm fucking tired. "Fuck!" I shout, turning around to look for April. "April?" I call out when I don't see her.

"She went to the car with Emilee," Titan reassures me.

I go to step off the sidewalk to the parking garage when Bones slaps his hand to my chest. "Was that true?"

I take in a long breath. "Why the fuck do you care?"

He sighs heavily, putting his gun away. "Grave ..."

"I'm just a druggie with a death wish."

APRIL

"COME ON," I say, helping Grave into his house. I had to drive him home from the hospital. His hand is swollen, and he hasn't said it, but I know he's hurting. He hit the concrete hard.

I was so pissed at him when the guy announced what Grave and Lucy did. And then he just kept going on, and I got angry for a different reason.

That's why Grave didn't want to go check on her. Because she had drugged him. That's why he wasn't nice when she cried in his lap on her bathroom floor. That's why she had said she was sorry. He knew what she did.

Why didn't he tell me? Was he embarrassed? He let me stand there and slap him over and over while I blamed him for being an addict. I know Grave has a past with drugs, but I never saw him high. I found it so off that he was always hanging out with me and then dumped me for her and drugs that night. And instead of questioning him about it, I turned on him.

We pull into the Kings compound and I park the car in his roundabout driveway. Not bothering with the garage. He gets out of the car before I can even help him. I walk behind him up his stone steps with my hands up hoping he doesn't fall down them. He unlocks the front door and slams it shut behind us.

"Here." I grab his left arm and throw it over my shoulders before he can even protest and start up the stairs to his second story.

I kick his bedroom door open and walk him to the adjoining master bathroom. He leans up against the white marble countertop. "You can take my car," he states.

I look at him in the mirror. "What?"

His blue eyes meet mine. "You can drive my car home. I'll have someone come get it tomorrow."

"Grave ..."

"You don't have to stay here with me. I'm fine." He turns his back to me and starts to walk over to his glass shower that sits over in the corner of his overly large bathroom. It has three sides made from nothing but glass so you can see inside of it.

I bow my head and let out a long breath. "I understand you're mad at me. I'm sorry for turning my back on you."

"I'm not mad," he says softly.

I look up at him through my lashes. "You should be."

He runs his left hand through his hair, keeping his back to me. "I hurt you. I lied to you. I did everything that I didn't want to do ... to you."

I walk up to him and place my hands on his back. He stiffens at the touch. I immediately pull away. "I shouldn't have assumed the worst."

He turns around. His eyes scan mine for a second before he looks away. "I'm an addict, April." My chest tightens at his confession. Hearing others say it just isn't the same as him admitting it. "You were right." His eyes come back to mine. "They are all right. You deserve better than me."

"I was wrong," I argue.

"No, you weren't," he says, and I fist my hands.

He's going to push me away. It's what I did to him. "Don't do this." I shake my head.

"Do what?"

"Stop!" I order, getting angry with him. Myself. "Quit pretending you don't know what's going on here."

His blue eyes glare down at me. "You may go," he states, dismissing me as though I'm nothing to him. As if the last month didn't happen.

I snort at his words. "I'm not leaving."

"April ..." he growls. "Turn around and walk away. You did it before without even thinking about it."

"I thought you cheated on me," I snap defensively.

"I fucking did," he yells.

"You thought she was me," I argue.

"And that makes you forgive me?" He snorts. "Thought you deserved better than that?"

I slap him across the face and instantly regret it when I see my handprint burning red on his cheek. "I'm sorry," I whisper, my hands cupping my face as tears sting my eyes.

"Aren't you tired of lying to yourself?" he asks. "Because I'm tired of doing it." He hangs his head, shaking it.

"Grave ..." I choke on his name.

"Leave, April." With that, he turns his back on me and opens the shower door to turn on the water.

I hang my head; the first tear runs down my cheek as I turn and exit his bathroom. I close the door behind me and lean back against it. My legs unable to move. My mind screaming not to make the same mistake twice. Emilee told me to communicate, and Jasmine told me to fight if I want it. And I know now more than ever that I want him. We made mistakes. I can admit that. That doesn't mean I want to give up.

I take a deep breath, square my shoulders, and open the bathroom door. Steam fills the large space as I stomp over to the shower and yank it open. "I'm not leaving!" I snap.

Stepping out from under the sprayer, he turns to face me. His blue eyes are tired, possibly sad. I'm not sure which at this point. "April ..."

"No, Grave! I will not let you ..." My words trail off as I spot his arm. Purple, blue, and black ink cover his right arm in a sleeve. "What ...?" My heart begins to pound in my chest. "Why?" It's the only word I can think of. "Why would you do that?" My eyes manage to meet his.

His eyes stare down into mine intently. "A woman drew this, and I thought it was so beautiful that I wanted to show it off to the world."

"It's me." I choke, those damn tears stinging my eyes once again. He makes me so emotional. "My drawing ..."

"It is." He nods once. "I had to have it."

"Why?" The first tear falls down my cheek.

"Because." He reaches out, grabbing my hand and pulling me into the shower. Clothes and all. "You are gorgeous, April. The most beautiful piece of art I've ever seen."

Another tear falls. "But we ... we broke up," I say.

"So?" He frowns. "You think that made me love you any less?"

My breath gets caught in my lungs. "You love me?" I whisper.

"More than anything."

I sniff, my chest tightening with remorse. I had so much I wanted to say to him. How I wasn't going to leave him. How I wouldn't allow him to do this to him or to me. But now the words mean nothing. "I love you. And I should have told you ..."

His lips crash onto mine, cutting off my rambling. I open for him, tasting my own tears. His hands go to my shirt, and I lift my arms above my head and pull away just long enough for him to remove the fabric.

"I love you," I mumble against his lips.

He growls, his hands yank my shorts undone and shove them down my legs. I kick them off. Spinning us around, he slams my back into the wall, shielding the water with his body. Then his lips are back on mine as he slides into me.

I throw my head back, pulling my lips from his to cry out. I forgot what he felt like. How big he was. He starts to move, after getting a better grip of my body.

My hands go around his neck, and I grasp his hair between my fingers.

He wraps his free hand around my neck, and my pussy tightens. My lips part, and I suck in a ragged breath.

I look at him through heavy eyes, and he's already watching me. The sound of our bodies slapping and the shower running fills the room along with our heavy breathing. My toes start to curl, and I close my eyes when the sensation takes over. "Oh, God." I gasp.

THIRTY-FOUR
GRAVE

HER PUSSY CLENCHES around my cock, and her body tightens against mine as she comes.

I lean down, attacking her lips with mine as I continue to fuck her, getting ready for my own release. I would love to take my time with her right now, but I can't. My body fucking hurts. I'm exhausted, but I couldn't not show her that I love her. That I'm sorry for what I did. How I reacted and that I let her think I truly didn't give a fuck about her.

I thrust one last time before coming. I lower her to her shaky feet but keep her pinned to the shower wall. "I'm sorry," I say. She'll never know how much I'm sorry for hurting her. I would give anything to take it back.

"Don't be," she whispers, running her fingers along my sleeve. "You did nothing wrong."

I place my forehead to hers, still trying to catch my breath. "I did." In so many ways.

She reaches up and cups my face and I lean into it. My eyes growing heavier by the second. I can feel the adrenaline from the fight dying off. I blink and her face grows with concern.

"Are you okay?"

"Yeah," I answer, taking a step back. "I just ..." I almost trip over her clothes and fall into the wall.

"Grave." She grips my upper arms. "Come on. Let's get you cleaned off and in bed."

I don't argue with her because honestly, I'm not sure how much longer I have left before I pass the fuck out.

She grabs my soap and washes me off, being careful with my busted hand. It's swollen, but it's stopped bleeding. I can't even make a fist with it right now. She finishes up quickly and turns the water off before she gets out and grabs two towels for us. She begins to dry me off and I take it from her. Then she walks over to the his and her sinks and starts digging under them in the cabinets. Slamming doors open and closed.

"What are you looking for?" I ask.

"Medicine. You need ..."

"No." I interrupt her, knowing where she's going.

She stops and stands, turning to face me. She hasn't even taken the time to dry off yet. Her towel still sits on the counter folded. Her wet hair clings to her naked chest and she still has some makeup smeared on her face. "Grave, you need to take something."

I shake my head. "I'll be okay."

She bites her bottom lip as if she wants to argue but I just told her I'm an addict. I have some tabs in my duffel bag in my closet but I'm not going to tell her that because I'm not going to take them. I can live with the pain. "I just need some rest." I assure her and walk over to the counter. "Will you stay the night with me?" I ask.

We've always stayed at her house. One, because I liked being at her house. It felt like home to me. And two, because I never wanted her up at Kingdom around the guys.

"Of course." She sighs, letting go of the fact I'm not going to take anything for the pain.

APRIL

I STAND IN the cooler at Roses when I hear the bell ring. "How may I help you?" I call out, walking behind the desk. The smile drops off my face when I see who it is.

Lucy stands there in a pair of blue jeans and a long-sleeve white shirt. Her blond hair is up in a high ponytail, and her face clear of makeup. Her brown eyes look sad, but she manages to give me a smile. "Hey," she says shyly.

"Hey." I cross my arms over my chest.

She bows her head, staring at her tennis shoes. "My brother told me that I owe you an apology and a thank you."

I just stare at her.

She looks up at me. "I'm sorry—"

"I'm not the one you owe an apology to," I interrupt her.

She lets out a long breath. "I told him I'm sorry."

It's been five days since we found her dying in her bedroom. Grave hasn't mentioned her once. But I think about her all the time. Wondering if she's okay.

"I was just jealous." She sighs. "I knew from the moment I saw you two together at the Airport the night of his fight that he loved you."

I feel what little anger I have for this woman fade. I walk out around the counter and over to her. I open my arms, and she all but falls into me. "I really am sorry." She begins to softly cry. "I just wanted him to love me like that. Like I loved him."

I rub her back, not sure what to say. You can't make someone love you.

"Thank you." She pulls away from me, rubbing her tears away. "I'm sober. And I understand what I've done is wrong." Her eyes meet mine. "I'm going to rehab. But I wouldn't have that opportunity if it wasn't for you."

I place my hands on her shoulders. "Don't let a man ever make you think your life isn't worth living, Lucy." She sniffs. "You're beautiful, and you need to put yourself first. Always." She really is pretty. Her blond hair brings out her big brown eyes. I hate that she put so much of her life into Grave's. But just because he doesn't return the feelings doesn't mean it's not worth anything. "I wish you the best, and I hope you find what you're looking for."

"Thank you," she says again, pulling me in for another hug. When she pulls away, she sniffs again. "You are what he needs. You're going to be the one to save him from himself." And with that, she turns and exits the shop.

THIRTY-FIVE

GRAVE

I SIT UP at my desk at Kingdom. I managed to sneak in without being seen. I was gone for almost two weeks when me and April broke up. Then I took some time off after Lucy's attempted suicide. I needed time to get my shit together. To decide the kind of life I wanted to have and how I was going to accomplish it. Plus, I just wanted to spend time with April. I helped her at the shop. She's been extremely busy playing catchup and getting ready for Emilee and Titan's wedding. It was a nice change of scenery. Not like anyone missed me here.

My door opens, and I hold my breath when I see my brother enter. So much for flying under the radar. I sit back in my seat, looking up at him.

He comes to stand at my desk. "May I speak to you?"

"If it's about rehab, no," I say simply.

He sighs and sits down, rolling up the sleeves on his button-down. "I'm sorry, Grave."

"Don't worry about it." I know my brother doesn't do well when it comes to talking about feelings. I don't want him to feel uncomfortable. He doesn't need to apologize. And I don't need to hear it.

His eyes go to my sleeve, and he frowns as he looks it over. Recognition flashes across his face when he realizes that face looks familiar. "So ..." He looks at me. "She's the one?"

I nod. "She's the one." April is everything for me. She's my accountability. My love and my hell. She's going to help me fight my demons every day by giving me all of her.

My office phone rings, and I pick it up. "Grave."

"Sir, you have a visitor," Nigel says into the phone.

"Who is it?"

"Tanner Mason."

I make my way downstairs, and I wasn't surprised when Bones insisted on coming with me. We step off the elevator into our private lobby. "Why are you here, Tanner?" It's the same thing he asked me that first night at the Airport.

He looks from Bones to me. "I, uh ..." He squares his shoulders. "I wanted to tell you in person." He pauses.

"Okay." I step toward him. "Tell me what?"

"Trey found Lucy in her penthouse this morning. She had passed away."

"I'm sorry to hear that." Bones is the first to speak. His words as sincere as you'll ever get from him.

My chest tightens, and I run my hand over my hair. "Cause of death?" I ask.

His eyes hold mine. You can tell he wants to cry, but he's holding it together the best he can. "It was ..." He clears his throat. "Suicide."

APRIL

I STAND NEXT to Grave at the graveside service for Lucy. "Fire Away" by Chris Stapleton plays softly in the background. The Mason brothers wanted to have a private service. Her death hasn't even been announced publicly since she passed away two days ago.

I still don't believe it. I just saw her. She came by the shop. She looked better, said she wanted to be better. Not three hours later she

238

was found dead in her penthouse apartment. It doesn't add up. Or maybe I just don't want to believe it. I've never known depression or addiction before. I don't pretend to even begin to understand what Lucy felt or went through.

I reach out for Grave's hand, but he pulls away from me.

I close my eyes and let the tears roll freely down my face. He's been this way ever since he found out about her death. Distant. Completely closed-off. No jokes. No nothing.

He blames himself. We all do. Even I feel like I could have done more to help her. To save her. She didn't deserve to die. Not this young and not this way. She had too much to give to this world. She was going to rehab. She had plans to change her life around. She wanted to do better for herself.

Opening my eyes, I see the three Mason brothers standing by her casket. Trey, the baby, openly sobs with his hand on the light wood.

Tanner stands next to him with his head down with his hand on his baby brother. I can see his shoulders shaking.

The only one I've never seen is Turner, but I knew who he was the moment I saw him. They all have a similar look about them. He stands there, head held high, and not a tear in his eye. His hands tucked in the front pockets of his suit. Sunglasses on top of his head. He looks out into nothing. And my heart breaks for him. At the inner battle he's fighting. There's nothing wrong with feeling something, especially when the loss is a sibling.

The song comes to an end, and a pastor steps back up to say a closing prayer. We all bow our heads, and I close my eyes, sniffing. I feel someone reach out to me on my left, and I pull the hand into mine. It's Jasmine. She was the last one I saw standing on that side of me.

"Amen." We say in unison.

I lift my head to reach out for Grave, but he's not there. I look around the cemetery and spot him over by the vehicles parked on the gravel. He stands in front of his flat black Zenvo STI, and Turner is right next to him. They're talking. Turner pulls out his cell, and they start watching something.

Grave nods a few times, and then Turner reaches out his right hand and shakes Grave's.

I immediately turn, looking for Bones. I spot him talking to Titan off to my left. "Bones?" I call out, running over to him. "What's going on between Grave and Turner?"

He looks from me to where his brother stands. "April ..." he starts.

"I'm asking you to check it out," I say. "I need someone to believe me."

He frowns. "Believe what?"

That your brother isn't the same person he was three days ago? That I see him standing in the kitchen while he stares at the bottle of vodka like he wants to down the entire thing at once. That I know, if he wanted, he could have a bottle of pills in his hands in a matter of seconds. That I'm afraid he's at the point of no return. I can only do so much. And if he relapses, I'm not sure I can bring him back.

"April, you ready?"

I spin around to see Grave now standing behind me. His sunglasses covering his eyes. I nod and walk toward him, knowing I'm on my own. They couldn't help him before, so they're not going to be of any help now. I'll do it by myself.

THIRTY-SIX
GRAVE

I STAND IN my closet back at my house, pulling a pair of jeans on.

"What are you doing?" April asks, entering the large space.

"I have to go to work," I say flatly.

"Grave, it's three a.m." She yawns.

"I know." I rip a shirt off a hanger and slide it on. Then walk past her, exiting.

"Grave ..."

"I don't have time, April," I snap at her, not in the mood to argue. I have somewhere to be.

"When will you be back?" she asks softly.

"Don't wait up," I say before I walk down the steps and into my garage.

I start my car, open the door, and back out, squealing my tires as I drive out of the gate. Heading toward the Airport.

I pull up to the back and park. I grab the bag out of my back seat and enter the building. I take the broken escalator two at a time and enter the room.

Turner sits at the table, waiting on me.

"Is he here?" I ask.

He nods. His eyes dropping to the bag. "Ready?"

We make our way downstairs to the underground tunnels. This existing, functional airport had a bomb shelter back in the seventies.

They have safe rooms that the Masons use as prison cells. They have their own law enforcement at the Airport. We make our way down through the tunnels and take a right at the end. Turner unlocks the master lock and yanks the door open.

A man sits in the middle of it, his arms strapped to the chair. He lifts his bloody face and looks at us. "Grave?" He fights the restraints. "What the fuck are you doing?"

"Jimmy Trust," I say with a smile.

His eyes narrow. "I knew you were into some sick shit."

Turner laughs. "I think that you're referring to me."

"What is this?" he demands.

"Gonna try to pretend you don't know why you're here?" I ask.

"Is this because I went and visited your girl?" I tilt my head to the side. "You can't blame me, right? That purple hair ..."

I punch him in the face, cutting him off.

His head hangs forward, and he spits blood onto the floor.

"What about my sister?" Turner asks.

"What about that whore?" he snaps.

Turner smirks. "Why did you kill her?"

"What are you talking about? She committed suicide."

"Did she?" he asks, pulling his cell out of his pocket. "Because after Grave here saved her life, I installed cameras in her penthouse."

His eyes widen, but he recovers quickly. "Like to watch your sister fuck, Turner? You Mason brothers really are sick fucks."

Turner places his phone in front of Jimmy and pushes play. The small room fills with Lucy's laugh.

"Let's get fucked up." You hear Jimmy's voice say.

"That's foreplay talk there," she tells him.

I've seen the video. Turner showed me at her funeral earlier today. The other brothers don't know. As far as they are concerned,

Lucy Mason committed suicide, and Turner wants it to stay that way. I'm not going to ask for his reasoning. His sister. His family. And his revenge.

Turner allows it to play. You hear them laughing and talking about nothing in particular as they swallow some pills and down some alcohol. Then you hear him say, "Let's fuck."

"I'm not in the mood." Her voice comes out soft. Like it took a lot of effort just to get them out.

"Come on, baby. It'll feel so good with the high." He grabs her by the waist and pushes the back of her legs to the edge of the bed.

"No." She places her hands on his chest.

"What about that foreplay you were talking about?" He reaches down and undoes her shorts.

"Jimmy ..."

He tosses her onto the bed, and she begins to fight him. But she's taken too many pills, had too much to drink. He's much more coherent than she is. She doesn't stand a chance against him.

"It'll be quick," he tells her, shoving her shorts down her legs.

"Not right now," she slurs, closing her eyes.

You can hear him slap her, and then there's very little struggle as he undoes his jeans, grips his hard dick and begins to fuck her. Her hands reach up and she tries to push him off, but he grabs a pillow and places it over her face, suffocating her to death. Jimmy makes sure to finish, though. Then when he gets off her, he takes what's left of the pills and flushes them, then sets the pill bottle next to her for it to look like a suicide, hoping that they didn't request an autopsy. A girl like Lucy—a drug addict with a suicidal background who was just released from a seventy-two-hour hold? They wouldn't think twice about it.

"What are you going to do?" he growls when Turner ends the video.

I lean down into my bag and pull out a roll of duct tape. I rip two pieces off.

"What the fuck ...?"

I place one over his lips diagonally while he tries to shake his head to prevent me from doing so. Then the other the opposite way. I go back to my bag and grab the tube.

"Hold his head," I tell Turner.

He walks over behind the chair he's restrained to and wraps his arm around Jimmy's neck, in a headlock, tilting it back. Jimmy tries to fight for his freedom, but he doesn't get it.

I walk back over to him. "You're gonna feel some pressure ..." I trail off and start to feed the tube down his nose. His body jerks, and he coughs behind the tape. His cheeks filling with air, and his eyes water. His hands clench and unclench. Once the tube is down his nose, I tip the bottle to the end and squeeze, the charcoal filling the tube. "I'm pumping your stomach, Jimmy. Just like they did hers. The only difference is that you're going to choke on your own vomit and die."

"Like the piece of shit you are," Turner adds with a sinister smile.

His body starts to convulse, and we both let go of him, stepping back. We watch his body turn on itself while he chokes on his own vomit. It shoots out his nostrils, and his eyes grow cold before his head falls forward, going limp.

Turner looks over at me. "Thanks for the help." He slaps my back.

I just nod. If it were up to me, I would have buried him alive, but this was Turner's revenge. I'm just happy he let me be a part of it.

He pulls a joint out of his pocket and lights it up. Taking a hit, he then hands it over to me. I stare at it for a long time, thinking about Lucy and how I let her down. How, once again, I wasn't there for her. I should have saved her. I don't love her the way she needed me too, but I did care for her.

APRIL

I SIT UP in Grave's bed the moment I hear the front door open and close. He's been gone for hours. The sun came up three hours ago, but I've stayed here, waiting on him. I wasn't able to sleep, and I've been sick to my stomach. Worried to death over where he went and what he was doing. Why he shut his cell off.

His bedroom door opens, and he walks in.

"Where have you been?" I demand, feeling both pissed and relived that he's okay.

He comes to a stop and looks up, his eyes meeting mine. My heart picks up at the look in them. They're red and I notice he stumbles. He's either drunk or high. Maybe both.

"Not sure how that is any of your business," he says.

"You left me here alone so you could go get fucked up?" I ask, trying to understand but not start a fight. I don't know how fragile he is right now. Lucy is dead, and I know he's hurting.

He doesn't answer. Instead, he sits on the end of the bed and removes his shoes. Then he stands and undoes his belt.

"Grave, we need to …"

"No, we don't, April. What I did and where I went is none of your business," he snaps.

"You're doing this again. You're trying to push me away."

"Then take the hint and leave," he growls.

I nod my head and lick my dry lips. "I know you're stronger than your demons, Grave. I just wish you'd realize that too."

He gives a rough laugh. "Don't start that shit with me. Next thing, you'll be telling me is to go to rehab like my brother."

I stand from the bed. "Grave …"

"Get the fuck out of my house, April!" he shouts, pointing at the bedroom door.

My bottom lip starts to quiver, and I try to swallow the knot that forms in my throat. I don't want to leave him, but I can't make him let me stay. This is his house and he obviously no longer wants me.

Instead of waiting for me to do what I'm told, he enters his bathroom and slams the door shut. Then I hear the sound of the door lock.

I run over and start banging on the door. "Open the fuck up, Grave! We're going to talk about this."

The shower comes on, but he says nothing.

I wrap my hand around the doorknob and start shoving on the door while my free hand pounds on it. "Grave! Open the fucking ..."

It swings open, jerking me into the bathroom in the process, causing me to run right into him. He stands before me shirtless and pants undone but still pulled up around his hips. His blue eyes glare down at me. I take in a shaky breath, not knowing what to do exactly. I don't want to push him, but then again, maybe that's what he needs. "I'm trying to help you." I soften my voice and place my hands on his chest. His heart pounds against my palms.

"April ..." he growls my name.

"Please, Grave." I plead with him. "I love you." I need him. What happened to Lucy was heart breaking and I'd hate to see him go down the same path. Maybe if her brothers had helped her, she wouldn't be dead. "You told me you loved me." He looks away from me and I see the tic in his sharp jaw. I'm not getting through to him. "Did you hear me?" I begin to slap his chest, growing desperate. "Answer me!"

Wrapping his hands around my wrists, he squeezes them, forcing me to stop. "I don't need your help!" he snaps. "And I sure as fuck don't need you." Then he shoves me out of the bathroom and slams the door in my face.

I begin to cry, knowing that he's too far gone. I'm not enough to make him stop. Lucy's death was hard on him and not even I can numb the pain. I run a hand through my hair and get dressed before walking out with my head down. Doing as I'm told, knowing that I can't talk him into letting me stay.

THIRTY-SEVEN
GRAVE

I SETTLE INTO the couch, my arms fanning the back of it, and look up at the ceiling. The room spins, and my vision goes in and out while "Sail" by AWOLNATION plays through the speakers. The words pound in my head like a drum. Two weeks I've gone without April, and it's been hell. But it's what I deserve. I was horrible to her. Just because I had a moment of weakness. I told her I didn't need her and to leave. She fucking left. What did I expect her to do?

"Man, it's gonna be fine," I hear Trey say as he snorts a line of coke off the coffee table. "You were fine without her before, and you'll be fine now."

I block him out, close my eyes, and listen to the thunder shake the walls. I draw in a long breath and fill my lungs with the tainted drugs. *It's not the same.*

The song changes to "Bury Me Low" by 8 Graves. It's always been my theme song.

"Grave? Man, someone is hollering at you," he says, shoving my arm.

"Fuck 'em." I take another hit, needing that high I was able to reach before April entered my life. I need to drown her out. Fucking bury her so deep it'll smother every thought of her I've ever had.

"Grave?" Trey sighs. "It's Titan."

"Fuck 'em," I repeat and take another hit.

Come on. Come on.

I need this hole to fill. The pain to go away. Just fucking knock my ass out.

"Grave, you sorry son of a bitch," Titan snaps. "Open the fucking door or I will break it down."

Maybe he'll hit me over the head with it. Memory loss would be better than this.

How long will it take ...?

I hear the door splinter and what's left of it bangs against the interior wall.

"Shit!" Trey hisses beside me.

Titans storms into the room, and I'm surprised he's alone. "Where are the rest of the bitches ...?" He punches me in the face so hard my head snaps back.

Blood instantly fills my mouth, and my face begins to pound.

"Fuck." Trey jumps up from his spot on the couch next to me.

Titan grips my shirt and yanks me off my ass, then shoves me to the floor.

"Stop, man!" Trey shouts.

I look up at my friend, already feeling my eye start to swell. "Fucking do it," I tell him, coughing up blood that's filled my mouth.

"Fuck, you're a piece of shit," Titan growls down at me.

I know I am. April knows I am. That's why she left me. "Just put me out of my misery."

"Get over whatever problem you have right now and move the fuck on."

"Easy for you to say." His woman didn't leave him. I wonder if he didn't share her with my brother, if she would stay with him? "I wonder who Emilee loves more?" I ask, thinking out loud.

"Grave," he growls. "Get your ass up. We have to go."

I close my eyes and welcome the darkness. "Fuck you, Titan."

He yanks me up by my shirt and hauls me out of the house. Then he's throwing me into his passenger seat. Squealing his tires, he pulls out onto the street and holds his phone up to his ear. "On our way." Pause. "Not well." He slides his eyes to mine. "Like shit. See you in a minute."

"Where are we going?" I ask. Maybe it's an intervention. I wouldn't be surprised if they throw me into a mental hospital and toss the key away. Everyone is tired of putting up with me. Myself included.

I blink, and my eyes grow heavy.

"How much did you have?" he grinds out.

"Not enough," I slur.

"Fuck!" He slams his palm down on the steering wheel. "I should leave you right here on the side of the motherfucking road."

"Do it," I dare him.

"Nah, that'd be too easy for you. You deserve everything that is about to hit you in the fucking face."

"Your fist? Hit me until I feel nothing."

He just shakes his head, ignoring my question.

We enter the gate for the property the Kings and I share, and he pulls into Bones's driveway. I groan. Pulling to a stop, he drags me out of the car and has to help me up the stairs. The moment we enter, Bones and Cross come up to us.

"This is a bad idea." Cross sighs looking me up and down.

"Leave us," my brother orders.

Titan lets go of me, and I fall into the wall. I blink, and then my brother is standing in front of me with his hand around my throat. "You were always fucking weak," he growls in my face.

"Fuck you, Bones."

"You don't deserve her."

I flinch at his words. I always knew that, but that didn't keep me from wanting her. From wanting to be better. She didn't believe in me. Just like the rest of them.

He steps into me. "You deserve to be alone for the rest of your fucking miserable life, which might be sooner rather than later." I know he's trying to hurt me on purpose, and I hate that it's working.

I go to swing at him but miss completely. He steps back, letting go of me, and I fall to my knees in his foyer. He kneels before me. "You can't stay high forever, Grave."

"Watch me."

He snorts.

"Why am I here?" I was perfectly content where I was. Getting lost in a drug-induced haze that didn't include a gorgeous woman with purple hair and the most amazing eyes that destroyed my heart.

Instead of answering, he turns and walks away from me, leaving me lying in the entrance to his house. I enjoy the cold black marble floor against my burning skin. Closing my eyes, I fall into the darkness that I've been praying for as the drugs do their job.

I WAKE IN A BED THAT I KNOW WELL. IT'S ONE OF MY BROTHER'S spare rooms. My head pounds, my jaw hurts, and I'm covered in sweat. I all but fall out of bed and stumble to the adjoining bathroom. I throw water on my busted face. I can't open my right eye, and my lips are busted. I feel like I was fucking hit by a truck.

Opening the glass shower door, I turn the shower on and strip out of my clothes before stepping in. My legs are too weak to hold myself up, so I sit down and lean my head against the cold tile.

"You shouldn't have brought him here." I hear Emilee's voice.

"Babe, he needs—"

"His ass needs to be in fucking rehab," she snaps, interrupting Titan.

The bedroom door slams open, and they must hear me in the shower because the bathroom door flies open next. She charges toward the shower as if she's seen me naked a hundred times. I make no move to cover myself. We all know how much she likes dick.

"You son of a ..."

"Em," Titan snaps and pulls her back to him.

"She's ..."

"It's not your place," he tells her.

She breaks down in front of me like a house of cards falling to the floor. Her body sags against his arms, and tears flow down her face. She sobs and covers her face with her hands. He spins her around, and she buries her face into his shirt.

I continue to sit on the shower floor watching her have a fucking breakdown. "And they say I need help."

She sniffs, spins around, and narrows her eyes on me. "She will never forgive you for this," she whispers, shaking her head. "She will never look at you and not hate you for what you did to her!" she screams.

That gets my attention. I sit up, and she turns, running out of the bathroom.

"What's she talking about?" I demand to Titan.

"Finish up in the shower and come downstairs."

"Titan—"

"April is here," he interrupts me.

Hope blooms in my chest. "She wants to see me?"

He shakes his head. "She doesn't know you're here."

I frown. "Why am I here?"

He runs a hand through his hair. "Because I believe in second chances. And ... I know the guy that you can be, Grave." My heart begins to pound. He sighs. He opens his mouth like he has more to say, but at the last minute, he decides against it. Then he turns around and walks out.

I finish up in the shower and find a Kingdom shirt and a pair of clean jeans on the bed. I pull them on and make my way downstairs. "Where is she?" I ask the moment I enter the kitchen. Everyone is accounted for except her.

No one looks up at me but Titan. He walks past me and down the hall. I follow him. He comes to a stop at a door, and he opens it quietly. My heart stops when I see April. She lies on her side, in the fetal position facing me. Her eyes are tightly shut, and her body shakes with soft sobs.

I rush over to her. "April?" I ask hoarsely.

She doesn't open her eyes. Instead, she begins to sob louder. Harder.

"What's wrong?" I ask, reaching out and running my busted knuckles down her tear-streaked face.

She buries her head into the comforter as her hands grip it. I pull away from her and get into bed where I can pull her into my lap. "April ..."

She sobs. I silently rock her back and forth while she breaks in my arms. "If it's because of me, talk to me please, baby." *Is she injured?*

She starts pounding her fists into my chest, and I let her.

"Tell me you're okay." Maybe it's just an emotional breakdown.

"I'll never be okay," she cries.

"April ..."

She jumps up from my arms and out of bed. I stand to follow her but stay where I am when I see she's just going over to her purse. She bends down, digging through it. And pulls something out. Coming back over to me, she shoves it into my chest. I grab it and look down. It's a pregnancy test. I swallow as I look at it.

She's pregnant.

I got her pregnant. Then I failed her. I showed her that I'm nothing. Just like her father. I can't be there for her. Not the way she needs. Now I'm going to be a father. "I ... I'm sorry." I swallow the lump in my throat. Looking back up at her, I take her hand in mine.

I believe in second chances, Titan had said. He knew. *She will never forgive you* ... so does Emilee. They all do. I'm the last one to find out.

Tears run down her face, and I lick my lips. "I can do better. I will be better. For you ... for the baby ..."

Her bottom lip begins to tremble.

"I know I can. I love you, April." She closes her eyes. "I ..."

"I can't trust you," she whispers softly.

My heart breaks at her words. "April ..." I try to tell her that she can, but my throat closes. My chest tightens. She's right. She can't.

"I'm gonna have this baby, Grave. But I won't raise him or her in a world where their father is always high."

She pulls away from me, and I allow it. I stand in the middle of my brother's spare bedroom while she crawls back into the bed and cries. I remain silent, unable to move. Barely able to breathe at the tightness in my chest.

She's right.

And it hurts like fucking hell. Minutes, maybe hours pass by before her cries stop, and her breathing evens out. She's fallen asleep, and I've just stood here. Numb. Without turning to look back at her, I finally get my heavy feet to move. I walk out the front door of my brother's house without bothering to say a word to anyone.

And Emilee's words finally make sense. *She will never look at you and not hate you for what you did to her!* She was also right. April will never forgive me, and I'll never forgive myself.

THIRTY-EIGHT
GRAVE

I stand next to the bed once again. My face is swollen and still pounds. I need a fucking hit, but I became a different man last night. I don't want to bury what I feel.

Leaning down, I kiss her forehead. She doesn't even stir. "I love you, April." Then I turn and grab the bag that I packed when I went home last night.

I walk through my brother's house again and out the front door. I walk over to my car and open the driver's side door.

"Running away?"

I look up to see Titan outside on his front porch. A coffee mug in one hand and his cell in the other. "You ever sleep?"

"Nope." He stands, and his eyes drop to my bag, but he doesn't say anything.

I run a hand through my hair. And my eyes meet his. I'm going to face this head-on. Taking in a deep breath, I say, "I need a favor."

He gets up from his porch and starts to walk over to his three-car garage. "Let's go."

I make my way to him and get into his car. We pull out of his driveway and through the gate. I reach up and remove my eyebrow piercing, lip piercing, and then my watch. I place them all in his center console.

He remains silent as he gets on the interstate. I look out over Las Vegas as the sun starts to rise, knowing that today is a new day and a fresh start. That second chance Titan was talking about to make things right. To be who she needs.

He pulls into the roundabout and comes to a stop. We sit in silence as I look over the building before us. It's white stucco with big bushes surrounding the building. It looks like a retreat. Somewhere I'd never go. But April has brought me here. She's going to save my life.

"You know ..." Titan breaks the silence, and I look over at him. "We may not be blood, but I've always considered you a brother."

I swallow through the tightness in my throat at his words.

He reaches across the center console and pulls me in for a tight hug. I slap his back, trying to hold back my emotion. I hate how much I feel. I've always tried to smother it, but not anymore. "Take care of her for me?" I ask him when he pulls away.

He nods. "Of course."

I pull my cell out of my back pocket and hand it over to him.

"Want me to walk you in?" he asks, looking over at the double doors.

I chuckle at that. "No. I think I can manage."

He looks over at me without an ounce of humor in his dark blue eyes. "I'm here for you, Grave. Whatever you need. Whenever you need it."

I nod, unable to voice my gratitude, again that knot back in my throat. Then I turn and exit his car, knowing I'm about to give up any freedom that I have.

APRIL

I open my heavy eyes and roll over. My head pounds, and my eyes are puffy. I'm pretty sure I cried in my sleep.

I'm pregnant. That's why I've been sick to my stomach. I just thought it was because of everything that has been going on, but then I realized I was late, so I took a test.

I don't know how it happened. I've been on birth control the entire time. I never missed a pill. But we never used a condom.

I place my hand over my face and take a deep breath. I'm going to do this on my own. All by myself. If I had a choice, I'd have him right beside me, but he's not ready. Not for me or a baby.

Sitting up, I see a folded piece of paper on the bed. I open it up, and my hands begin to shake.

> My beautiful April,
> I'm sorry I had to go. I'm going to get the help I need. I'm sorry I wasn't big enough to do it on my own. It took you entering my life to show me that I needed it. I've failed you. And it kills me to know that I hurt you. I don't expect you to wait on me, but just know that you're all I want. I love you and our baby more than anything in this world. I'm going to be a man and prove it to you.

The words become blurry, and I sniff. I hear the door open, but I don't look up. I try to read the letter again to understand what he's saying. But when I feel a hand on my shoulder, I lose it. I begin to cry.

"It's okay." I hear Emilee's voice. "You have us. We're here for you."

"Yeah, we're not going anywhere," Jasmine adds before I feel her rub my back.

"He left," I manage to get out between sobs.

"He'll be back. For you and the baby," Haven speaks.

He went to rehab. He did what he needed to do for us. And I couldn't be prouder of him.

THIRTY-NINE
GRAVE

I SIT IN an uncomfortable chair in the center of a room with seven other people. It's group therapy time.

I hate this shit!

It's not that I haven't had a hit in three weeks. It's not that I haven't had a sip of alcohol either. I don't miss the high at all. It's because I miss April. I thought I knew what addiction was. I didn't, but I do now.

It's a fucking hole in my chest. I can't sleep at night. I can't function during the day. She consumes me more than any drug ever did, and it feels like a weight on my chest that I can't remove.

It has nothing to do with sex. And everything to do with her voice, her smell, the way she smiles. I wonder if she's okay. Is the baby okay?

I'm like a hamster running on a wheel getting nowhere.

"Grave?"

"Hmm?" I look up from my seat to see Jessie sitting in hers with a warm smile on her face. She runs this show. "Would you like to share?'

Fuck no! "What is it we're sharing?" I ask, trying to not think of

April and what she's doing. I know the Kings are looking out for her, but that's not enough. They can't be there twenty-four seven like I could.

"Whatever you feel comfortable with," the brunette adds. She's got to be midthirties. If I saw her on the streets, I would say her brown hair and dark eyes are attractive. But since I didn't know her until I checked myself in here, I think her cheerful smile and bubbly attitude are annoying as shit.

I sit back and run a hand through my hair. "Well ... I once partied for a solid two weeks," I offer.

The guy by the name of Jenson snorts from beside me. This place is not your average rehab center. Harbor Heights is catered to the rich. The only thing I could compare it to is a country club.

"And?" she asks.

"And what?" I shrug.

"What did you take from that experience?" Jessie asks.

"To always make sure your plane has fuel before takeoff."

The woman to my left laughs and I take a look at her. She's a replica of a Playboy Playmate. Bleach blond hair that doesn't stop until it hits her ass, bright blue eyes, long tan legs and big fake breasts. She reminds me of Lucy in a way. Back when she took care of herself.

"Now this I have to hear," Jenson says.

I sigh, focusing back on the group. "I got in a fight with my father. I decided to go to Vancouver for the weekend to party. Well, what was supposed to be two days ended up being two weeks. Most of it was a blur. But Cross came after me when I didn't return and found me in a run-down motel alone. Turns out I had lost over five hundred thousand in a poker tournament and had crashed my private jet because I hadn't put fuel in it. Thankfully, I had parachutes and managed to get to one and bail out before it crashed." Most of it is still blurry but what I was able to put together was that I crashed shortly after take-off on the way home to Nevada. And that's why I ended up spending more time in Vancouver than I had originally intended.

And when I didn't return on time, my brother had sent Cross to fetch me.

"Oh, my gosh," Jessie places her hands to her face. "Was anyone hurt?"

"Nope. It's lying at the bottom of the Pacific Ocean." I know I got lucky. I believe that someone was looking out for me that day.

Two years ago

I sit at the conference table on the thirteenth floor of Kingdom, drinking Pedialyte out of the bottle. I haven't even been to bed yet. Partied all night with Cross last night, and just when I was headed home to go to bed my brother messaged me to meet him here.

"Where is everyone?" I ask, looking through my sunglasses. My eyes are sensitive from the partying. And the bright fucking sun beaming in from the floor to ceiling windows are making my head pound.

"It's just us," he answers, staring down at his cell while sitting at the head of the table.

I lean my head back and pull my hoodie up and over my face for more eye protection. "Why are we here?"

"Dad wanted to meet us."

I place my hands on the armrests and push to stand, knocking the hood off my face. "I'm out."

He jumps to his feet. "Grave ..."

"Save it," I interrupt him. "I don't give a fuck what Dad wants." He knows that. That's why he didn't tell me that.

I step in front of the glass double doors to exit the conference room right when they open. My father steps in and I stiffen when my eyes go to what's standing next to him. It's a woman. My father always has them coming and going. But he never brings them to Kingdom. And he sure as shit makes sure to never be seen with them in public. Too many eyes and ears always watching to look for the next big story.

"Who the fuck is this?" I ask, ripping off my sunglasses.

261

My father smiles at me and it makes my skin crawl. He's called me here just to piss me off. "This ... is Francesca." He lifts her left hand and I see a massive fucking ring on her ring finger. "My new wife." His smile widens, his blue eyes light up with excitement. "And your new mother."

I had never wanted to fucking kill him more than I did right then. For some stupid reason, Bones stopped me from ramming my fist in his face until he was no longer breathing. I ran out of the conference room, jumped in my car, drove to our private hangar and took off in my jet. I had my pilots license. Now I wish I would have taken the time to hire someone. Maybe I wouldn't have crashed my seven-million-dollar jet trying to get back home.

My father and Francesca's marriage was annulled by the time I got back from my two week binge in Canada. Turns out, she found him in bed with her sister and his airtight prenup saved him from having to give her a fucking penny.

"I think that's enough for today," Jessie says with that fucking smile on her face.

I can't figure out if I'm moody because of lack of drugs, or because I feel like a caged animal here in this elite daycare.

"Want to share more?"

"Huh?" I look over to the Playboy Playmate. "What did you say?"

Her blue eyes look around the room. "Everyone left, but you just stayed seated. I thought maybe you had more you wanted to share." Her eyes come back to mine. "If so, I can listen."

"Oh, no." I notice we are the only two left in the room. "No, I'm done." I hate a lot about this place, but most definitely the group sessions. I don't need to tell these strangers anything about me. Most they have read in headlines.

I stand and walk out of the room and turn to the right, exiting the side door. I stand out on the patio that overlooks the tennis courts and golf course.

"Want a cigarette?"

I look over to see she's followed me outside. "No, thanks. I don't smoke." Not anymore, anyway.

She gives a soft chuckle. "Yeah, me either." Lighting the end of the cigarette, she takes in a drag and blows it out. "But when they take everything away, you have to find something to pass the time."

"How long have you been here?" I ask.

"Five days." She holds out her right hand to me. "They call me Bex."

"Grave." I shake it, wondering if that's a fake name or not.

She nods quickly. "I would say it's nice to meet you but not much is nice about this hell hole."

I laugh. "It could be worse, I guess." Could be dead.

She snorts. "Speak for yourself."

"I'm guessing you didn't check yourself in?"

She shakes her head and tucks her bleach blond hair behind her ear. "My father is getting married to his fifth wife in three months. Walked in on me fucking my soon-to-be stepbrother on his desk. Next thing I knew, he was dragging my ass out of bed the next morning and had a car deliver me here. This is my home for the next five weeks."

I nod, dropping my head. "There's nothing wrong with admitting you need help with addiction. Drugs can take over your life." I haven't been this sober in this amount of consecutive days in I don't know how long. The first five days here I felt like shit. My body trying to learn to live without them. I didn't do them when I was with April, but the temptation was still there. I just chose not to. Now that I know I can't, my body craved it. Or maybe that was just my mind wanting to bury my feelings and the heartache. I've always known I had a problem, but I never wanted to admit it.

"I wish my problem was drugs." She brings the cigarette to her lips.

I frown. "You're in rehab but don't have an addiction?"

She shrugs. "They say I'm a sex addict." Turning her head, she winks at me while biting her bottom lip. "I say I just like cock." Her eyes drop to my jeans.

I laugh. "Who doesn't enjoy sex?"

"Right?" She throws her head back and laughs. "See, someone gets it."

I nod. "Yeah, I do."

"Grave?"

We both turn around to see Jessie walking toward us. She frowns at Bex smoking a cigarette but doesn't voice her opinion about it. "You have a phone call," she tells me.

I begin to walk away from the railing as Bex calls out, "See you around."

APRIL

I STAND INSIDE the wedding chapel, looking over the flower arrangements that the girls and I put together. It took six weeks of nonstop work, but it looks amazing, if I do say so myself.

The wedding is tomorrow. We've been here for the past three hours for the rehearsal, and it couldn't have gone any better. I should be ecstatic, but a part of me is still so sad. Grave has been gone for over a month now. I haven't had any kind of interaction with him whatsoever, and that's been the hardest part. No phone calls, no visits, not even a letter. I get all my updates for him through Titan, but even that, he keeps short. He visits him once a week with multiple phone calls. I know Cross and Bones also have contact with him, but I'm not close with either one of them to ask what they know.

Titan walks up to me, and I give him my fake smile. He doesn't buy it, but at least he pretends he does. "The flowers look amazing. Thank you."

"Thank you, but it was a group effort." Titan was adamant that I do the wedding, but my little flower shop wasn't equipped to handle such a big order. So the girls spent days and nights at Roses helping me, and when we ran out of space, we moved over to Emilee's and his house.

"I spoke to Grave yesterday."

My heart starts racing at the mention of his name. "Is he okay?" I ask. That's my greatest fear, that he's in pain. I've seen documentaries that show someone going through withdrawals and how excruciating it can be.

He nods. "He gets to be here tomorrow for the wedding."

My eyes widen. "What? He's getting out?" I thought he was doing a six-week program.

"No. He gets a day pass. He didn't want to miss the wedding. And we want him here." He smiles at me. "He asked me if I'd come pick him up. I lied to him and said I would."

I frown. "Why would you do that?"

"Because you're going to be the one there."

I shake my head quickly. "I ..."

"Titan, your bride-to-be is looking for you," Jasmine tells him, coming up to us.

He nods. "Duty calls."

I nod, but hate to be left hanging. I want to know more. Is he going to be excited to see me? Like I will him? I turn and notice Bones standing there. His hands shoved into his dress pants. "You should be the one to pick him up," I say.

"I'm the last person Grave wants to see right now," he answers.

My brows knit together. "You don't forgive him?" Grave hurt me, but I haven't known him all my life. I can't imagine how hard it must have been for his brother and best friends to see him hurt himself over and over.

"You do?"

I sigh. "Grave is ..."

"An addict."

"I was going to say trying to get better. We need to support that decision." I rub my growing stomach. It's not much, but even if others can't tell, I can.

"Are you still going to forgive him when he relapses?"

I take in a long breath. "He won't."

"He will." He nods. "I know my brother." He says it with such conviction. Bones truly believes his brother won't be able to stay sober.

My hands fist. "People can change."

"No, people replace one addiction for another."

"What does that mean?"

He looks away and his jaw sharpens. "I love my brother." His eyes come back to mine. "But you and my niece or nephew are my main priority."

Tears prick my eyes as my hands go to my stomach once again.

"If you need anything, call me. Day or night. Do you understand?"

I nod and mumble, "Thank you."

FORTY

APRIL

I STAND OUTSIDE the facility, leaning up against his Challenger. I drove it, thinking he would want to drive, to feel in control again. I know how much he loves it.

I watch the front door open, and he steps outside. My heart pounds at the sight of him. He wears a black V-neck Kingdom shirt with a pair of ripped jeans and black boots. And he's got his sunglasses on. I know the moment he spots me because his entire body tenses.

Pushing off the car, I take a couple of steps toward him but stop. Doubt fills me when he comes to stop on the bottom step. Maybe I shouldn't have come. Titan said Grave called him. That's who he wanted here.

He begins to walk toward me, and I let out a shaky breath.

My hands shake, and my heart pounds. Blood rushes in my ears. What if he no longer wants me? What if without the drugs, he doesn't love me? What if ...

"What are you doing here, April?" he asks.

I swallow nervously at the sound of his voice. "I ... uh ... I thought ..."

He reaches out and cups my face. I lean into his soft touch, and like a dam breaking, tears spill from my eyes and a sob comes out.

He wraps his strong arms around me and pulls me into him. My hands grip his shirt, and my face burrows into his chest. "I'm sorry," I cry.

"April." He sighs. "I'm the one who is sorry."

"No, no, no," I say quickly and pull away, sniffing.

He pushes his glasses to the top of his head, and my breath catches in my lungs when I see them. They're so blue. No drug-hazed fog.

"I'm sorry, April." He swallows and brushes the tears from my cheeks. "I destroyed me. I destroyed us. But I promise you, I'm going to be better. I owe you that." His hand comes down to touch my stomach. Fresh tears fill my eyes. "And our baby. I'm supposed to work for forgiveness ..."

"Grave, I already forgive you." It's true. This man is trying to be better. And I know he can.

He wraps his arms around me and kisses my forehead. I half laugh, half cry. I don't know what will happen in three hours or three years, but I do know that this man is my king, and I will be his queen and protect him at all cost.

GRAVE

I WRAP MY arms around her, pulling her into me. I inhale her scent and let out a long breath. She pulls away first and gestures to my car. "I thought you would like to drive it." And then hands me the keys.

Taking them from her, I walk over to the car and open up the passenger door for her. She thanks me and slides inside. I close the door and make my way to the driver's side.

"I hope you weren't disappointed that Titan wasn't the one who picked you up," she says softly, looking down at her hands knotted in her lap.

"April." I reach over and cup her face, lifting her chin so she has to look over at me. Those ice blue eyes that I see every time I close mine, stare at me. They're swimming in unshed tears. I'm not sure if they're tears of joy, sadness, or regret. I hate that I can't read her right now.

I move in closer to her, leaning over the center console. Her breath hitches when her eyes drop to my lips. I go to kiss her when her cell starts to ring. I pull away and start up the car as she answers it.

"Hello?" she answers, her voice shaking. She clears her throat and tries again as I pull out of the parking lot. "Hello?"

I sit back in the seat, letting my shoulders relax. I didn't expect her to be the one standing outside of Harbor Heights, but she was the one I wanted.

"Yeah, we're on our way," she speaks.

My left hand grips the steering wheel while my hold tightens on the gear shift.

"Okay, I'll let him know." She hangs up. "That was Titan. He has your suit at the church."

A silence falls over the car and I want to ask her a million questions at once. I want to kiss her for hours. Hold her for days and love her until I die. I have to earn that privilege. I have to show her what she means to me.

"I ..." She gets cut off as her phone goes off again. "I'm so sorry." She sighs, picking it up.

"Don't be sorry," I tell her, giving her a quick side-eye.

"It's Jasmine, the girls ..."

"It's a big day for Emilee," I say with a nod. "I'm sure they're wondering where you are." I'm not sure if they know that she was going to pick me up or not. But I can only imagine they're either drunk or on their way to it. Starting the celebration early. The wedding is in two hours. "We can talk afterward." I don't have to be back until eight tonight. And I only plan on dedicating a few hours of my day to this wedding of the year. The rest will be with her.

THE MOMENT WE ARRIVED AT THE CHAPEL, WE GOT SEPARATED. She went to go get dressed and have her hair done. I was shoved down a long hall and into a room where a tux was hanging in a garment bag that had my name on it.

I'm sitting in the corner high-back chair tying my shoes when the door opens. I look up to see Titan enter. "Hey." I stand.

He immediately opens his arms and walks over to me, pulling me in for a man hug with a slap on the back. When he pulls back, he keeps his hands on my shoulders. "You look great." He smiles at me.

"You sound surprised," I joke.

He pulls away and runs a hand down his freshly shaven face. "It could have gone either way."

I laugh because we both know that's true. I was either going to rot in that place or decide that I needed to change who I was and what I wanted out of life. April is the new me. The future that I want. What I never even knew could possibly exist.

His face goes serious and he lets out a long breath. "Seriously, Grave. You look great." His eyes roam over my face. "Decided to leave the piercings out?"

I nod. "Yeah."

He grips my face. "Makes you look like a baby."

The guys always joked that I had a baby face. We both begin to laugh, and the door opens. I immediately stop and clear my throat when I see my brother enter.

Titan looks over at him. "Once you're done, meet me at the altar," he tells me.

I nod. "Wouldn't miss it."

He turns and exits, not saying another word. Bones closes the door once he's gone and faces me. He doesn't say anything. He just stands there with his arms crossed over his chest and his usual scowl on his face.

I bow my head, fixing my suit jacket, unable to meet his eyes.

"You can save the big brother speech. You can't tell me anything that I don't already know." I'd be lying if I said I wasn't embarrassed or ashamed of the things I've done.

He remains silent.

I keep my eyes down and start to walk to the door, ready to get this over with, but at the last minute he grabs my upper arm and brings me to a stop. My eyes snap up to look at him. "Bones ..."

"You're wrong," he says. "There's something that I can tell you that you don't already know."

My first thought is April. She's found someone else. Five weeks without someone is a long time. She's moved on. Found someone to treat her the way she deserves.

He places both of his hands on either side of my face, pulling me closer to him. I watch his hard blue eyes soften and I hold my breath, preparing for the worst.

"You know, we both lost a mother," he starts, and a knot instantly forms in my throat. "But you know what else I lost?" I don't answer. "A brother. A best friend." I swallow. "I lost you the day that we buried Mom. And I've been losing you every day since to your addiction."

He's right. I've pushed everyone away, even April. And I need to be a man and take responsibility of my mistakes. "I'm sorry," I choke out.

"No." He grips my shoulders tighter. "I'm sorry I let you down. But I won't do it again."

I sniff and he pulls me in for a hug.

"I'm so proud of you," he whispers. "And Mom would be proud of you."

My throat tightens at his words.

"I ..." He clears his throat. "I didn't realize until this morning that I was your biggest problem ..."

I pull away quickly, frowning. "No."

"I let you go too far."

I sigh. "You couldn't have stopped me."

"That's where you're wrong," he argues. "I realize I failed you in the worst way a brother could fail. But I promise you, Kyle. I will not fail you again. Do you understand me?"

I nod once, my throat tightening, unable to form a word.

"I love you," he says.

I can't even remember the last time my brother said those words to me. After Mom passed, the words just weren't spoken in our house. I didn't realize how much I missed them.

"I love you, Kyle. And that woman out there." He pauses and my chest tightens. Here it comes. The blow that's gonna bring me to my knees. "That woman carrying your child loves you too. And it took her to make me see that together, we can overcome anything."

I let out a shaky breath. "I was afraid you were going to tell me her boyfriend was here, and you were going to kill him for me."

He pulls away laughing. "She's not going anywhere. For some reason she wants to stick around. Could be because you knocked her up."

My mouth falls open. "Did Dillan Reed, a.k.a. Bones, just make a joke?"

He shrugs. "You're not the only Reed who can make people laugh."

"There are hundreds of people who will disagree with you."

And just like that, I feel a weight lifted off my shoulders. A cloud that no longer hovers over me. I feel twenty pounds lighter. Forgiveness and love are more powerful than any drug you can take.

I've always had a death wish, but for once I have something to live for.

FORTY-ONE
APRIL

"W E'RE READY." THE wedding coordinator that Emilee hired calls out, entering the bridal room.

Emilee spins around, smoothing her hands down her Marie-Chantal Miller wedding dress. She looks like royalty in the white lace material. It's an off-the-shoulder, backless dress with a royal train. It was made for a queen. "How do I look?" she asks nervously.

"Gorgeous," Jasmine tells her before taking a sip of her champagne.

"Absolutely stunning," I say with a smile.

"Thank you." She walks up to me and takes my hands in hers. "I couldn't have done this without you."

My cheeks heat up as I look around the room full of women that quickly became my best friends. "I didn't do anything."

"Yes, you did." She let's go of my hands and pulls me in for a hug. "You took my dream and turned it into reality."

I pull away and try to fight back the tears that want to fall. "I couldn't have done it on my own." She makes it sound like I planned this entire thing from the ground up. All I did was make flower arrangements. I didn't even do it on my own. Me, Haven, Jasmine, and Emilee worked day and night on these. Even Alexa helped me when she had free time.

"Come on, ladies. It's time to go." They start to usher us out of the room. I hear my cell ringing in my purse and I quickly grab it and walk out with the girls.

I press ignore but it instantly starts to ring again and this time I press answer. "I can't talk ..."

"April, I've been trying to reach you." I hear a familiar voice on the other end.

"Now is not a good time," I whisper, coming to a stop with the girls in front of the closed double doors.

"I'll make it quick."

"I ..."

"They took your offer," she interrupts me.

My mouth drops open at her announcement. "What?" I ask, making sure I heard her.

"They accepted your offer, April," she repeats excitedly.

"That's ... amazing." I breathe.

"It is. I know you're busy; I just wanted to tell you the good news." She hangs up before I can even respond.

I pull the phone away from my ear and then Sarah, the wedding coordinator, snatches it out of my hands, pocketing it.

"You okay?" Jasmine asks me, her green eyes full of concern.

I nod. "Yeah, I am."

GRAVE

I sit at the long bridal party table at the head of the ballroom. I watch Titan dance with his wife on the black dance floor in front of two hundred and twenty people. I look over their faces, recognizing most of them. Some I couldn't even guess who the fuck they are.

Titan has always been a showoff. And that's exactly what he's doing with the reporters and guests here. He's showing the world that he is one of the luckiest Kings on earth, marrying Emilee. Because they're not here for Emilee. She couldn't care less.

My brother sits next to me. A glass of bourbon in his hand. He speaks to a guy by the name of Avery and his brother Tristan. The Decker brothers are friends of his.

Being sober shows you how alone you truly are. I never got close to anyone. They'd see who I really was.

I take a sip of my water as a woman I know well walks up to our table. Marsha Wells. A reporter who slept her way to the top in Vegas. She's always the first to break a juicy story. Her pussy has gotten her all the best connections.

"Bones?" Her eyes stare at him hungrily. I'm pretty sure he's fucked her before. But I could be wrong.

"Marsha." He nods to her, throwing back his drink.

The Kings have always been in the media spotlight. Our fathers started Kingdom—The Three Wisemen weren't any better than we are. I can't even count the stories that have been written about us. Some true. Some not. I ignore them. They don't mean anything to me.

"I was wondering if you had anything to share with me?" she asks him.

He tilts his head to the side and looks her up and down. His eyes starting at her pink heels and running up her cream-colored dress before meeting hers. "I might have something."

She smiles and he gets to his feet, buttons his suit jacket, and walks around the table. "Excuse me, gentlemen," he tells the Decker brothers. Taking her hand, he leads her to the dance floor.

I take another sip of my water as my eyes catch the most beautiful woman here. April stands across the ballroom. Her dark purple hair styled in an updo. Pieces falling down and framing her face. She wears a strapless, black silk dress.

I swallow nervously and stand, wanting to talk to her. I make my way around the dance floor and over to her. She has her back to me, talking to Jasmine.

Jasmine looks up and spots me coming. She brings the glass of champagne to her lips and tilts it back, winking at me. "I have to go," she tells April the moment I get close.

"What? Where do you have to go all of a sudden?" she calls out to Jasmine's back.

"She's my wingman," I tell her. Jasmine has always had my back. She understands that we're not all the same. That some of us feel too much while others don't feel at all.

April spins around and looks up at me. I reach my right hand out. "Dance with me?" I hold my breath. Still unsure how she feels about me. The horrible situation I've put us in. Sitting alone in a room with nothing but your thoughts for weeks on end hasn't been good for me.

She doesn't say anything, just takes my hand, and I pull her into me. God, I missed this. Holding her. Everything about her was addicting.

But what little hope I had dies when she speaks. "I can't."

I let go of her and run a hand through my hair. "Okay," I say, hating that I've hurt her. I understand that just because I'm trying doesn't mean I deserve the chance to make it right.

"I mean." She sighs. "I need to talk to you, Grave."

Her words don't help the bad feeling in my gut that I've gone too far. I did too much. She isn't Lucy. April demanded all of me and what I gave her was a watered down, drug induced version. "Yeah, sure. I guess there is a lot we need to discuss ..."

"I didn't get pregnant on purpose," she rushes out.

I frown. "I never said that you did." That thought never even crossed my mind. It took the both of us to make our baby. I knew the possibilities when I chose not to use a condom.

"I've been going crazy thinking. Finally I remembered that a few weeks before you came into Roses, I was sick. I was on antibiotics. I didn't realize they could disrupt birth control." She licks her lips. "I'm sorry. I wasn't thinking ..."

"Hey, it's okay."

"I don't want your money, Grave. And if you want to walk away, I understand," she adds.

"What?" I blink.

"I don't want you to be stressed. If you don't want to be part of his or her life, I also understand."

She's not making sense. What the hell has she been thinking while I've been in rehab? I should have reached out to her. But there was a very short list of people who I could have contact with. I wanted her to focus on the baby, not my recovery. "April ..."

"I know things aren't ideal." She sniffs and averts her eyes to her heels.

I place my hands on either side of her face and she looks up at me, her ice blue eyes full of tears. "What are you talking about?"

"I don't want to put any pressure on you," she whispers.

"You're not." I assure her. She's the only thing that I know I can't live without. I need her more than any hit I've ever craved.

She bites her bottom lip. "I'm afraid." Her watery eyes dart around the room.

"Of what?" My chest tightens. "Of me? I promise you, April. I will be better for you and our baby," I quickly reassure her.

"That's what I'm afraid of." A tear rolls down her face.

"What do you mean?" Her bottom lip begins to quiver. "Hey, talk to me. Please." Whatever it is, I'll do whatever it takes to make things right. But I can't guess what she's thinking.

She lets out a shaky breath. "I'm afraid you won't love me sober."

My tight chest constricts like a vice at her confession. How could she think that? What have I done to make her think I could love her any less? I love her more. I did this for her. I'm demanding more of myself because she deserves that. "April ..."

"You almost kissed me in your car but stopped," she adds, interrupting me. "And I realized that maybe you don't want ..."

I cut off her insane words by pressing my lips to hers. Her arms immediately wrap around my neck as she parts her lips for me, allowing me to deepen the kiss. My hands tangle in her hair, loosening her updo, and I tilt her head back to give me better access to her lips. I devour her. Drink her in as if she is the cure to a disease.

I pull away and she opens her heavy eyes, lips parted as she sucks in a breath. "I'm going to spend the rest of my life proving to you that I love you."

EPILOGUE

APRIL

I T'S BEEN A month since Emilee and Titan's wedding. Grave went back to rehab that night, and a week later I picked him up knowing that he wouldn't have to return like Cinderella at midnight.

Things have been crazy busy since the wedding. Titan had every news crew in Las Vegas there and there was a picture of him and Emilee that ended up on the cover of a magazine. The title read *The King found his Queen*. It was gorgeous. I blew it up and hung it inside of Roses.

Turns out, that wedding got a lot of publicity, which in turn gave me exposure. Emilee and Titan had done an interview that was published in the magazine as well and dropped my name along with the shop as their florist. The calls started rolling in.

And that call that I got right before we walked with Emilee down the aisle? It was from my realtor. After what Emilee and Titan had paid me for their wedding, I had enough to make an offer on the boutique that was for sale next to me. They accepted it.

Me, Jasmine, Haven, and Alexa spent the week that Emilee was away for her honeymoon tearing down the wall that divided the boutique from Roses. Who knew a sledgehammer and some beers would be such a great stress reliever? Well, being the mom-to-be, I had Capri Suns. But there was still something very therapeutic about it, nonetheless.

Ethan is staying out of trouble for the most part. He's been at the shop every day showing me that he's dedicated and trying his best. He told me that he wants to work off his debt to Grave the right way. I respect that. And so does Grave.

Grave is doing well. He doesn't seem much different from the man I fell in love with. He's always going out of his way to make me laugh. He's home every night after he leaves Kingdom and at work every morning. I can't say he's on time because I always seem to be making us late.

I moved in with Grave after he got out of rehab and gave Ethan our mother's house. He tried to refuse it, but it was the right thing to do. Although he comes over to our house once a week and drops off his laundry. He can't understand the concept of sorting colors.

"I know. That's what I said." Grave speaks into his cell as he enters the kitchen. He comes over to me, kisses my hair and takes a pancake from the plate. He nods his head to himself while he stabs the peanut butter jar with a knife, spreads it across the pancake and then folds it in half before shoving it in his mouth. "Mmmm hmm." He mumbles to his phone before swallowing it. "It needs to happen now. We're losing money every day," he tells whoever he is talking to.

"Hello?" I hear a female voice call out.

"In here," I answer, reaching over and grabbing the tray that has the raw steaks on them off the island. "I seasoned them," I whisper to Grave and he takes them from me, mouthing *thank you*. After another kiss in my hair, he's gone, continuing his conversation.

"I brought the syrup," Jasmine announces, entering.

"Thanks," I say, taking it from her. "I didn't realize we were out."

"Where are Haven and Emilee?" she asks, jumping up to sit on the island and starts peeling a banana I had sitting in the glass bowl.

"Haven messaged me that her and Luca would be thirty minutes late," I answer.

She rolls her eyes. "They're having sex more than me. Every time I talk to her, she's like *gotta go fuck his dick because we want a baby.*" Then Jasmine sticks the banana in her mouth biting it almost in half.

I snort. "And Emilee is in the bathroom down the hall."

"Is Alexa going to make it?" she asks, shoving what was left of the banana down her throat.

"No. She said she was going to use this day to catch up on sleep."

For the last month, we've all gathered at Grave's and my house every Sunday for brunch. The guys grill streaks in the outside kitchen while me and the girls cook inside. Once everything is finished cooking, we sit down in the formal dining room and eat until we all have to waddle out of the room.

I never thought this would be my life—living with a King. But I couldn't imagine it any other way. I don't know what brought Grave into Roses that morning, but I like to think that fate knew what it was doing because it brought me the man that I'm going to spend the rest of my life with.

THE END

Thank you for taking the time to read **Grave.** Did you enjoy the Dark Kings? Read on for the prologue from **Cross...**

WANT TO KNOW MORE ABOUT *THE DARK KINGDOM SERIES?*

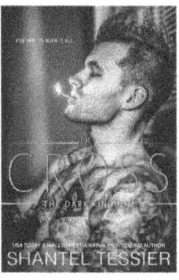
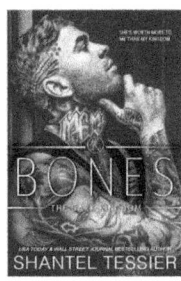

CROSS

THE DARK KINGDOM

PROLOGUE

CROSS

Thirteen years old . . .

"HAPPY BIRTHDAY, SON," my mother says softly to me while we stand at the entrance of Oak Grove, my father's church.

I hate being here after hours. It gives me the creeps. The walls creak, and the wind always makes the old, stained windows rattle. It gives me a feeling so deep down in my bones that I'm cold for hours after I leave. I can't explain it, but it feels like evil is inside these walls. Which is stupid since this is a place of worship where people come to heal—God's house. My father says it has power, but I have yet to see that. I have never witnessed a miracle that couldn't be explained by science.

I step back from her, forcing her hands off my shoulders, and take a quick look around the empty structure. "Why are we here?" I ask, my hands shaking nervously. It's past midnight and officially my thirteenth birthday. She woke me from my bed and said we had to go for a drive.

Lowering her eyes, she sighs deeply, forcing my heart rate to speed up. "Mom ...?"

"Son," my father's voice booms behind me, and I spin around to see him walking our way. He's dressed in his business attire—a black button-down shirt with black slacks and a matching suit jacket. His dark hair is slicked back, and his face is freshly shaved. You wouldn't know just by looking at him that he's worth billions of dollars.

He comes to a stop and removes his hands from his front pockets, crossing them in front of him. The black ring in the shape of a crown on his right ring finger tells the world that he's a member of the Three Wisemen. It's a reminder that my father may play the martyr, but he does the work of the devil.

He and his two best friends started Kingdom—the largest, most corrupt hotel and casino here in Sin City. They each play their part outside their gilded cage. The only difference is they asked for their prison sentence. My father likes to pretend he's a disciple of God. That he does his work of ridding the world of evil. When the truth is, he creates it. He takes whatever the sinners have to offer and promises redemption, but instead, he feeds it to the devil as an offering.

Their sins are his currency. Knowledge makes you rich and powerful.

I take a step back from him, needing the space, and bump into my mother. Sidestepping quickly, I move to where I can see them both at the same time, whipping my head back and forth. "I wanna go home," I manage to get out, trying to calm my nerves when I want to scream. Why am I here? My father makes me attend church on Sundays when the congregation is present. That way, he can show off his perfect family along with the other Three Wisemen and their families. Appearance is everything in this city. Without a kingdom, there is no need for a King to rule.

"It's time," he states, walking over to me.

"For what?" I ask. My voice squeaks, and I want to punch myself for acting like such a little bitch.

Placing his hand on my back, he ushers me through the double doors and down the aisle. "The Lord forgives all sins until we reach the age of thirteen."

I look over my shoulder to see if my mother has followed us, and she has. She stands at the back in front of the double doors, just staring at us. "Yes, Father." But I've been saved since I was three. He reminds me every day that I'm a son of the Lord.

He looks down at me, giving me a kind smile, but it doesn't ease my fear. His green eyes look even brighter from the candlelight. I got his eyes, and I hate it. I wonder what he sold in order to get a son—an heir to continue his legacy once he's passed. His death can't come soon enough if you ask me. "Today, you have reached that age—age of accountability."

I have done a little research on this, but as far as I can find, there is no such thing in the Bible that states we must be saved by the age of thirteen. But I will never tell him that. No one argues with my father. His word is as strong as God's. "Yes, Father," I agree once again.

"You must repent for your sins."

My body begins to tremble at his choice of words, and I pray that he doesn't notice. *Sins?* What have I done? He is the one who pretends. I hear the stories around town. The way kids look at me and my friends at school. Evil doesn't just walk among us. It also lives in our houses. It intertwines itself in our everyday life so you can't break free. We're being trained, conditioned to take it over one day. We don't have a choice. We will be the Kings. The question is, what will we do with it?

My eyes go back to the scene before us. I've seen it before. The first time I was nine. I shiver from the memory of that night and the scar that reminds me of it.

We come to a stop, and he reaches up, grabbing the chain around his neck and removes the silver cross that my mother got him when he became a priest as if that was supposed to mean something. It might have once, but it no longer does. Not to me. It's his weapon of choice.

He hasn't always been a religious man. He and my mother weren't this way when I was born. The Three Wisemen took an oath and must do whatever it takes to uphold it.

"You must allow the Heavenly Father into your soul, son."

"I have, Father." My voice shakes, and I cross my arms over my chest, trying to shield my body. Not again. Why tonight? Why this birthday?

He sighs heavily, clearly not happy with my answer. "Remove your shirt."

I swallow the lump that forms in my throat. "Dad ...?"

"Remove your shirt, son," he demands. The echo in his voice bounces off the walls and cathedral ceiling.

I grip the white fabric and slowly pull it over my head. He reaches out for one of the candles. "But why ...?"

"Shh." He shushes me. "I'm going to save you, my child."

He runs the candle along the back of the silver cross. The flame licks the precious metal. Without looking down at me, he speaks. "Down on your knees."

My heart pounds, and blood begins to rush in my ears. There's no stopping what's to come. Either I will willingly do as I'm told, or he will force me, which will just make it worse. With shaky knees, I slowly lower myself to the cold floor.

"Place your chest to your thighs and reach your hands out in front of you."

Tears begin to blur my vision, but I blink them away, refusing to cry or look weak. To him, weakness is a tool. Something useful. I heard him once say, "A man must willingly sacrifice himself with dignity."

I hear him set the candle back and my body shakes as he places his hand flat on my back, holding me down while kneeling beside me.

"Dad—" My voice breaks as I try to catch my breath.

He interrupts me. "Bless him, Father, for he does not know what he does." Then he places the burning metal against my back, and I bite down on my tongue, refusing to scream into the silent church. The smell of burning flesh hits my nose while blood slips between my lips and onto the floor under me. Every muscle in my body is taut while I hold my breath. "But he will. Being a King has a price that very few are willing to pay."

Sucking in a breath through gritted teeth, he removes the hot cross, and I sag to the floor.

"You must learn to endure pain, son," my father says, pulling me to my feet.

I sniff and quickly rub the back of my hand under my nose to catch the snot. When I swallow, I taste the lingering blood.

"People don't understand what it takes to be us." He goes on, and I look at my shoes, unable to meet his eyes. The shame I feel right now is too much.

My back is on fire from the branding he just gave me. As if a fucking cross is going to guarantee me a trip to heaven.

"You will see, son." He taps my shoulder, and I pull away from him.

He turns and walks away, leaving me standing alone at the front of the church. Moments later, I hear my mother's heels clap on the floor as she makes her way to me.

"He is teaching you to be better," she states, coming to stand next to me.

Lifting my head, I glare up at her, hating her for marrying him and for having me. Why would anyone want this life? Why would anyone want to hurt the innocent?

"Happy Birthday," she says once again. Reaching into the pocket of her jacket, she pulls out a small rectangular box.

I just stare at it.

"Go ahead and open it." She holds it out to me.

I take it from her hand and gently unwrap the white paper and see it's a black Zippo. *A lighter?* My birthday present is a lighter?

"We all have a cross to bear," she reads what's engraved on the back. "Fire is a symbol of the Holy Spirit." She goes on to explain. "Fire can bring warmth, but it can also be uncontrollably dangerous." I look up at her. "You've always been fascinated by fire, Cross. Just like your father." I flinch at that thought. I hate being like him. "This is your faith. Your redemption. A reminder that we must all do what needs to be done." With those words, she takes my hand and guides me back down the aisle of the church.

WANT TO DIVE INTO THE LORDS WORLD?

CONTACT ME

Facebook Reader Group: Shantel's Sinful Side

Goodreads: Shantel Tessier

Instagram: shantel_tessierauthor

Website: Shanteltessier.com

Facebook Page: Shantel Tessier Author

TikTok: shantel_tessier_author

Store: shanteltessierstore.com

Shantel Tessier's Spoiler Room. Please note that I have one spoiler room for all books, and you may come across spoilers from book(s) you have not had the chance to read yet. You must answer both questions in order to be approved.